THE NARROWBOAT ORPHANS

DAISY CARTER

Copyright © 2023 Daisy Carter
All rights reserved.

This story is a work of fiction. The characters, names, places, events, and incidents in it are entirely the work of the author's imagination or used in a fictitious manner. Any resemblance or similarity to actual persons, living or dead, events or places is entirely coincidental. No part of this work may be reproduced, stored in a retrieval system, or transmitted, in any form or by any means, without the prior permission of the author and the publisher.

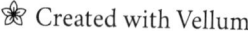 Created with Vellum

CHAPTER 1

he West Country, England - 1844

THE APPETISING SMELL of mutton and vegetable stew roused Ruben Hinton from where he had been dozing in the sagging armchair next to the hearth. He yawned and leaned forward to add a couple more pieces of wood to the fire before rattling the poker in the embers to help the flames take hold. A spark flew out with a popping sound, landing on the rag rug, which he hastily flicked back onto the flagstones before it burnt the faded fabric. He needed to cut more wood, and it was tempting to let the fire die down, but the stone cottage could still feel chilly on a spring evening, and the walls would be running with damp again soon enough if he let the fire go out. Little Amy had only just got over another chill which had left her with a shuddering cough which shook her skinny frame. He didn't want to risk her getting sick again.

"Are you going to eat with us tonight, Pa?" Dolly asked. Tendrils of her raven-dark hair fell in unruly curls around her face, where it had escaped from the braid that hung down her back. There was a questioning look in her big brown eyes, and one eyebrow twitched up in a way that sent a pang of loss through Ruben's heart. Dolly was the spitting image of Anne, Ruben's childhood sweetheart and wife. Except now Anne was buried in the graveyard of Middleyard Church. Doctor Skelton had fought valiantly to save her life on a stormy night five years ago, when she had given birth to their last child, Amy. But to no avail. Anne had drawn her last breath just as the sun edged over the eastern hilltops painting the scoured land pink, leaving him a widower, brokenhearted, with four children depending upon him.

Ruben ran a hand through his thick brown hair and shook his head. "Just leave me some in a bowl on the range for later, our Dolly. I've got a bit of business I need to see to."

He stifled another yawn and thrust his feet into the leather boots, which were still steaming gently in front of the fire from where he had propped them up on the hearth earlier. The soles were worn thin enough to make him wince if he stood on a sharp stone, and he'd been meaning to get them mended at the cobbler's, but he would try and get by for a little bit longer, stuffing some rags and scraps of sheep's wool into them. The weather would soon dry up. Besides, the children's threadbare clothes needed mending, so he would have to spend a few pennies on the services of old Mrs Epperson to keep them looking half-decent until the children were old enough to sew their own clothes, and there wasn't enough money to do both.

He eyed each of his four children, trying to see them as an outsider would. Dolly, at ten years old, was growing fast. The ragged hem of her dress was halfway up her bony shins, but given that she was such a tomboy, she probably didn't mind.

Next to her, Jonty was his only son, three years younger than Dolly. His head was bent in concentration over a sack of pebbles he'd spent the afternoon picking from the fields. Clearing stones for Farmer Baggins earned them a few extra coins at this time of year, and then Jonty used the smaller pebbles in his catapult to keep the crows and pigeons off the newly emerging shoots of his wheat crop.

His heart softened as he glanced towards his two youngest children. Gloria, aged six, always took it upon herself to care for little Amy, who was a year younger. She had hitched Amy onto her lap and was haltingly trying to read her a simple story from one of the books the church ladies had lent them. Amy snuggled closer to her, giggling every so often when Gloria embellished the tale to make it more interesting. The three older children doted on Amy ever since they'd noticed that she kept bumping into things, and Doctor Skelton had informed them that her eyesight was very limited, possibly due to the difficult labour which had taken Anne too soon.

Glancing around the cramped cottage, he noticed the thin film of dust on the dresser and the muddle of wool in the basket in the corner with some half-darned socks poking out. He was gripped by the usual sense of guilt that he wasn't doing a good enough job of looking after them.

The place needs a woman's touch to make it feel like home again. It was a familiar thought, but he pushed it away, knowing it might make him feel maudlin. He knew that some of the villagers thought his high-spirited children would benefit from having a stepmother to take them all in hand, but he couldn't bring himself to start looking for another wife. Not yet.

"...Pa! Did you hear what I said?" Dolly's insistent voice pulled him out of his introspection. "Are you going out poaching, I asked?" She looked troubled as she put the four bowls of stew on the table and started slicing the heel end of a loaf.

Ruben hesitated and then gave a small nod. "No point pretending otherwise, our Dolly." He grinned, trying to look as though it was normal. "You're old enough to know that times are hard at the moment. If I can catch a few rabbits up on the estate, or even a couple of pheasants if I'm lucky, it will put a few more meals on the table for us."

"But what if Mr Granger sees you, Pa?" Jonty sat to the table and reached for a piece of buttered bread. "Give over, Dolly," he grumbled, as she slapped his hand away, making him wait politely until they were all ready to eat.

"Yes, Pa, aren't you worried about what might

happen if you get caught?" Dolly handed out the bread, making sure that Amy had the piece with the most butter on it. "Miss Clark at church told us that Percy Higgs got transported to Australia for stealing a cabbage."

"He got sent away for helping himself to a cabbage?" Jonty looked shocked and shivered. "I heard Mrs Higgs saying Percy had been chosen to be an under-butler to a grand family in Cheltenham. She must have been too ashamed to tell what really happened."

"Poor Percy. He'll never see his ma again." Gloria blinked back tears and looked beseechingly at Ruben. "Please stay home with us tonight, Pa."

"Let's not get all het up about nothing," Ruben said firmly. Perhaps he should have pretended he was going out for a sup of ale instead of telling them what he was really up to. He tugged his threadbare old jacket on and checked the sharpness of his pocketknife on his thumb before folding the blade away. There were two large pockets sewn into the lining of his jacket, which were plenty big enough to conceal a couple of rabbits or pheasants if anyone chanced to see him. "Mind you get to bed straight after dinner, and if anyone comes to the cottage asking for me, tell them I've gone to The Woolpack."

"Don't be late, Pa," Gloria mumbled through a mouthful of stew. "Amy frets if she thinks you're not here."

Ruben bent over and planted a kiss on Amy's cheek, chuckling as his whiskers tickled her baby-soft skin. It had come to something that he had to go poaching to keep his family fed instead of actually enjoying a pint of ale at the village tavern. But seeing as Lord Longton hadn't raised his wages for as long as he could remember, he would just have to take his payment from the estate in other ways, he told himself.

Dolly ran to the door after him and turned her face up for a kiss as well. "I'll look after the little 'uns, but promise me you'll be careful Pa." Her dark eyes were clouded with worry, as if she could sense that something bad was going to happen.

He pushed away his own sudden feeling of foreboding, ruffling her hair and grinning as he buttoned up his coat. It was normal for Dolly to be worried because she'd been old enough to remember losing her ma.

"I'll be back before you know it, our Dolly. Besides, Evan Granger has known me since we were nippers. Just because he's Lord Longton's gamekeeper now doesn't mean he'll forget twenty-five years of friendship if he happens to bump into me."

He strode away into the approaching dusk of evening, whistling softly under his breath.

As Ruben walked along the familiar cobbled streets of the village, the setting sun cast a warm glow on the honey-hued cottages. The village green, with its duck pond at the centre, was surrounded by the grander houses of the local gentry, but he stuck to the back lanes where the cottages jostled together in a more haphazard fashion. Woodsmoke curled up into the still air, and the church clock tolled the hour, making him walk faster.

With a bit of luck, the snares he'd laid the night before would have worked, and he could bag some rabbits and be home before darkness fell. He might even have one to spare that he could take round the back of The Woolpack. The landlord, George Lloyd, didn't ask too many questions, and he could almost taste the hoppy flavour of the mug of foaming ale his wife, Ruby, would give him, along with a couple of coins for his trouble.

He climbed over the stile and set out across the

fields towards Oakridge Wood. Come the autumn, the air would be filled with the sound of gunshots as Lord Longton hosted shooting parties for his well-to-do friends from London, but tonight he hoped to have the woods to himself. Yellow cowslips nodded in the grass, and the first few swallows swooped low over the ground with their distinctive whistling call, but Ruben barely paid any attention to them. His head was filled with thoughts of Evan Granger, his childhood friend, and now Lord Longton's gamekeeper. Or more to the point, about Evan's wife, Stella.

"What did she have to go and tell me for?" he muttered to himself. A worried frown creased his brow, and the questions which had been keeping him awake the last few nights started nagging at him again.

He'd always had his doubts about Evan falling head over heels in love with Stella. She came from Lechford village, on the other side of the valley, and her sparkling green eyes and russet-coloured curls had set plenty of hearts aflutter back when he'd been courting Anne. But Stella had a restless way about her. She'd made no secret of the fact that she wanted more than the plodding life the country boys who vied for her attention at the midsummer fayre could promise her. That's why it was a surprise when Evan had triumphantly told Ruben he'd tamed her into agreeing to marry him.

"It'll come to no good," Anne had said darkly, in a way that implied she knew more about Stella than Evan was willing to face. "She'll break his heart, you mark my words."

But Stella had calmed down, it seemed. Evan's job as a gardener on the Minsterly Estate came with a small cottage, and she had dutifully produced a son, who they had christened Joe, two years before Dolly was born. And then, several years later, little Billy arrived, making Evan happy to prove all the naysayers wrong.

Ruben could remember Anne's happiness that their children would all grow up together, continuing the friendship from one generation to the next as was the way of their tight-knit community.

The trouble had started last Michaelmas when a travelling troupe of performers came to Middleyard. Under the silvery light of the barley moon, as the villagers gathered to celebrate the end of harvest, Stella was plucked from the crowds to sing with the performers. Her voice had soared like a nightingale's holding everyone spellbound, and Ruben had to admit to himself that she came alive in a way that he'd never seen before.

"That's the most beautiful thing I've ever heard," Ruben said as she rejoined Evan afterwards with a dreamy expression on her face. "You should join the church choir."

"Or how about doing singing lessons at the village school," Evan had suggested. "Even though Lord Longton has promoted me to be his head gamekeeper, a few extra shillings each month would be a great help."

Ruben had thought no more of it in the months that had passed since. That was until Stella had sought him out when he'd been picking the mud out of the Clydesdales' hooves after a long day of ploughing a week ago.

"Evan doesn't understand," she had whispered, looking furtively over her shoulder. "I told him after Michaelmas that I want to move away from the village and try my hand on the stage in London, but he won't agree."

Ruben had straightened up, unable to keep the shock off his face. "Go to London? What sort of work would you expect a gamekeeper to get there, Stella? And what about your two boys? Them's country lads through and through." He'd shaken his head, wondering whether she'd had a nip of gin to be talking in such a way.

Stella had tossed her coppery curls defiantly. "Who says I want Evan and the boys to come? I'd stand a better chance without them."

"Well...you certainly have a wonderful voice, Stella. And perhaps if your life had taken a different path, you could have been on the stage. But you can't just up and leave." Ruben had peered at her more closely. The colour on her cheeks was high. Perhaps she was sickening for something.

"I've been told I've got real talent," Stella continued. She eyed the muddy fields beyond the farmyard with a disdainful sniff. "I'm only telling you so that if something...changes, it won't come as too much of a surprise."

"What do you mean? Are you leaving Evan? How would you support yourself?" Ruben had heard the anxiety in his voice, but Stella airily waved his questions away.

"All in good time." She had smiled to herself. It was a look Ruben recognised from when Stella had declared she was first in love with Evan all those years ago, and he felt a shiver of misgiving.

. . .

A BARN OWL SUDDENLY GLIDED out of the trees in front of him, snatching Ruben's attention back to the present. He couldn't afford to let his concentration wander thinking about the strange conversation with Stella. Not when he had snares to check and rabbits to catch, hopefully without being seen by anyone.

Should I tell Evan? Still, the question troubling him the most insisted on popping into his head again. *Maybe nothing will come of it.* He didn't want to ruin a good friendship, and he sighed, wishing Anne was still alive. She would have known what to say. It was probably just a fanciful daydream of Stella's that Evan would chuckle about the next time they enjoyed an ale together at the pub.

Ruben managed to put his worries aside as he walked quietly through the woods.

Within an hour, he had two rabbits inside the pockets of his jacket, and only one more snare to check. The trees provided a dark canopy against the moon, which was just rising over the hill, and his spirits started to lift at the thought of being able to provide enough meat for a few hearty meals for the children over the next few days.

Suddenly his ears caught the sound of muffled

clopping, and he was surprised to see a horse trotting steadily along the track towards him.

"Stella? Where are you going?" Ruben was alarmed to see that she was riding one of Lord Longton's horses. He knew the man would be furious if he found out. "Does Evan know you're here?"

Stella glanced nervously over her shoulder, but the shadows under the trees revealed nothing. "I'm leaving him," she stated boldly. "I've met someone new...someone who believes in me."

Ruben's worst suspicions were confirmed, and his heart clenched with sadness for Evan, and the scandal Stella was about to unleash. "But what about the children? That's no way to treat your family." Ruben hurried towards the horse, hoping to grab the bridle and talk her out of it.

"You can't stop me," she cried. The echo of her voice under the trees startled a pheasant, and it clattered out of the undergrowth in front of them, making the horse rear in fright. Her scream pierced the night as she tumbled off the horse, landing in a crumpled heap on the ground.

"Stella, are you hurt?" Ruben rushed forward and hastily knelt down by her side.

"I...I think I'll be alright," she said shakily. "I

need to leave before Evan finds out. I'm riding to Gloucester, where Mr Portiscue is meeting me. We're going to take the train to London."

Stella stumbled as she tried to get to her feet, and Ruben bent down to steady her. He put his arms around her shoulders and helped her stand up. "I don't know who this Mr Portiscue is, but what you're doing is wrong," he began. He had to try and stop her, for Evan's sake and for their young boys. "Evan will be heartbroken—"

Before he could say another word, a shout went up. "Come back, Stella. You can't mean what you said about leaving us." Evan was running down the track towards them, his face dark with anger. He skidded to a halt, and his eyes glittered with desperation as he looked at his wife in Ruben's arms.

"She fell off the horse," Ruben said urgently. He stepped away from Stella, not knowing what else to say.

"And it just so happens that you were here to comfort her?" Evan snarled, turning on his friend.

"I thought she'd hurt herself. I just helped her stand up, that's all. I came hoping to catch a rabbit, Evan; it's not what you think."

Evan shook his head in disgust. "You wouldn't

be the first man she's had a dalliance with," he said, his voice dripping with sarcasm.

"It's not a dalliance," Stella said indignantly, backing away from him. "Fred Portiscue loves me, and he's going to help me become a great success on the stage in London. I told you, he's the theatrical agent for the travelling performers, and he can give me the life I deserve."

"So not only are you thinking of leaving us to chase some foolish dream of becoming a singer, but you don't care who gets hurt. Have you been cuckolding me with Ruben behind my back as well?"

"Don't be so silly," Stella scoffed. "And what if I was? At least Ruben told me I have a beautiful voice, and I should have been on the stage."

Evan rounded on Ruben, his fists clenched by his side. "What sort of friend would condone my wife leaving? It's all your fault. You encouraged her…filling her head with these ridiculous dreams."

He charged towards Ruben with his head lowered like an enraged bull, landing his fist on Ruben's jaw before he had time to move out of his way and then raining blows on his ribs in a frenzy.

"I've been trying to tell her to stay," Ruben

yelled, breaking away from Evan. He rubbed his hand over his jaw, feeling shocked that Evan was taking out his anger on him.

"You mean you knew she was thinking about running away with this...this charlatan?" Evan stumbled around in a circle, talking to himself. "What will become of us...leaving to become a singer on the stage...it's ridiculous...the shame of it...what will Lord Longton think..."

Ruben suddenly noticed that Stella had used the distraction of the fight to get back onto the horse. She gathered up the reins and cast a pitying look at Evan. "I should never have married you," she said coldly. "You and the boys will be fine. Forget all about me, Evan. Marry some mousy little village woman who's more suited to you. I don't belong with you...don't come and find me."

As she kicked her heels into the horse's flanks and galloped away, Evan turned back to Ruben. The rage and frustration of Stella's actions were distilled into pure hatred. "You knew, and you didn't tell me." The words came out like the bellow of a wounded animal, and Evan charged towards him again, knocking him to the ground.

Ruben felt a sudden crack of pain in his ribs as he landed heavily on a log hidden under the brambles. He managed to get onto his hands and knees, crawling a few yards, and then dragging himself upright again. "You can't blame me," he croaked. He could smell the iron tang of blood and tore his neckerchief off to press it to the cut on his head.

"I will always blame you, Ruben," Evan cried angrily. "You encouraged her in this folly, and now Joe and Billy will have no ma, and I have no wife." He kicked a rotten log, sending splinters flying. "You should have told me, but you didn't. I'll never forgive you for as long as I live."

Ruben blinked as his vision blurred. "We're friends," he mumbled. "You must know I would never wish any harm on you and your family." Suddenly the thought of his own four children swam into his mind. "I have to get home to Dol—" He shook his head as he struggled to articulate her name. A dull ache started to spread across his chest, and he felt bone weary. All he wanted to do was get back to the cottage and crawl into bed. He turned his back on Evan and trudged away. They would have to find a way to make it up, and he would help Evan however he could, but for now, he wanted the blessed relief of sleep.

CHAPTER 2

*D*olly stretched under the soft, worn, patchwork quilt, taking care not to wake Gloria and Amy, who shared the bed with her. She turned her head slightly and smiled to herself at the sight of Jonty's unruly hair sticking up in tufts in the other truckle bed. His mouth was slightly open, and there was a small sound in his throat with each breath as his chest rose and fell. She tentatively stuck one leg out from underneath the quilt, wondering why the room felt so cold. The bedroom she shared with her three siblings was under the sloping eaves of the roof, and usually, her father banked the fire up to keep it ticking over during the night, and the warmth would trickle through the floorboards beneath their rickety beds. Stifling a yawn, Dolly slipped out of bed to get dressed, carefully standing on the rag rug so her feet wouldn't get cold. She tugged on her woollen socks, then pulled a cotton shift over her head, followed by the plain grey dress, which had been patched so many times it had splashes of colour that made it look more cheerful. Her hair was a tumbling mass of curls, still tangled from being asleep, but she decided that brushing it could wait.

"Is it time to get up already?" Gloria opened one eye and smiled with relief as Dolly shook her head.

"You can have ten more minutes," she whispered. "Best not to disturb Amy; she could do with a bit more rest. I'll shout for you when the porridge is ready."

Dolly tiptoed down the steep stairs, avoiding the fourth step down, which always creaked. She couldn't hear any sound of movement from downstairs, so if her pa had had a late night and was still asleep, she didn't want to be responsible for waking him up. The grey early morning light filtered through the thin curtains at the kitchen window. Either the sun had not come up yet, or it was an overcast day; otherwise, there would have been a puddle of golden light on the flagstones.

Glancing at the clock on the mantle shelf, she saw that it was still early, but she didn't feel tired.

"Why did Pa let the fire go out, Bob?" Dolly smiled as her young rough-coated terrier pup jumped up from his blanket in the corner and trotted over for a fuss. They had found him abandoned in a hessian sack near the river before Christmas, and Dolly had pleaded with their pa for them to keep him.

"We'll fill the bucket with water first, shall we?" Bob wagged his tail and started prancing under her feet before rushing to the door, eager to get outside and go hunting in the garden for all the enticing smells left behind by passing foxes and badgers.

She picked up the old bucket that lived under the crooked cupboard next to the sink. It wouldn't take long to fill it up at the water pump in the back lane, and then she could get the fire going again. She would need to rake out the ashes and hope that there were still a few embers glowing underneath for the sticks of kindling to catch alight again.

"What—" Dolly gasped as she stumbled over Ruben's boots which had been left abandoned in the middle of the floor in front of his armchair.

She scratched her head, feeling puzzled, noticing the clumps of mud in their trail. *Even when Pa's been to The Woolpack, he never leaves his boots like that, and he never forgets to add more wood to the fire.* The thoughts felt disquieting. Something strange was going on, and she felt a trickle of alarm shiver down her back. The sense of heavy quietness in the cottage reminded her of the first evening after her ma had died, and she didn't like it.

She peered up the steep staircase, calling to him in an urgent whisper. "Pa...Pa, is everything alright?" She crept back up the stairs, this time turning left on the small landing into the other bedroom. She pushed the door open tentatively, expecting to see Ruben sitting up and yawning widely. But instead, he was still shrouded under the blankets. "Did you get back from the estate late, Pa?" she whispered, tiptoeing closer. "The fire's gone out, but I'll have it going again in no time, and I can bring you a mug of tea if you're feeling tired."

Behind her, Bob whined and slunk back out of the room, tail between his legs. His claws tapped sharply on the wooden treads of the stairs as he escaped.

In the half-light, Dolly wondered why the room

seemed so quiet. The oil lamp was still flickering on the dresser where her ma's tortoiseshell combs still lay with some ribbons, but there was no other sound.

She shook his shoulder, but it was cold and stiff under her small hand, and his face had a terrible grey pallor. "Pa, wake up."

Dolly knew that something was very wrong, and a sob burst from her lips as she clattered back down the stairs and ran out of the house. Her legs started trembling, and she sat on the doorstep, pulling her knees tight under her chin, not caring who saw the tears running down her face.

"Dolly? What is it, child?" The vicar's round face under his black hat loomed over the wall at the front of the garden. "What's making you so upset?"

She had always been rather afraid of the vicar because of how his black robes flapped about him in the wind, making him look like a bird of prey, but as she rubbed the tears from her eyes, she saw that his expression was kind.

"It's P...Pa," she stammered. "He's upstairs in bed, but I can't wake him up, and his face doesn't look right. The little 'uns are still in bed, and I don't know what to do."

The vicar looked alarmed and hurried up the path. "I'd better go up and see him." She felt the weight of his hand on her shoulder as he briefly squeezed it to reassure her.

Dolly stayed sitting on the doorstep as she waited. She could hear the cows mooing at Tuppley Farm as Mr Baggins called them in to be milked, and a cockerel crowed as the village slowly awakened. The rising sun caught the steeple of the village church, making it glow, which she found comforting. "Maybe Pa's just poorly," she murmured as Bob nudged her arm and curled up in the folds of her dress. She scratched his wiry fur, glad of having him next to her. "A nettle tea will make him better, surely."

A moment later, she heard the vicar's heavy tread behind her. "Your papa is with the Lord now, Dolly," he said in a grave voice. "I need to fetch Doctor Skelton. He'll check to confirm what I've told you, but I'm sure it's just a matter of formality."

Fresh tears stung Dolly's eyes, and she blinked them back hastily. "Do you mean that we are orphans now?" A violent shiver gripped her. Even at her tender age, she knew nothing good would come of being orphaned.

"I'm afraid so, child, but try not to worry about it too much. The folks of Middleyard Village like to take care of their own, so you won't be abandoned."

Dolly nodded mutely, not knowing what to say. The little cottage was all she had ever known, and she couldn't begin to imagine living anywhere else. A thought struck her. "What about the others? What should I say to them? Poor Amy's been ever so ill…I'm not sure she'll understand."

The vicar had already started walking away, but he turned back. "Get the other children up and light the fire to make breakfast. It will be an upsetting time for them, but I know your pa would have wanted you to try and continue with your day as normal." He stepped aside to let a horse and cart rumble past. "Don't let them go into his bedroom. Doctor Skelton and I need to prepare the body for the undertaker."

After a flurry of tears when Dolly explained what had happened, the younger children seemed to accept that they had lost their pa, automatically turning to Dolly to follow her lead. She had been a mother figure to them since their ma had died, so in some ways, it didn't feel very different.

"'Tis just the way of things," Dolly said with a

sigh as she helped Amy put her dress on. "Pa did his best for us, but as long as we can be together, we'll get by." Although her heart was aching, she squared her shoulders, determined to keep things as normal as possible.

"You'd better chop some more kindling for us, Jonty," she said once they were all downstairs. "The wood basket is almost empty, but mind you take care with that axe."

"I'll make the porridge," Gloria piped up. The tip of her tongue poked out in concentration as she riddled the stove and then measured oats into the pan before pouring water over the top.

"Amy, why don't you play with the pegs?" Dolly sat her under the kitchen table and placed the peg bag on her lap, glad that she was still too young to really understand what had happened.

The next minutes passed in a blur of their usual morning chores. It felt strange to Dolly that everything had changed, yet life continued on as normal. The kettle was soon whistling merrily on the trivet, and she put a pinch of tea leaves into the pot and fetched their mugs from the dresser.

Doctor Skelton was always a jovial sort of fellow, which was why Dolly found it disconcerting to see him looking so serious when he arrived with the vicar, and the two men hurried straight upstairs with barely a word of greeting.

"What are they doing, Dol?" Gloria's dark eyes scrunched with worry as she helped Amy eat her breakfast.

Jonty helped himself to more porridge, making Dolly smile. He was always hungry, it seemed, no matter how much he ate. "I'm not rightly sure," she said, bustling back and forth with mugs of tea for them. "Hush a moment, and let me listen and see what I can find out."

She tiptoed to the bottom of the stairs as the others fell quiet, hoping to overhear what the two men were discussing upstairs. Snatches of conversation drifted down to her, and she tilted her head slightly, trying to make sense of their sombre words.

"...'tis a terrible shame for a man to be taken in his prime like this," The vicar's rumbling, deep voice was just loud enough for her to hear.

"Aye, he's had a nasty bump on his head, but I doubt that's what took him." There was a pause before Doctor Skelton continued. "Thinking back, I recall that Ruben's father died young as well from a weak heart. I'm willing to bet Ruben's gone the same way, looking at the pallor on his skin. Probably not helped by being malnourished."

"Another unfortunate soul who has worked himself into an early grave...no thanks to Lord Longton's miserliness."

Dolly jumped when the floorboards creaked above her head as the men walked around the bed. Every so often, they would stop, and she hoped that they were looking after her pa.

"What's to become of the children?" Dr Skelton asked in hushed tones. "St Joseph's Workhouse, I suppose, seeing as there's four of them. Or perhaps Gloucester orphanage?"

The blood ran cold in Dolly's veins. If they were sent to the workhouse, she doubted whether Amy would survive. She had heard the rumours about the forbidden building at the end of the valley. They would be split up, and she felt panic rising in her chest at the thought of it.

"I rather foolishly promised the eldest daughter that folks in the village would take care of them," the vicar replied. The bedroom door suddenly swung open at the top of the stairs, and the vicar looked awkward as he wondered how much of the conversation she had overheard.

"Please don't send us to the workhouse, Doctor

Skelton," Dolly pleaded once the men came back to the kitchen. She glanced towards the other children, who had all stopped what they were doing, their eyes rounding in worry.

"What's a workhouse?" Gloria asked, her chin starting to tremble.

"Now then, Dolly, you shouldn't have been listening in on something which wasn't intended for your ears." Doctor Skelton looked flustered as they all stared at him.

"I was wondering…" The vicar cleared his throat in a distracted fashion. "Miss Clark is a very godly woman and a great believer in doing charitable acts." He exchanged a look with the doctor, which Dolly couldn't fathom.

"We're not a charity, sir," Dolly said firmly. Her only dealings with Miss Clark were at the Sunday service in church each week, and she had always got the impression that the woman didn't like children very much. She had a tendency to fuss over the slightest thing and glare at them if they were noisy.

"Perhaps that was a clumsy turn of phrase, but it will take a kindhearted person to want to take four of you on." The vicar surveyed them with a slight shake of his head that made Dolly want to put her arms protectively around her siblings.

"We don't need nobody's help," Jonty said stoutly. "I know how to chop wood and scare the crows off the corn. An' Dolly could go cleaning in the big house."

Doctor Skelton tutted. "High-spirited children, as well, Vicar," he muttered under his breath.

Undeterred, the vicar gave them all a strained smile. "Wait here. I'll be back with Miss Clark by lunchtime after she's finished tending to the old folks in the almshouses...such a generous woman she is. I'm sure she won't turn away in your time of need, Dolly."

"I have my rounds to do. It's a busy day for me visiting patients, but I'll stay in the village," Doctor Skelton said. He patted Dolly on top of her head, happier now that the vicar had come up with a plan. "I expect you all have chores to be getting on with?" he asked.

"Yes, Doctor Skelton." Dolly bobbed a little curtsey obediently and followed him to the door as both men left.

"Can we have a cup of hot chocolate?" Jonty asked as soon as they were alone again. "It feels strange without Pa telling us what needs doing."

Dolly took a deep breath. Part of her wanted to run and hide under the patchwork quilt again and hope it had all been a bad dream, but her siblings needed her to be strong. "We'll have a hot chocolate for a treat, and then we all need to clean the cottage until it's spotless. If Miss Clark is going to look after us, she'll want to live in a tidy house. We might not be well off, but I won't have anyone accusing us of being mucky."

CHAPTER 3

Miss Clark pulled her lace gloves off with sharp little movements and placed them in the reticule hanging over her arm. "Don't slouch like that, Jonathan." She pressed her thin lips together, and her pale blue-eyed gaze swept around the kitchen, taking everything in.

"His name's Jonty," Dolly said. She noticed Miss Clark sigh quietly with annoyance at being corrected as she looked at the threadbare fabric of the armchair, and the shrivelled potatoes and carrots on the side waiting to be cut up to add to the stew.

"Sorry, Miss Clark," Jonty muttered. He sat up straighter and then squawked and got to his feet when Dolly gave him a sharp nudge and mouthed for him to stand up politely.

"I've discussed your situation with Miss Clark, but she would like to speak to you all first before making up her mind." The vicar's Adam's apple bobbed up and down in his throat as he swallowed. Dolly couldn't help but think that he sounded a little less sure of himself than he had that morning.

"I expect you all know, I'm a very busy woman," Miss Clark said piously. She looked at Dolly with her eyebrows raised, waiting for her to nod in agreement. "My charitable works are very important to me, and I don't want to let the vicar down." She gave him a doting look, and a faint flush of pink coloured her gaunt cheeks.

"Quite right, Miss Clarke. You're a stalwart of the church; I really don't know how I would manage without you. Middleyard village has much to thank you for."

"We'll be on our best behaviour," Dolly said. She had been thinking all morning about what the woman might want to hear and was willing to say practically anything if it took away the terrifying prospect of being sent to St Joseph's Workhouse. "We're all used to doing chores, so we won't be any bother."

Miss Clark sniffed and attempted a smile. "That's what I like to hear." She strolled slowly around the kitchen and ran a finger along the dresser, turning it over and pulling a face when she saw the dust on her fingertip.

"I'm sorry...the chimney's been smoking lately, and I forgot to clean the dresser, what with finding Pa dead this morning." Dolly felt tears pricking at the back of her eyes again and gripped the edge of her apron to stop herself from crying.

"It's nothing more than I would have expected. Your mother always struck me as someone who didn't pay much heed to cleanliness." She sniffed again. "Your pa never disciplined you as much as he should have either, especially her," she added, looking pointedly at Amy.

"I don't know what you mean," Dolly bristled. "Pa raised us right, and Amy's too little to understand about being silent in church. Besides, what has a bit of dust got to do with anything? We'll polish it before you move in. At least Ma never had a bad word to say about anyone."

"Oh...no...I think you've got the wrong idea, Dolly," the vicar interjected, hastily. He had expected the children to be fawningly grateful, not answer back like this. "Miss Clark wouldn't be moving into your cottage; you would go and live with her."

"We don't want to leave our cottage," Gloria said, stamping her foot. "We like it here because it reminds us of our Ma."

"Goodness me. Beggars can't be choosers, child." Miss Clark turned to look at the vicar with a horrified expression.

"We ain't beggars," Jonty shouted.

"I can see they need to be taken in hand immediately, and I consider it my Christian duty to drum some manners into the little terrors. I'll have my work cut out, but it's not a moment too soon."

"Gloria, I don't feel very well." Amy tugged on her sister's sleeve. "Where's the bucket…I'm going to be sick."

"'S'cuse us, Miss." Jonty elbowed Miss Clark out of the way and grabbed the pail, getting back to Amy just in time to catch her wretches, which splattered all over the woman's dress. Miss Clarke stumbled backwards in horror, standing on Dolly's toes, which made her yelp with pain. In all the commotion, Bob shot out from his bed in the corner and nipped Miss Clark on her ankles.

"Get that dreadful creature off me," she shrieked, flapping her reticule at the dog and grabbing the vicar's arm. "I've never seen such an ill-behaved family in all my days, Vicar."

He handed her a clean cotton handkerchief, and she fluttered it in front of her face, which had turned scarlet with outrage. "I think they're just feeling a little overwhelmed by events," he said soothingly, patting her hand.

"But…they're so…" Miss Clark searched for the right word. "They're wild…and downright insolent. And as for that creature biting me." She shrank back against the vicar again as Bob pranced around her buttoned boots, yapping excitedly at this wonderful new game.

"He's not a creature; he's our dog," Gloria cried, swooping across the room and picking Bob up.

"I can assure you, he won't be coming with you," Miss Clark snapped, recovering her composure. "I expect he's riddled with fleas, and I don't believe in children having animals. It distracts them from their studies."

"We're not going anywhere without Bob," Dolly said defiantly. "Please, Vicar, it's not that we're ungrateful, but we love our dog, and we've already lost Ma and now Pa." She wracked her brain for a better solution to their problem. "Could we live with Doctor Skelton instead? I'd be happy to be a housemaid, and Jonty could carry on doing odd jobs for Farmer Baggins. Gloria and Amy will behave, I promise."

"As if the good doctor would want a rabble like you living with him," Miss Clark said with an incredulous splutter. "It's a preposterous idea. He's a busy man, and his wife has quite enough on her hands."

Dolly felt the fight go out of her. "Can we just stay here? I've always looked after the little 'uns. It won't be so different." She tried not to think about how they would pay the rent. She'd find a way somehow.

"No, my mind's made up. I'm willing to overlook the fact that you've been insufferably rude today, and we shall start anew." Miss Clark gave the vicar another simpering smile again. "It's my duty to raise them better than their parents did, even though it will come at a great personal sacrifice to me." She shot Dolly a chilly look, all pretence at charm gone in an instant. "You may bring one or two things from this cottage with you, but I don't like a mess, and I'll ask Farmer Baggins to deal with that wretched dog." She pulled her lace gloves on again, eyeing Bob warily.

Before Dolly could think of how to reply to

Miss Clark, there was a rat-a-tat at the door. "Hello! Anyone home?" The doorway was suddenly filled by the welcome sight of Beryl Stump, their neighbour, and Dolly felt a wave of relief. "I did hear such a commotion coming out of the house; it sounded like you were fair being murdered in your sleep Miss Clark," she said with a chuckle.

"I'm just informing the children that they'll be coming to live with me."

Dolly eyed the two women, who couldn't be more different if they tried. Where Miss Clark was angular with a permanent expression of disapproval, Beryl Stump was plump, and her brown eyes twinkled as she bustled into the room.

"How are you, ducky?" Beryl ignored Miss Clark and swept Dolly into a tight embrace. "I heard the terrible news about your pa…such a generous man, 'tis a terrible loss for you."

Dolly gulped as Beryl's kindness threatened to make her cry again. "We're alright," she replied quietly. Beryl lifted Amy and settled her on her broad hip, smacking a big kiss on her cheek, which made her giggle.

"Anyway…there's no time for this," Miss Clark said bossily. She looked at the vicar for support.

"It's time to go, Dorothy. I expect Lord Longton will want to fumigate this cottage before new tenants move in, and we should start on some studies this afternoon."

"The poor lambs only just lost their pa this morning, Miranda," Beryl said. Her generous bosom wobbled as she sighed and jiggled Amy on her hip, wiping a fraying handkerchief over the little girl's chin where a smudge of hot chocolate remained. "Why are you in such a hurry to take them away from the only home they've ever known?"

Miss Clark looked affronted. "Someone has to take them in hand. It's not as if they've had a very good upbringing so far."

"Miss Clark has offered, out of the kindness of her heart." The vicar quailed slightly as Beryl rolled her eyes.

"I'd have taken you in, Dolly, you know that," she said. "But my house is already bursting at the seams with my six children, and Sid home more since he got bronchitis."

"Exactly," Miss Clark said, shooting her rival a triumphant look. "They've got no family now, so either they come with me, or we can send them to the workhouse. I'm sure Dolly will choose wisely if she knows what's good for her."

"That's not strictly true," Beryl said. She grinned broadly and chuckled. "Ain't you all forgetting about Verity and Bert? Perhaps the children would prefer to live with their aunt…they are family, after all. And not as hoity-toity as you, Miranda, by a long way."

Dolly stared at Beryl. The day was getting stranger by the minute. "We have an aunt? But Pa never mentioned any other family."

"That's because your aunt Verity married a river rat." Miss Clark's voice was laden with scorn. "If you go and live with them, you'll be tarred with the same brush, Dolly. River rats, the lot of you. You might as well become beggars for the sort of upbringing that would be."

"We're not beggars…or r…rats." Dolly stammered. She couldn't understand why Miss Clark was being so mean about these mysterious people she'd never heard of before.

"Aye, don't listen to her," Beryl said with an amused chuckle, patting Dolly on her shoulder. "All she means is that your uncle Bert lives aboard *The River Maid*, on yonder canal."

"The River Maid?" Dolly echoed. "Did you

know about us having other relatives?" She turned to the vicar, feeling as though everything was spinning out of control. "Why have we never met them?"

"I believe there was a falling out between your ma and her sister in the past." The vicar looked flustered again. "The canal folk live by their own rules. They don't come to church, or have much to do with the villagers, which is why I never thought to mention them."

"Then we must find them," Dolly declared. "Tell me where they are, and I'll take little 'uns to meet them."

"I don't think that's a good idea," Miss Clark said. She lunged forward and grabbed Dolly's arm in a vicious grip. "You're coming with me. It's for the best otherwise, who knows what sort of ruffians you'll all turn into? You need to forget all about your aunt and uncle...dreadful canal-dwellers that they are." She shuddered as though the idea was too aweful to think about.

For a split second, Dolly was too stunned to speak, but then she screamed and tried to pull away. All it seemed to do was make Miss Clark more determined. "You can't force us to come with you...help!" She screamed again, this time even louder, and Bob snapped at Miss Clark's ankles again.

"What's going on in 'ere, then?" A shadow appeared in the doorway, accompanied by the booming voice of Constable Redfern as he burst into the cottage.

Dolly gaped up and him and stumbled backwards, landing hard on the flagstones as Miss Clark released her and folded her arms defensively.

"These children are resisting my charity, and trying to attack me, Constable. You got here just in time. I've a good mind to tell you to arrest them and throw them in jail for the night to teach them a lesson."

Constable Redfern scratched his head, looking perplexed. "I ain't here to arrest nobody. There were two people loiterin' outside, but before I could ask them who they are, I heard your caterwauling."

"Dolly?" The room suddenly became even more crowded as a small woman squeezed past the bulky frame of the constable and came rushing to Dolly's side. "It's me, Dolly...your aunt Verity... your ma's sister." Tears filled her brown eyes as she helped Dolly to stand up again. "We heard about your pa. Bless you all, our Dolly…we've come to offer our help. I just hope we're not too late."

Dolly looked up at the woman in shock, wondering how she had known to come right at that very moment. Verity's brown hair was threaded with silver at her temples and pulled into a loose bun at the nape of her neck. She wore a green cotton blouse above a long grey skirt which was dusty on the hem, topped with a peacock-blue shawl. Her face already bore the lines of age and hard work, but there was a startling likeness to her ma, which made Dolly yearn to be hugged again.

Miss Clark was suddenly galvanised into action. "Tell her, Vicar, the children are coming with me." She looked down her nose at Verity. "It's already been decided. The vicar asked for my help, not yours."

"But these children are part of our family." Verity sounded indignant and looked at the constable expecting him to agree.

"A family who never spoke to you once you married Bert Webster. I expect your sister was ashamed of you for becoming a river rat. We all know that canal folk are mostly petty thieves and criminals."

"Now, you look here—" Although Verity was

short, she drew herself up to her full height, and the two women glared at each other. "Are you going to let her get away with slandering us, Constable? She can't call us criminals, and if Anne and I fell out, it's none of her business."

Dolly's head started to spin, and tears rolled down Gloria's cheeks. "It's our Pa who died…we should be allowed to choose what happens to us."

Miss Clark's eyes gleamed greedily. She was determined to get her own way, just to prove the point. "Come here, Dolly. I won't be spoken to like this. Your aunt turned her back on your family a long time ago. If she thinks she can swan in and take you—" She reached out and grabbed Dolly's arm again.

As quick as a flash, Verity put her arm around Dolly's shoulder and tried to pull her away. "Anne and I never fell out…not really, ducky. She used to bring you to visit us on *The River Maid*, you just can't remember it because you were too young. 'Twas just a storm in a teacup, and Bert had to work on a different part of the canal for a while, which is why we haven't seen you lately."

"So you say…but you know they'll have a better life with me," Miss Clark shrieked. She tugged Dolly's arm again.

"If this doesn't stop right now…I'll be arresting the lot of you," Constable Redfern bellowed suddenly. He looked around the room and shook his head. "The undertaker hasn't even taken Mr Hinton away yet, and you're tussling over this poor little mite as though it's the summer fayre tug o' war."

"Bert and I were never blessed with children. If it's what Dolly wants, we'd like to look after them." Verity looked shamefaced. "I was terrified we'd be too late, but we came as soon as the lad from the village brought word. I don't want them to end up going to the workhouse. It wouldn't be right."

Constable Redfern mopped his brow and took a deep breath. With so many people in the room and the fire crackling in the hearth, it was getting too warm for him. He bent down and looked Dolly in the eye. "What do you want to do? It sounds as though nobody's asked you yet, but you're old enough to have an opinion, I reckon."

Dolly took Amy out of Beryl's arms and went and stood next to Gloria and Jonty. She lifted her chin as all the adults watched them, their expressions ranging from eager to perplexed. "Will you let us bring our dog, Bob?" she asked her aunt.

At the sound of his name, Bob spun in a circle,

trying to bite the end of his tail, before bouncing over to pull the laces of Jonty's boots.

Verity's expression softened at the puppy's antics. "Of course, ducky. You've all been through so much, it's the least I can do. It will be a tight squeeze on the narrowboat, but he's only little. He'll help keep the mice down, too, I shouldn't wonder."

"What about Joe and Billy," Gloria asked. "They live in the gamekeeper's cottage on the estate, and they're our best friends in the whole world," she explained to Verity.

Dolly felt a sudden pang. If they moved out of Middleyard, she might never see Joe again. She wondered why he hadn't been to the cottage. Their news was bound to have travelled around the village like wildfire, and she had a sudden longing to see his bright blue eyes and cheerful smile. Everything always felt better in Joe's company.

"They can come and visit on the boat any time we're in Thruppley," Verity reassured them. "You won't lose touch with folks from the village, don't worry."

Dolly glanced at her siblings, feeling the weight of knowing she needed to make the right decision for all of them. "Your offer was very kind, Miss

Clark, but I think Ma and Pa would have wanted us to live with Aunt Verity and Uncle Bert, even if it is on a narrowboat."

"That's all settled then," Constable Redfern said firmly before the women could start bickering again. "Are we all in agreement? Vicar?"

"Yes…that seems sensible." The vicar shot him a grateful smile, glad that someone else had been able to take responsibility for the situation. "Perhaps you could still bring the children to church sometimes," he asked Verity hopefully.

"I'm sure we will if we're not too busy with work. It's not an easy life, but we'll raise them to be honest, I can promise you that."

Dolly heaved a sigh of relief. It wasn't in her nature to be rude, and she felt a pang of guilt at Miss Clark's crestfallen expression. "It was kind of you, Miss," she said hastily. "But Pa gave Bob to us, and he's all we've got to remember him by."

"Very well." After a moment wrestling with her conscience, Miss Clark extended a bony hand and shook hands with Verity. "If you ever need help with them, you only have to ask."

"I appreciate it. And Anne would have been grateful for your offer if we couldn't have taken them in." Verity broke into a broad smile as she turned to the children. "Ready to see *The River Maid*?"

Dolly nodded, and the other children scurried away to start packing their few belongings. It was hard to believe they had lost their pa and their home, but she knew she couldn't dwell on the past. They were setting out to a new life on the canal with an aunt and uncle she never knew existed, and she only hoped it would work out for the best. Her siblings were depending on it.

CHAPTER 4

The magnolia tree in the garden of the gatekeeper's cottage at the entrance to Minsterly Grange scattered pink blossoms on the ground as a gust of wind rippled through the village.

"I hope you don't mind a bit of a walk," Bert Webster said jovially as he strode ahead of the four children, setting a brisk pace. "Verity managed to persuade one of the farmers to bring us to the village in his horse and cart when we heard your news. Perhaps if we see one passing, we'll be able to hop on to get back too, but until then, it's Shanks's pony."

"What does he mean, Dolly? I don't see a pony anywhere, other than them on the common."

Gloria whispered. She had stopped to pick some golden celandines from the hedgerow, and she ran to catch up, holding the flowers tightly in her fist.

Verity chuckled. "He just means we're walking back to the narrowboat, ducky. Don't mind Bert, you'll soon get used to his expressions. We'm boat people, you see. We've got our own little ways that them on the bank don't always understand."

"On the bank?" It was Jonty's turn to sound puzzled. He puffed slightly as he tried to keep up.

"Aye, that's what we call the folk who don't live on board their narrowboats," Verity explained patiently. "Villagers and the people who live in normal houses, although the boat is normal to us."

Dolly felt a pang of what she thought must be homesickness as they left the edge of the village and started heading over the common. She had spent her whole life in Middleyard, and even though the canal was only a few miles away, it felt almost like a betrayal to their pa to be leaving on the same day he had died.

"I expect it will all feel a bit strange for the first few days, but you'll find that boat people are friendly. Some of them have already heard you're coming to live with us. They're looking forward to meeting you." Verity's dark eyes crinkled as she gave Dolly a sympathetic smile.

"Why did Miss Clark call us rats?" Jonty asked. He pulled a face and kicked a pebble in the road.

"Because she doesn't know any better." Bert pulled his pocket knife out and cut a hazel stick from the hedge, trimming the foliage off the top, and whittling a small indentation to make it a thumb stick. He held it up next to Jonty to measure it against his height, with a small wink, and then whittled a bit more off the bottom to make it shorter, before giving it to him to use as a walking stick. "It's just a nickname some of them on the bank call us. When I was a boy, my family worked the boats on the River Severn, and we were called river rats. Now I work on the canal, it's a bit different. Some folks do call us cut-rats because the canals have been cut out of the land."

"They make it sound like something dirty or nasty," Jonty said, swinging his stick happily and sending a cloud of dandelion seeds floating away on the breeze.

Verity shrugged, but a shadow crossed her face for a moment. "People often fear those who aren't like them." She sighed and shook her head. "That's what happened when Anne and I fell out," she said slowly.

"It's all in the past now, dear," Bert said.

"I know, but I owe it to the children to explain what happened." Verity walked on in silence for a moment, as though she wanted to choose her words carefully. "There were eight years between your ma and me. When I fell in love with Bert, our parents disapproved. They thought the river folk were little more than water gypsies, always travelling, and rough and uneducated. They said I was marrying beneath myself."

Dolly shot a worried look at Bert, thinking he would find this comment hurtful, but he slipped his arm around Verity's shoulder and squeezed it comfortingly. There was nothing but affection in his eyes, and Dolly couldn't help but think that Verity was lucky to have met a man who loved her so much.

"My parents cut me off," Verity continued. "They never spoke another word to me since the day Bert and I got married. My mother had a vicious tongue, and she turned Anne against me. I used to miss her so much."

Two fat pigeons landed on the track and waddled ahead of them, flapping clumsily away again when Bob barked. "When we had the narrowboat near Middleyard, I used to try and sneak into the village to talk to her, but she believed the lies that Ma said about the boat people."

"Thankfully, all that changed once your ma had you, Dolly," Bert said cheerfully. "It broke my heart to see my Verity cut off from her family."

"Yes, once our parents had passed away, and Anne had you, she used to bring you down to the canal if she knew we were in these parts. Sadly, our work took us away from the area for a while, but I was very glad that we'd made up before little Amy was born. It was as if the falling-out never happened."

Dolly wondered why her father had never mentioned Aunt Verity and Bert.

As if reading her mind, Verity carried on talking. "Ruben never felt quite the same way…he was always suspicious of us narrowboat folk. Lord Longton and the workers on the Minsterley Estate swore blind that because we were travellers, we would go poaching on his land. Us and the Romanies are tarred with the same brush, thought to be thieves and vagabonds just because we aren't tied to one place."

Dolly raised her eyebrows at hearing this and felt she had to say something. "I'm sorry Pa felt like that."

"Don't you worry, ducky." She tapped the side of her nose and grinned. "I know when times were hard, your pa wasn't averse to helping himself to a few rabbits or the odd salmon and pheasant from Lord Longton's estate. 'Tis just the way of things. It's what us less well-off folk have to do to get by." Verity shrugged again, happy to forgive and forget whatever slights they had been dealt in the past.

Bert whistled a jaunty tune and tipped his hat at a farmer riding by, heading back to the village. "Funnily enough, we saw your pa a couple of months ago. For the first time in years, we had a nice chat. I think he would have been happy to know that you were coming to live with us on *The River Maid*."

"That's why we came as soon as we heard the news," Verity said. She lifted Amy onto her broad hip, seeing that the little girl was getting tired. "I couldn't have slept at night knowing you weren't with family. It wouldn't have been right."

As they trudged along the dusty road, Dolly's spirits started to lift. She could see the canal ahead sparkling in the sun with the cottages of Thruppley village beyond, and knew that whatever the future held, living with their aunt and uncle was infinitely better than being dumped in the workhouse.

THE WATERWAY WAS busy with people bustling along the towpath and the general hubbub of a tight-knit community where folks lived and worked in close proximity to each other. Tall reeds rippled in the breeze on the water's edge in places, and two swans swam serenely along, paying no heed to the boats.

"Home sweet home." Bert's voice was tinged with pride as he gestured towards a colourful narrowboat moored on the edge of the canal. "There's her name, see." *The River Maid* was painted in swirling script on the bow of the boat.

"It reminds me of the gypsy wagons that camp on the common," Dolly said as they stood in a row on towpath. Her hand flew to her mouth as she realised her aunt might take that as an insult. "I mean…it's so pretty the way you've decorated the outside." The narrowboat was painted green, with red trim, but it was the decorative art on the sides of the cabin which really captured her imagination. Intricate floral designs of roses with ivy wound through gave the boat a jaunty air, and there were tubs of herbs on the roof, along with several shirts pegged on a piece of rope strung between two poles to dry.

Verity smiled. "Some of our traditions are similar to the Romanies. Just because we'm on the water moving from place to place doesn't mean we don't like things kept nice."

"Your aunt likes everything spick and span," Bert said, leaning over and smacking a kiss on Verity's cheek that made her blush. "There ain't much room, so you'll soon learn that we have to make every inch of space count."

"I promise we'll do our best to keep out from under your feet," Dolly said hastily. The other three children nodded solemnly when she looked at them with her eyebrows raised.

"We'll all rub along just fine, I know it." Verity picked up her skirts and raised them slightly to jump nimbly onto the narrowboat. "Are you coming aboard then? Welcome to *The River Maid*." Her eyes misted with emotion as she held out her hand to help Amy onto the small deck area.

"You must stay close to one of us, Amy," Dolly said. "If we're living on the water now, it's important." She shot her aunt a worried look, thinking they might regret the decision. "She's not blind. She can see hazy shapes, and she's a clever little 'un. Pa said she was blessed with a goodly amount of common sense to make up for not being as clear-sighted as the rest of us."

"I don't doubt it," Bert said. He was already busying himself further along the boat, rearranging his cargo. "We used to have a horse pulling the boat that lost an eye. I swear Prince could hear ten times better than any other horse." He nodded towards Bob who was standing with his paws on the side, wagging as some coots glided past under the opposite bank. "Don't worry about the dog either. He'll learn to keep himself safe soon enough. One dunking in the canal will be enough, you'll see."

"I reckon we all deserve a nice cup of tea, and then we'll get you settled in," Verity said once all the children were aboard. "Jonty, go up front with Bert, and he'll show you where we keep the coal for the stove. We likes it ticking over all the time, to keep the damp out, so how about that could be your job?"

Jonty grabbed the coal scuttle and hurried away

to where Bert was stacking crates, eager to show that he could be trusted.

"Down the steps, and this is the cabin," Verity continued as she opened two small wooden doors and beckoned them in.

Dolly took the opportunity to have a proper look at their new home as they went down into the belly of the narrowboat, and was surprised that it seemed more spacious than she'd imagined from when they were standing on the towpath. There was a small wooden table with bench seats around it, a black pot belly stove in the corner, with all the pots and pans neatly hanging from hooks or stowed on shelves. A copper kettle was on the side, resting on a trivet, and there was a cupboard for crockery and food. The long narrow windows had patchwork curtains sewn from offcuts, tied back with braided ribbons during the day. Everywhere was a myriad of rainbow colours, with cleverly designed storage under the benches, and hooks to hold all manner of items, from Bert's ale mug to oil lamps, and a milk jug.

"We sleep through there," Verity said, jerking her head towards a thick curtain which partitioned off the main living area from what lay beyond.

"You'll have to share, but you'll be as snug as bugs in a rug."

"We're used to that," Dolly said quickly.

"It won't be forever. I expect young Jonty might want to follow his pa and get a job on the land one day, and there's plenty of chances for you girls to get housemaid's work in the future, but for now, this is your home…for as long as you want it to be."

A MOMENT LATER, Verity reached for the hessian sack Bert had been carrying and pulled out two skinned rabbits, with a twinkle in her eye. "These will do nicely for a stew tonight," she said.

"Did you…were those at the cottage?" Dolly asked.

"It was the first thing I spotted when we came to find you, ducky. What with all the commotion with Miss Clark, I don't think anyone else had noticed them, but we thought it would be prudent to take them away. We don't want Lord Longton or the constable finding any reasons to paint your pa's name in a bad light for poaching, God rest his soul."

"Tell me what I can do to help," Dolly said. She

was grateful that her aunt had removed the evidence of her pa's poaching expedition, and in a practical sense, folk like them could not afford to waste good meat, especially now that Verity had four more mouths to feed.

No sooner had Dolly started scrubbing potatoes and chopping turnips to make the stew than a cheerful shout came from the towpath.

"Cooee, Verity," a voice called. Two buttoned boots and the bottom of a brown skirt appeared in the doorway of the cabin, followed a moment later by the rosy-cheeked face of a plump woman as she bent to peer inside. "I brought you a twist of mint humbugs for the little 'uns and some milk for your tea because you were away when the farmer's lad brought his produce round on the cart."

"Come in," Verity said. The woman squeezed down the steps into the cabin, needing no further encouragement. "This is our friend Sadie Pendle, she lives on the narrowboats with her husband, Isaiah."

Sadie handed each of the children a humbug and beamed as she looked at the three girls sitting politely at the table. "Well, Verity, aren't they the dearest children, and they certainly share the same looks as you and Anne. 'Tis the dark hair and dimples. I'd have picked 'em out as your kin, that's for sure."

Dolly and Gloria exchanged smiles. It was nice to know they belonged.

"It's a terrible shame that you lost your pa," Sadie said to Dolly, enclosing her hand and squeezing it to show her sympathy. She pulled a handkerchief out of her sleeve and brushed it across her eyes as they misted over. "Verity and Bert always longed for a family of their own…if you ain't already realised it, you won't find two more kindhearted people than them to take care of you."

Verity reached for another mug and poured everyone a cup of tea, adding a splash of milk to each one before handing them around. "I never imagined I would be blessed to have children."

"Aye, but that gypsy fortune teller said your life would change, didn't she." Sadie blew on her tea and took a noisy slurp that made Gloria giggle.

"Yes, she did." Verity turned her hands over and looked at her lined palms, as though she could still hear the words spoken when the Romanies had pitched their wagons on the common last summer. "I didn't for one minute think it would be this. I wish it hadn't been in such tragic circumstances, but I'm certainly thankful that we happened to be at this end of the canal when we got the news. The vicar was all for giving the children to Miss Clark, one of the most hoity-toity ladies from the village." She wheezed with sudden laughter. "You should have seen the poor woman's face when I told her we were more than happy to welcome the little 'uns into our family."

"I can imagine what she said." Sadie's plump face creased with a broad grin that revealed several gaps in her teeth. She tilted her nose into the air and clutched her hands together, adopting an outraged voice. "'You're going to take them to live on the canal? What a dreadful fate for them'." Her generous bosom quivered with mirth as she laughed until tears came to her eyes, and she pulled her handkerchief out again to wipe them away. "Don't worry, Dolly, you'll soon learn not to let people's rude comments about us narrowboat folk bother you."

"We're not bothered," Dolly said stoutly. "We were already used to people looking down on us after Ma died. Some of the ladies in the village used to gossip about Pa not looking after us properly by himself, but it wasn't true. Even if it wasn't the tidiest cottage, Pa did his best."

"You'll fit right in," Sadie said, taking another slurp of tea. "I can see they've got your high-spirited nature as well, Verity." She turned to Gloria and Amy. "What do you think of Jester, then?"

Gloria wedged her thumb into her mouth and burrowed against Dolly, feeling suddenly shy. "I don't know who Jester is," she whispered.

"I clean forgot to tell you about him," Verity said. "He's our horse. He's grazing on the common land over yonder at the moment. You'll all meet him in the morning when Bert gets him back in harness. We've got a delivery to make to Selsley Mill tomorrow, so you'll see exactly how we work."

"You're off again already, are you?" Sadie looked disappointed. "Ah well, 'tis a busy time of year for us all. Hopefully, we might see you at Frampton Basin in a week or so, and I'll get to spend some more time with the little 'uns and see how they're faring." She leaned over and patted Gloria's hand. "If you like sewing, I've got some nice scraps of material. My daughter left the boat to marry a cobbler, and they live over the shop. I miss having children around."

Gloria brightened immediately. "Dolly's been teaching me how to sew buttons on. Maybe I could learn how to do mending to help Aunt Verity earn some pennies."

As soon as she had finished her tea, Dolly got back to making the stew, letting the conversation between the two women wash over her. There would be a lot to get used to in this new way of life, but if Sadie's visit was anything to go by, it seemed that the narrowboat dwellers were friendly. *We need that,* she thought. Her heart squeezed with sympathy for her younger siblings. *Will they even remember Pa and our old life in Middleyard Village when they grow up?* She felt the weight of responsibility to try and keep the memories alive for them, but also to make sure they weren't a burden to Verity and Bert.

"Good luck to you all," Sadie said a little while later as she gathered her shawl around her shoulders and clambered back up the steps. "You'm one of us now, remember that. We look out for each other, especially when them on the bank make things hard for us."

Her parting words left Dolly feeling comforted as another wave of homesickness swept over her. There was a sense of belonging, and she knew that whatever happened in the future, it could never be taken away from them.

"Are you two coming in to have a bite of dinner?" Verity called, sticking her head out of the cabin. "Your uncle will talk until it's dark unless I make him come inside," she said with a chuckle, shaking her head. "Get some spoons out of the drawer under the cupboard, Gloria."

Dolly peeked through the window and was surprised to see that it was getting dark already. The day had flown by, and it already felt as though the cottage was from a lifetime ago. Bert was deep in conversation with a man a little way along the towpath, and she felt a shiver of foreboding as Bert suddenly turned and ran back towards *The River Maid*, his face creased with worry.

"What's wrong?" Verity paused in the midst of putting out the plates, as Bert clattered down the steps.

"It's true, love." Bert shook his head, absent-mindedly taking his cap off and running a hand through his thatch of greying hair. "Isaiah just told me. They're closing Nailsbridge Mill…the owners are saying there's no call for the cloth they make down 'ere no more, not now they're making it cheaper in Yorkshire."

Verity gulped and sat down heavily before collecting herself a moment later. "We'll be alright," she said brightly. "We've been through worse, and now we've got the little 'uns to consider; something better is bound to come up."

A vision of the forbidding tall walls of the workhouse swam into her mind, and Dolly hoped her Aunt Verity was right.

CHAPTER 5

The mist was just rising off the canal as Dolly came outside the following morning. She had slept surprisingly well, given everything that had happened, and wondered if it was because of the faint movement of the narrowboat on the water. A trio of ducks quacked as they paddled past, making her smile, followed moments later by an indignant gaggle of coots who skittered across the water after being disturbed by a stealthy tabby cat stalking the canal bank.

"You go and help Bert get Jester in his harness, and Gloria can help me make breakfast." Verity handed Dolly her shawl. "Pop that around your shoulders until the sun comes up properly; I don't want you catching a chill."

"Can I go with them?" Jonty asked eagerly. He shoved his feet into his worn leather boots, ignoring the fact that his big toe was poking out of a hole in his socks, and hastily pulled his shirt over his head at the same time.

"The more, the merrier," Bert said good-naturedly. He stood up and put his jacket on, before gulping down his first mug of tea of the day. He patted his stomach and winked at Jonty. "A man can't do a proper day's work on an empty stomach. By the time we get back from the common with Jester, your aunt will have bacon and eggs frying for us. I always say she's the best cook on the canal, and my mouth is already watering thinking about those tasty rashers sizzling in the pan with a thick slice of bread."

"Get along with you, Bert Webster; never mind sweet-talking me as though we're still courting," Verity said, laughing. She shooed the children up the steps and out into the crisp morning air.

Bert grabbed a couple of old carrots from the shelf where Verity kept her vegetables and stuffed them in his coat pocket on their way out. "Jester is partial to a carrot or an apple. You can each give him one, which will help him trust you. He's a good horse, but most animals are a bit wary of strangers, which is what you are to him at the moment."

"How old is Jester?" Jonty asked as they headed off over the common land where anyone was allowed to graze their animals. Bob was already scurrying ahead of them, darting from one tuft of grass to the next to sniff out delights which only he was aware of.

"He's going on six years old now," Bert said. "I had Prince for years, and he was a loyal horse who served us well, but one winter, we had terrible weather." Bert shook his head at the memory. "Rain? I thought it would never stop, but it was cold with it, as well. We rugged him up, but it wasn't any good. The chill got into him, and then in the blink of an eye, it turned into colic. It was a sad time. I walked him for hours, and we dosed him with Verity's herbal tincture, but there was nothing we could do to save him."

"Poor Prince. Did you have to stop work until you could get a new horse?" Dolly lengthened her stride to try and keep up with her uncle. There was so much to learn, and she wanted to know it all.

"Aye, it's funny you should mention that. By rights, Prince should have lasted a good few more years, so I wasn't especially looking for a new one.

But the previous summer, when the gypsies were in town, one of them offered me Jester for a good price. He was still a bit green, and the fellow didn't have time to give him the training he needed before they were moving on again. It turned out to be a stroke of good fortune for me. Prince helped Jester settle with us... they do learn from each other, you see. I got him trained up in no time and planned to sell him on again to make a few shillings, but then...well, we lost Prince, and so it became Jester's time to be our horse."

"Do you have to ride him when he's pulling the narrowboat?" Dolly asked, thinking of the ragged boys she had seen larking around on sturdy ponies on their way here the day before. She hoped her uncle didn't mind all the questions.

Bert chuckled, and his eyes twinkled with amusement. "I'm getting on a bit to be riding a horse these days, but there's no reason why you shouldn't be able to in the future when he's not working. But as for pulling *The River Maid*, no, we just walk with him on the towpath. It's a bit like how your pa would have walked with the horses ploughing the land," he added, trying to explain it in a way they would understand. "There he is. That's our boy, Jester, near the silver birch trees."

Dolly felt a surge of pleasure as she saw the stocky piebald horse that Bert had pointed to. He was dozing in the morning sun, with one back leg relaxed under his barrel-shaped belly. His lower legs and hooves were covered in long hair, the characteristic feathers of his working breed, and his mane was kept long and natural, not hogged. "He's not as big as I thought he would be."

"Remember, he has to fit under the canal bridges," Bert explained patiently. "I know your pa was more used to working with Shire horses and Clydesdales, but our horses need to be smaller. Mind you, they work hard, and Jester is as strong as any horse you'll meet. You'll see that some folk use mules or a pair of donkeys, but this lad suits us just fine." His voice was full of affection as he slipped a head collar onto Jester and scratched the horse's neck as he woke up.

Jonty hung back, and Dolly could tell that he was nervous. "Don't worry," she said, "he looks kind. Don't be afraid, Jonty."

Bert gave them a carrot each. "Hold your hand flat and let him sniff you, and take the carrot from you."

"I...I don't think I want to," Jonty blurted out. "I think I'd rather help you with other jobs on the narrowboat, loading and unloading," he muttered, handing the carrot to Dolly.

"There's no rush," Bert said easily. "If you're not used to working with horses, 'tis best to take your time." He tousled Jonty's hair and gave him a warm smile. "You'll make friends with Jester all in good time, and until then, you're going to be a great help to me with all the other little jobs on the boat."

Dolly took a deep breath and held her hand out as her uncle had instructed. At first, Jester was hesitant, sniffing suspiciously. "Nice to meet you, Jester," she murmured gently. "There's a good boy," she added, stepping slightly closer. His whiskery pink nose, as soft as suede, tickled the palm of her hand as he daintily took the carrot and crunched it, with a small groan of delight. "You liked that, did you?" Without hesitating, she stepped a little closer and stroked the side of his neck, before resting her cheek against him, breathing in the sweet horsey smell of his coat. Jester snickered and huffed noisily in her ear before sniffing her apron, looking for another carrot. Dolly had never been allowed to go near the mighty horses at Lord Longton's estate where their pa had worked, but standing with Jester, she had never felt happier.

"I can see you have a way with animals," Bert

said, looking at her thoughtfully. "You're a natural if ever I've seen one. It usually takes Jester a while to get used to strangers. I ain't never seen him take to someone as quickly as he's taken to you, Dolly."

Dolly felt a warm glow in her chest at her uncle's words. "I'm glad," she said. She squeezed Jonty's shoulder, not wanting him to feel left out. "If Jonty can help you on the boat, and I can help with Jester, we'll be happy to know that we are contributing to say thank you for taking us in."

"Never you mind about needing to keep thanking me and Verity," Bert said. His voice cracked with emotion. "You poor little mites have been through more than enough, and it's our pleasure to look after you." He cleared his throat and handed the lead rein to Dolly. "We need to walk him back to *The River Maid* now and get him in the harness. Are you ready for a lesson in how to do that?"

Dolly nodded, and the three of them set off back towards the narrowboat. She noticed several other children watching them and felt a burst of pure happiness, knowing she had found something she seemed to be good at in a most unexpected way, as Jester clopped sedately behind her.

Within an hour, Jester was happily back in his

harness, and Dolly's mind was whirling with everything new that she had learnt. She had helped Bert lift the padded collar over Jester's head so it sat comfortably around his shoulders, and then they had attached the traces from the collar to the single tow rope, which, in turn, was attached to the narrowboat's towing mast. A set of wooden rollers, called bobbins, were fitted on the trace ropes to prevent chafing on Jester's flanks, as well as a spreader bar to keep the ropes apart, so they wouldn't press against Jester and cause any discomfort.

"You'll see that some horses wear blinkers to stop them from being distracted or frightened by something they see out of the corner of their eyes, but we don't use those with Jester," Bert explained. "He's a steady sort of horse, not given to spooking. And the last thing we'll do before we set off is check his feet." He handed Dolly a hoof pick and showed her how to run her hand down Jester's leg and gently tug his feathers for him to obligingly lift his foot so she could pick out any stones which might make him lame.

"We'll see you soon," Sadie called from the towpath as they set off after breakfast. "Looks like you found your calling in life," she added, watching

Dolly with an admiring glance as she walked proudly next to Jester.

Dolly gave her a jaunty wave and fell into step next to Bert, ready with a stream of questions to try and learn everything she could about the narrowboat way of life.

"I've been carrying coal for these last few years," Bert explained. "We take it to the unloading yard at Selsley Mill; it's one of many of the mills in the valleys around here that weave broadcloth for the fancy gentlemen's suits and the scarlet wool broadcloth for military uniforms. But it's smaller than Nailsbridge, the one I mentioned last night."

Dolly wondered whether she dared ask her uncle about what had troubled him so much the night before. She chewed her lip for a moment and then decided that if she was going to be as helpful as she could, it would be best to know. "Are you sure they might close the mill? What will you have as your cargo instead?"

Bert plucked a long piece of grass from the hedgerow and stuck it in the corner of his mouth, taking a while to answer. "Isaiah and I have heard many rumours these last few months. The times are a-changing, you see, Dolly. All these newfangled inventions, nipping at our heels, and changing our way of life. The Great Western Railway line will be coming to these parts soon, and from what I've heard, the cloth mills in Yorkshire are using steam-driven machinery to produce twice as much cloth in half the time." His shoulders lifted in a small shrug, but Dolly could tell he was troubled. "Some men call it progress, but I ain't so sure," he muttered.

"I hope you're not worrying too much," Verity called from behind them on the stern of the boat. She was standing with her hands on her broad hips, and their conversation must have drifted back to her.

Bert lifted his hand in acknowledgement and shot her a guilty smile. "Just telling her how it is," he replied.

The next few hours flew by, and Dolly enjoyed the way that everyone they met on the canal called out a cheery greeting or stopped for a chat. It seemed that the boating community was abuzz with gossip about the rumour that Nailsbridge Mill was potentially closing.

"Now it's time for your second lesson of the day," Bert said cheerfully as they came to a halt behind another narrowboat. "Your Aunt Verity will teach you what we do at the locks. You're too small to do it by yourself for now, but you may as well learn."

As if summoned by his words, Verity suddenly bustled towards them along the towpath, with Jonty a couple of steps behind her. "You're doing a grand job with Jester," she said.

While they waited for the boat in front of them to get through the lock, Verity took the opportunity to give Dolly and Bert some ham sandwiched between two doorsteps of bread with a scrape of butter to eat. Dolly was quickly discovering that living on the canal meant that the day was governed by the rhythms of not only nature, so they could make the most of the daylight hours, but also needed to fit in with what the other boat owners were doing, and taking turns to get through the locks, which were dotted along the canal. Meals and rests fitted around all of that, but still, it felt like a pleasant way of life, even though she wasn't naive enough to realise that it would be tough during the winter.

"What do you think will happen when yonder mill stop producing cloth?" a wizened old man asked them as he hobbled from the narrowboat waiting behind them. He gave Dolly a toothless smile and accepted a piece of fruit cake from

Verity. "Could be it's Nailsbridge first, and then the rest of them. Once one closes, who's to say what might happen?"

"I can't see them letting a building like Nailsbridge go to ruin, can you?" Bert said. He looked gloomy as he bit into his sandwich and pushed his cap to the back of his head, a gesture which Dolly had come to learn meant that he was thinking.

"What do you think you'll do, Arthur?" Verity asked. "Will you try and get work taking a different load somewhere else?"

The old man shook his head. "Ain't much call for someone my age to be leaping into something new," he said philosophically. "My Prudence has been hankering for us to leave the canal life behind since our son went to work in Bristol docks. I reckon we might sell *The Skylark* and go live with him and his wife." He raised his eyebrows, looking between Dolly and Verity. "All the hard work is worthwhile if you have someone coming along behind you to take over, but you know as well as me, this is a hard life if it's only to line the pockets of them as would be our masters."

Before Dolly had a chance to listen to any more of the conversation, Verity had already beckoned for her to help her get through the lock. Snatches of the conversation between the old man and Bert drifted towards her between the clanging of metal and shouts of other boatmen.

"...what about carrying crates of vegetables from the market down to the city? The more folks who come and live here to get away from the bad air in London...that might be something?" Arthur said.

"...got to think of the children now...there wouldn't be enough money in that for a family of six," Bert replied in a low voice, not meant for Dolly's ears.

"Are you ready, Dolly? Follow my lead." Verity pushed her sleeves up and gave her a nod once the boat in front of them had gone. "We need to take the windlass and put it into the lock spindle," she said, brandishing what looked to Dolly's untrained eye like some sort of metal handle. "Come and stand with me, and you can wind it…it ain't too hard once you get the knack."

Dolly placed her smaller hands within Verity's calloused ones and gripped the handle, leaning into it with all her strength, and straining against the stubborn mechanism. Slowly the metal teeth turned, and the wooden lock gates creaked open, revealing the yawning chamber beyond them.

"Put your back into it." There was a snigger of laughter from nearby, and Dolly was startled to see two young men lounging nearby, watching her efforts with amused expressions. Their fashionable frock coats told her they were well-to-do, and she wondered why they weren't at work.

"Pay them no heed," Verity muttered. "They'm just nosey parkers with nothing better to do." She hurried away and took up her place at the narrowboat's tiller again, guiding the boat into the lock with practised ease while Bert continued to talk to the other canal folk. Stopping at the locks was a time to catch up on business, and Dolly could see that Verity was more than capable of taking care of their progress meanwhile.

"Now we let the water into the lock chamber," Verity said, jumping out of the boat again.

"Why do we need to do that?" Dolly followed her to the sluice paddle and helped her open it, marvelling as Verity explained that the water would raise the narrowboat so that they could go up the small hill ahead of them.

"Look at them, Horace. Scurrying around like water rats, don't you say?" One of the men had pushed himself off the nearby footbridge and strolled towards them, examining Dolly with a cold-eyed gaze as if she was an outlandish creature with no feelings of her own. He twirled his silver-topped cane and came closer, still talking to his friend. "This is why there's still so much drunkenness and petty pilfering around these parts. People like these have no morals, you know." His clipped tone marked him out as well-educated.

Dolly bristled at his comment. "That's not true," she said, spinning around to glare at him. "My aunt and uncle are kindhearted, hard-working people."

"Hush, love," Verity whispered, pulling her back. "It's best to leave the folk on the bank alone. We'll be on our way shortly and probably never see them again."

The man gave a bark of laughter. "We've got a feisty one here, Horace. Thinks she can talk back to us."

"We should be on our way, Dominic," the one further away said. He grimaced slightly, as though he was uncomfortable with the way the conversation was turning.

Dolly looked at Verity, who gave a small shake of her head. She stood in silence, as the narrowboat seemed to miraculously rise up on the water in front of her eyes, stealing a glance at the two men every now and again.

"How interesting," Dominic said. He was staring into the back of the narrowboat, watching Amy who was fumbling with old cotton bobbins in Verity's sewing basket under Gloria's watchful eye. "It seems the child is blind perhaps…yet they keep her penned on the boat like a hobbled goat."

Verity was already leaning against the balance beam at the lock's exit as the water slowly guided the boat onwards, and in the rush of the water, she didn't hear the hurtful words. But Dolly couldn't bite her tongue for a moment longer. Not when someone was being mean about little Amy.

"She's not a goat, you horrible man," she said scornfully, lifting her chin in defiance. "That's Amy, my little sister, and we put the rope around her waist for a few days while she learns where everything is because she can't see very well and she doesn't know how to swim."

"Exactly. You're keeping her like a hobbled animal," Dominic said with a disdainful curl of his lip. He wagged his finger. "People like her are a burden, she should have been—"

"What?" Dolly cried, cutting across his words. She wanted to make sure that Amy wouldn't hear whatever despicable thing he was about to utter. Tears pricked the back of her eyes, and she blinked them back. "Don't you dare say what should happen to our Amy. It's none of your business." She strode off, feeling her cheeks burning with anger and shame.

Why do people pick on us? What harm has Amy ever done to him? The indignant questions pounded through her head, making it ache. Now she understood what Verity and Sadie had meant when they said people made terrible assumptions about the narrowboat people, just because they lived a different way of life. It seemed so unfair, but she knew she would have to get used to it.

"Ready for the next stretch?" Verity called cheerfully, unaware of the exchange. She hopped back onto the narrowboat and took up her place at the tiller again. "Come on, Bert, time's getting on."

Bert waved goodbye to his companion and ambled ahead, happy for Dolly to lead Jester now that they had got past the lock.

"Come on, boy," she said softly. She stroked the horse's neck, feeling her anger drain away again. "What do they know? We're happy, and we have a roof over our heads." The sun glinted off the water, and she reached down to pick a primrose flower, threading it through the top button of her dress and smiling again as the towpath meandered past some watermeadows with pied wagtails hopping from one tuft of grass to the next catching flies.

A sudden pounding of feet behind her caught her attention, and her heart sank as she saw it was the man called Horace running after her. "I suppose you've come to have another go at us, have you?" she said curtly.

"No…quite the opposite." He took his hat off and gave her a small bow. His blue eyes looked hesitant, and the breeze lifted his non-descript brown hair. Dolly realised he was not as old as she'd thought, probably about eighteen, or thereabouts. "I'm Horace Smallwood, and you must forgive us. My brother, Dominic, has aspirations to become a social reformer in Parliament when he's older. He likes to observe those who aren't as privileged as us, and sometimes he speaks his mind too frankly without appreciating that it might hurt people's feelings."

Dolly regarded him coolly. The apology had taken her by surprise, but she didn't want him to know that. "I see. Perhaps he could start by understanding that we're just doing our best to earn a crust for an honest day's work."

"Of course. It's admirable that so many of you squeeze into such a small space…and that you work with this horse at such a young age." Horace stumbled backwards in alarm as Jester suddenly nuzzled his pocket for a treat, making Dolly chuckle.

"Don't mind Jester," she said. "You probably smell of food, even in that fancy frock coat."

"We just came from a rather good coffee shop, and I must confess to eating a hearty bowl of vegetable soup for my lunch."

"That's probably it," Dolly said. She spied another lock in the distance and saw Bert giving her a questioning look. "I need to get on now," she said.

"Perhaps I could walk with you again one day?" Horace looked worried as Bert suddenly turned and started walking back towards them. "I'd like to know more about your way of life. Papa owns one of the mills, and I've often wondered what it must be like on the narrowboats."

Dolly shrugged, thinking he was just being polite to make up for their earlier rudeness. "I'm new to this, but Aunt Verity says we go up and down this stretch regularly. You can walk with us if you like. Maybe bring some food with you next time, 'tis hungry work doing this," she added with a grin.

Horace threw back his head and laughed. "Touché. I'll keep a look out for when you're next on this part of the canal, and happily pay you in food if you don't mind talking to me. What's your name, by the way?"

"Dolly. Dolly Hinton," she said. "But all you have to do is look out for *The River Maid*." She watched as he loped away, not sure whether she had made a friend or not. Her aunt had said they shouldn't mingle with folk on the bank, but there was something about Horace that seemed kind-hearted, unlike his brother. He hadn't needed to run after a girl her age to apologise, yet he had, and it had felt genuine. And if he was willing to bring them food in exchange for learning more about the narrowboat people, it would help Verity, she hoped.

CHAPTER 6

"I was expecting you an hour ago," Mr Tebbett, the foreman of the yard at Selsley Mill, glowered at them from the bank, where he was standing with his arms folded.

Bert pushed his cap back on his head and gave the man an apologetic nod of acknowledgement. "Sorry, there was a problem at one of the locks earlier this morning. The lockkeeper said that ruffians from down Bristol way have been hanging around causing trouble. They damaged the lock spindle, and it took him a while to mend it."

Mr Tebbett sniffed disparagingly. "If there was trouble, it was more likely to be from folk travelling through. Maybe even one of the narrowboat owners? There always seems to be something you lot are falling out about."

Dolly gave him a sharp look. She was about to ask why he thought they were the problem until she saw Bert's good-natured shrug. A month had passed since she and her siblings had come to live on *The River Maid*, and she still took her cue from her uncle on how to deal with the people they did business with.

"Well, we're here now. Best we get on and unload this coal for you, eh, Mr Tebbett? Do you want it in the usual place?"

Tebbett paced back and forth, looking flustered. "Just put it over there for now," he said, pointing towards a storage shed. "Mr Farringay is in high dudgeon today, thanks to losing out on an important contract. Those mills in Yorkshire have a lot to answer for…we'll all be out of business if it carries on like this."

"It's troubling times, indeed," Bert replied. Although it was nothing unusual for the mill owner to be in a bad mood. "How is Mrs Tebbett doing?"

The foreman's expression softened for a moment. "She's got her hands full, what with just having our seventh child. That's why all this talk of the mill closing is the last thing I want. Seven hungry mouths to feed...I can't afford to be sent packing. I've worked here since I was a lad, and it's the only thing I know." He stuck his hands in his pockets, looking morose as he glanced back at the large building behind him. There was a constant rumble of machinery from the weaving shed where rows of women and children toiled over the looms, and smoke belched from the tall chimney beyond, carried down the valley by the breeze.

"Come on, Jonty, look lively." Dolly grabbed her brother, and they hurried away to get the handcart to help Bert unload the coal from *The River Maid*. Hearing Mr Tebbett's comments, she realised that it wasn't just the narrowboat families who were worrying about the rumours of mills closing and the new railway lines taking away their business. It seemed to her that the owners of the mills could make whatever changes they liked, but they would never have to worry about where the next meal was coming from.

"Move that horse of yours along a bit further," Mr Tebbett snapped a few minutes later, just as Jester's head was starting to droop as he dozed under the hot sun. "The next narrowboat needs to come alongside, so you can both unload at the same time."

Bert looked troubled at his request. "It ain't helpful you trying to rush us," he said sharply. "You know we always unload one at a time. Why change something that's always worked just fine?"

The foreman harrumphed, ignoring Bert. "Did you hear me, girl? Get that beast moved further along the towpath." He glared at Dolly, nodding his head in Jester's direction. "Mr Farringay said we need to be more efficient here in the yard. He reckons there's too much time being spent with you narrowboat people dawdling and chatting when you should be working harder."

"Come on, Jester," Dolly said, keeping her voice calm. Mr Tebbett's flustered demeanour was creating an air of tension in the yard, and she could tell that the horse didn't like it by the way he twitched his ears backwards and fidgeted uneasily in his harness. "Just a few more paces, boy. That's it." She stroked his neck and encouraged him to move forward, talking to him all the time in a soothing way before slipping him a piece of apple.

"Next one! Move up closer," Mr Tebbett yelled, stomping back along the path to the narrowboat waiting behind them. "Are you even awake, Mr

Dimmock, or have you been supping too much ale?" He rapped on the roof of the cabin, rolling his eyes and muttering under his breath that Mr Farringay was probably watching and he'd be out of a job by teatime at this rate.

Dolly tried not to stare but risked a quick peek as she manoeuvred the handcart closer to the canal edge. She hadn't seen the boat behind them before, and the paint was peeling off its hull, giving it a rather neglected air.

"You were late with our payment last time." The owner of the boat jumped onto the towpath. His face was red, and he jutted his jaw forward with a mulish expression, striding up to the foreman and jabbing him in the chest with a grubby finger. "It's all very well you telling us to work faster, but why should we listen to you when that skinflint Farringay is trying to cut our pay at every opportunity?"

A mousey-looking woman holding a wailing baby to her chest emerged from the cabin and scurried to join her husband. "Don't make trouble, Fred," she pleaded, trying to pull him away. "It's not Mr Tebbett's fault. He has to do as he's told, just like the rest of us."

Dolly didn't recognise the family and

wondered if they were some of the incomers who had been trickling into the area from down near Bristol, as Verity had mentioned recently. Their boat was pulled by a scruffy chestnut horse in need of a good brush. It pranced nervously near *The River Maid* as Mr Tebbett threw his hands up in the air at Fred Dimmock's accusations.

"You'll have to take that up with Mr Farringay," he said, seething with irritation. "Just hurry up and unload your coal; I don't have time for all these shenanigans."

"Never mind worrying about them," Bert said quietly to Jonty, who was watching the scene unfold. "Let's get our load off, and we can be on our way again."

Jonty huffed and puffed with exertion as he dragged the sacks of coal to the edge of the narrowboat with Dolly's help. They had a good rhythm going, with Bert heaving them out onto the towpath and then lifting them onto the handcart. It was a warm day, and sweat trickled down Bert's brow, carving lines in the coal dust which had settled on his skin.

"Run, Davey...'afore he grabs us!" There was a sudden commotion on the other side of the yard, and two young boys clad in ragged clothes burst out of the door on the side of the weaving room.

"Oi! Come back 'ere, you little toerags!" A man ran after them, heavy-footed, with a face as red as a beetroot, and Dolly recognised him as the manager of the mill, Mr Watson. "Stop them, Mr Tebbett!" he yelled. "They've been stealing from the master's office, if you please."

Tebbett spun around and tried to head the two boys off, but they were too quick for him, weaving and darting in opposite directions, so he didn't know which way to turn.

"You ain't going to catch us," the smaller of the two boys cried. "Besides, we're only taking what's rightfully ours."

"Your pay was docked for being lazy," Mr Watson roared indignantly. "You both deserve a clip around the ear and being taken to jail to think about mending your thieving ways." He lunged towards one of the boys, determined to stop him, but before he could manage to get a proper grip on his arm, the lad wriggled free again and sprinted towards where Dolly was standing.

"Out of my way!" he cried. His eyes were wide with fright because he knew that if he was caught, he'd be carted off by the constable in no time.

"Catch him, Bert!" Tebbett shouted. "He's as slippery as a fish, but he ain't going to get away with this."

Bert made a half-hearted attempt, holding his arms wide, but yet again, the two boys confounded everyone by suddenly changing direction again and running towards the narrowboat behind *The River Maid*.

"Lookout, you're frightening the horse." Dolly watched with horror as the mill manager's flapping arms, and angry shouts suddenly spooked Fred's horse. The animal whinnied and reared, its eyes rolling with terror. "Whoah there, boy," she said, torn between trying to grab its reins and staying calm in the hope that it would settle again.

"Don't let those boys get away, whatever you do," Watson shouted even louder. He grabbed a handful of coal and threw it at the nearest boy, hoping to knock him over.

"Stop it," Dolly cried. It was too late. The horse reared again and then bolted forward, thundering into Bert and knocking him flying.

"Sorry, mister, we truly are," the boys shouted, pausing for a split second. They sprang onto Fred Dimmock's narrowboat, bounded across the cabin roof, and then there was a splash as they jumped into the canal and swam across as quickly as they could, emerging on the opposite bank and vanishing into the long grass.

"Bert, are you alright?" Verity picked up her skirts and jumped off *The River Maid*, rushing towards where he was lying groaning on the floor. The horse was still prancing nervously nearby until Dolly and Fred managed to lead him away.

"'Tis my own silly fault…I didn't…get out of the way fast enough…he landed on me good an' proper," Bert gasped. He tried to sit up, but the blood drained from his face, and he collapsed back onto the ground, his mouth twisting in pain.

"Oh, Bert, I thought for one terrible minute you were dead." Verity knelt down next to him. "Don't try and get up, my love. Just lie there and catch your breath." She whipped her shawl off and bundled it up to make a pillow for his head.

"I don't think I can walk." Bert tried to lift his head again and groaned. "Perhaps it's just a sprain, and I'll be alright shortly." He sounded hopeful, but his face fell when he saw Verity shaking her head.

Dolly's stomach roiled with nausea as she saw the peculiar angle of Bert's foot in his boot. It was twisted unnaturally to one side, and she could tell from Verity's expression that his injury was serious.

"Please send for Dr Skelton, Mr Tebbett," she said firmly, scrambling to her feet again. "I'm worried he's broken some bones, and he needs the right help for it."

"If I see them boys again..." Mr Watson was still looking angrily across the canal, scarcely glancing at Bert.

"Never mind that," Verity snapped. "I know us narrowboat folk don't mean anything to you, but my Bert is in agony. You shouldn't have chased the boys; anyone could see that horse was spooked."

"I'll be alright," Bert said, managing to push himself up into a sitting position. He shot Verity a weak smile, not wanting to get on the wrong side of the men who paid them. "It's nobody's fault, just an accident. I'm sure Doctor Skelton will have me right as rain again in no time."

"I ain't so sure." Tebbett looked queasy as he gazed down at Bert's mangled foot, before coughing as he caught the manager's eye. "I suppose that'll be you and *The River Maid* out of work for a while." It was a statement, not a question. "We'll have to tell one of the other men to take on your deliveries instead, we can't be without the coal for the mill, and every load counts."

Dolly saw the worry on Verity's face and rushed forward. "No," she said firmly. "We'll carry on and bring your coal, just as normal. The other narrowboat owners will help us, so please carry on giving us the work we need."

"Aye, Mr Tebbett," Fred said, coming to join her. "My wife and I will help these good folks unload this cargo, so they can be paid." He lifted his grubby cap and gave Verity and Dolly a nod. "I'm sorry my horse caused this."

Verity pursed her lips but then nodded her thanks back in return. "We look after our own," she said, turning back towards Mr Tebbett and the mill manager. "As Dolly said, we'll team up with one of the other families until Bert is back on his feet again. We'll carry on bringing your coal as though nothing has happened, so you be sure that Mr Farringay pays us accordingly."

"I suppose I have to take your word for it," Mr Watson said curtly. His gaze travelled over Dolly and then Gloria and Amy, who were sitting quietly on the boat deck, keeping out of the way. "I'm still shocked that those two boys stole money from Mr Farringay. If anyone was going to be light-fingered, I thought it would have been one of you narrowboat urchins."

Dolly put her hands on her hips, ready to answer back, but then remembered they needed to be on the man's good side in case Mr Tebbett decided it would be easier to allocate their work elsewhere. She bobbed her head, swallowing the retort that was on the tip of her tongue. "You can rest assured we're not thieves, Sir. And we'll do our very best to keep the deliveries coming as though nothing had happened."

The mill manager was already walking away, preoccupied with how he was going to break the news that two boys he was meant to be in charge of had pilfered money from Mr Farringay's heavy mahogany desk when they should have been keeping the loom fed with bobbins of wool. He threw Dolly a parting look, which was still laced with suspicion. "Be sure you do," he griped. He couldn't resist one parting sneer. "I'm fed up with all the problems people like you cause."

CHAPTER 7

Dolly waved to Doctor Skelton as he clambered off his horse and hitched it on the side of the towpath. A week had passed since the accident, and *The River Maid* was moored up in Thruppley village. She turned her face upwards for a moment, enjoying the early morning sunshine. It was market day in the village, and she could hear the cries of the costermongers jostling for the best spots in the cobbled square, already eager to sell their wares.

"I thought I'd call in and see how Bert is doing," the doctor said. He lifted his hat and dabbed a handkerchief on his forehead before reaching across to hand Dolly the black leather bag which contained the tools of his trade. "It's been a long night. First, I had to visit Ruby at The Woolpack, because her youngest child is suffering from whooping cough, and then I got called out to help Mrs Charles, the baker's wife in Thruppley, who has a terrible case of gout, not to mention her niece, who gets an attack of the vapours at the slightest provocation."

Verity appeared in the cabin doorway and smiled broadly. "Come aboard and join us for a cup of tea and some breakfast, Doctor."

Dolly held out her hand to steady him as he stepped onto the narrowboat. She was so accustomed to jumping from the bank to the boat's deck herself now that she forgot how people found it alarming stepping off the bank. "Gloria, take Amy to play on the towpath for a little while. It will be too much of a squash on board otherwise." She ushered the two younger girls out of the cabin and wondered what else she could do to help.

"Bert is feeling better, but he still hasn't been able to stand up properly yet," Verity said in a low voice. "Not being able to do anything is getting him down. He hates feeling this helpless, especially when he's worked every day since he was a boy."

Doctor Skelton squeezed through the doorway and into the cabin, unclipping his bag and pulling out a new bottle of laudanum. "I'll leave this for you, Mrs Webster."

"I don't need to take any more of that stuff," Bert called from behind the curtain. "I'm sure if you can make me some sort of splint, I'll be able to get up again with a crutch. Verity might have to cut my boot open to be able to get it on my foot, but I can't just lay around here when there's work to be done."

Verity attempted a smile, but the two furrows between her eyebrows gave away her true feelings. She was worried; it was clear to see. None of their friends were on this stretch of the canal at the moment, and they had already lost a week's pay. She had been buying vegetables that were past their best from the farmer's lad to try and stretch their meals further, but they needed to start earning proper money again if they were to survive.

"You'll have to let me be the judge of that," Doctor Skelton said firmly. He leaned over Bert's leg and gently pressed his fingers against the swollen purple skin, feeling his way carefully around his ankle and foot. "Does this hurt?" He applied a tiny bit of pressure against the bottom of the foot.

In spite of his protestations that he was on the mend, Bert yelped in pain. "Steady on, Doctor," he gasped. Beads of sweat appeared on his brow, and his lips were clamped together in a thin line. "If I could just get my leg down off this bed," he grunted.

Dolly could see Bert trying to sit up with his fists clenched tightly as he tried to move his leg, only to fall back on the bed with a sigh of frustration. His face had turned an alarming shade of grey, and his breath came in ragged gasps.

"Has he been trying to do this since I saw you at Selsey Mill last week?" The doctor straightened up and gave Verity a firm look. "I thought I told you he had to have complete bed rest. I suspect he has broken some bones in his ankle, but it's hard for me to tell while everything is still swollen. He needs to keep his leg raised so the swelling can go down."

"He can be a stubborn sort of man when the mood takes him." Verity rested her hand gently on Bert's shoulder and smiled down at him, to show that she meant no malice by her words. "It's hard for a narrowboat owner to see the other boats going past and stay lying here, knowing there's nothing he can do about it. He has been trying to get up, in spite of me telling him that you said he was to rest."

Dolly poured a mug of tea and added two rashers of bacon to the frying pan. They barely had any bacon left, but she knew her aunt would be too proud to tell the doctor this. She hoped that perhaps Doctor Skelton would accept the breakfast in lieu of payment, especially when she saw him take an appreciative sniff as the smell of the sizzling meat wafted through the boat.

"I know it's hard, but trust me, if you can bear to rest now, I promise that your foot will get better faster in the long run. Take the laudanum drops to manage the pain, keep your foot up, and I'm confident that the bones will heal."

"Alright, Doctor." Bert looked resigned to his fate. "If that's what I have to do. Are you sure I can't just—"

The doctor held up his hand, giving Bert a rueful smile. "You're very lucky that the skin wasn't broken, but there is a lot of bruising. In fact, it could have been a lot worse. You might have a limp, but with a horse that size landing on you, it's a small price to pay."

"Cooee, Verity. Cooee Dolly...are you there?" Sadie's greeting drifted into the cabin

"Oh, thank goodness, Sadie," Dolly said, looking up to see their friend. "We've been wondering when you and Isaiah might get back to Thruppley. Did you hear? A horse at Selsley Mill spooked and landed on Bert. He's broken his foot...leastways, that's what Doctor Skelton thinks."

"Gracious me, we only went down to Frampton Basin to collect a load of sand, and all this has happened since then," Sadie exclaimed. The curls peeking out from under her bonnet bobbed with alarm as she came aboard.

"I'm so glad to see you," Verity said. A look of relief crept into her eyes, replacing the gnawing worry which had been there since the accident. She turned back towards Doctor Skelton. "We'll be alright now; I know Sadie and Isaiah will be happy to help so that Bert can rest and get better properly."

"You make sure he does," Doctor Skelton said again. "I know you depend on him, which is why I insist he has to do what I say." His eyes lit up as Dolly handed him the bacon, folded between a thick slice of bread, with the bacon fat drizzled over the top. "I'll have this and be on my way," he said, giving Dolly a smile.

"How much do we owe you for the visit?" Verity

reached for the tin on the top shelf where they kept a few coins for emergencies.

"A bacon sandwich and a mug of tea should just about cover it," the doctor mumbled around his mouthful. "I was passing anyway."

"Bless you, Doctor. You're a good man."

Doctor Skelton hastily gulped down the final mouthful of bread and drank his tea standing up. His eyes twinkled as he saw Gloria and Amy playing on the towpath. "I see the little ones have settled well into life on the canal," he said, "and you too, Dolly. And it looks like Jonty's being a helpful boy as well."

"We love it here," Dolly said. She thought about how close they had come to being handed over to Miss Clark and tried to imagine what it would have been like to live in her quiet, tidy house, where no noise or mess would have been tolerated. "Aunt Verity and Uncle Bert are the kindest family we could have wished for."

"I'm glad it worked out well. It can't be easy being orphaned so young, but you keep making the best of things, Dolly and you'll go far. Now… I'd better be on my way."

"So, what can we do to help you?" Sadie asked

once the doctor had left. "Just say the word, and we'll happily do it."

The colour had returned to Bert's face now that he had had a cup of tea with two drops of laudanum in it. Verity plumped up the pillows behind his back so he could sit up and join in the conversation.

"I trust Dolly completely to do everything that's needed with Jester," he said slowly. "But the problem is loading and unloading the coal. Jonty does his best, bless the boy, but he's still only a young 'un, and it's too heavy for him. And I don't want Verity struggling with it either, even though I know she would if she thought I wasn't looking."

"I should think not," Sadie said with a chuckle. "That's what friends are for, isn't it? We'll work in tandem. Isaiah was just saying he fancied working up this end of the canal for a couple of months anyway, instead of going back down towards Bristol. This stretch is nicest during the summer, so it suits us nicely to stay here."

"Are you sure?" Verity asked. "The money's better down Bristol way."

"Never surer of anything," Sadie said, giving Verity's hand a quick squeeze of sympathy. She nudged Dolly and pulled a twist of humbugs out of her apron pocket. "These are for you and the little 'uns. And while we're working together, I'm going to start teaching Gloria some proper dressmaking, like I promised. The few times she's been helping me with some sewing, I can see she has an aptitude for it, even at her young age."

"Sadie is as good as any of the dressmakers in the village," Verity told Dolly. "She's too modest to say so, of course. It will be good for Gloria to learn from her. I'd suggest it for you too, but I know your heart's set on working with Jester instead."

"Thank you, Sadie." Dolly felt a wave of gratitude at how kind-hearted their new friends were. If Gloria could learn a skill like that, it would give her a better chance of employment when she was older, which would be one less thing to worry about. She knew that Jonty would always be able to find work on the land, but it was harder for the womenfolk on the narrowboats to get proper jobs.

"What would we do without you?" Bert said. He smiled to himself as the laudanum started to take effect, making him sleepy. "It was a great blessing when Dolly and the little ones became part of our family. And a double blessing to have friends like you and Isaiah."

"That's all sorted then," Verity said. She pulled

the curtain across to give Bert a chance to rest. "We'll pick up another load of coal tomorrow and head off towards Selsley Mill again, shall we?"

Sadie nodded. "I need to go into the village to stock up on supplies from the market, but that sounds like a good plan. It will give our horse a chance to rest for the day, and then we'll be ready to go again in the morning."

"I'm going to take Jester onto the common to graze for a few hours if that's alright?" Dolly stood up and tidied the mugs away.

"Of course, ducky," Verity replied. "We'll be busy again starting from tomorrow, which will make Bert happy. You and the little 'uns make the most of having a day off today so that we're all fresh in the morning." She reached for the tin again and pulled out a couple of coins, handing them to Dolly. "How about you buy some fresh milk and eggs from Farmer Latham's lad if he's on the common with his cart? As long as I know we're getting paid again next week, we can have a hearty dinner tonight. I think we all deserve it after the week we've had."

CHAPTER 8

Dolly unhitched Jester and called for Gloria and Amy to join her.

"Can we ride on his back?" Amy asked, skipping along the towpath with Bob at her heels. She had a daisy chain around her narrow shoulders, wearing it like a necklace, while Gloria was bent over, watching a blue dragonfly flitting through the reeds with fascination.

"I don't see why not. Jester is used to you now; just make sure you hold on tightly to his mane." She paused for a moment to watch Jonty, who was sweeping up small pieces of coal on the front deck of the narrowboat. "Do you want to come with us?"

Jonty tipped his cap to the back of his head and wiped his brow, which made Dolly smile. He had picked up Bert's habit without even realising it. "No, I'm going to get on with this to help Uncle Bert. I want it nice and tidy so that horrible Mr Tebbett can't find anything to complain about next time we're down at Selsley Mill."

"I love Jester," Amy said happily a moment later. She sat proudly with her little legs gripping onto the horse's broad back, with Gloria sitting behind her, holding her tightly around her waist. Her fingers wound through the coarse hair of Jester's mane, and she clicked her tongue against her teeth, the way she had seen Dolly do countless times. "Walk on, there's a good boy."

Jester's feathered hooves clopped steadily along the path which led to the common, sending up small puffs of dust in their wake. It had been dry for the last two weeks, and the ground was baked hard, but there was still good rough grazing to be had on the common, which was all Dolly was concerned about. It was fortunate that they could feed him without any cost during the summer. It would be a different matter in the winter, though. Bert had told her that they would need to buy hay and increase his rations of oats to get through the long cold months, which was why it was all the more important for them to get as much work as possible, even while Bert was laid up.

"Is Uncle Bert going to get better? He's not going to—" Gloria left the sentence hanging, as she looked down at Dolly from Jester's back. Her fine, dark eyebrows were drawn into a frown of worry, and Dolly was struck with the thought that perhaps her younger siblings thought they might lose their uncle, the same way they had already lost Ma and Pa. To their innocent minds, they had already experienced too many people dying, and she could have kicked herself for not guessing Gloria would be scared.

"He definitely is," Dolly said brightly. "Doctor Skelton was very reassuring, but we have to do everything we can to help him rest."

Gloria nodded solemnly, and the look of worry eased. "I'm going to ask Sadie if I can sew something for Uncle Bert to make him feel better."

Two buzzards wheeled overhead, riding the warm air with nothing more than the occasional flap of their wings to keep them circling higher and higher in the blue sky. Gloria tilted her head backwards to watch them with a smile on her face.

"I think Uncle Bert would like that very much." Dolly was grateful that there was always something on the canal or the surrounding countryside to catch their attention and that her sisters had readily accepted her promise that Uncle Bert would be fine. Once they had arrived at their usual spot, she opened her arms to catch Amy and then Gloria as they slid off Jester's back with a giggle. "We'll tie him up here and then walk back. Aunt Verity wants us to buy some milk and eggs, but I need to make sure Jester is secure first."

She attached the long rope they used, which would give him the freedom to graze without wandering off too far. There were already numerous sturdy horses dotted all along the common, doing the very same thing, which she was used to seeing now, thanks to Bert putting her straight. "'Tis our right to graze on this public land, and thankfully, people respect that, and we don't have to worry about anyone stealing our horse," Bert had told her the first time he had shown her how to tether Jester safely.

"Look, there's Joe and Billy." Gloria ran ahead of her over the undulating hillocks on the common and pointed excitedly towards the spinney of trees near where the common met the canal a little way further along from where they moored *The River Maid*.

"So it is," Dolly said. "I wonder what they're doing down in Thruppley." Even though it was only a couple of months ago that they had left Middleyard, it came as something of a shock to see people from their old life. Dolly felt a surge of happiness as she saw Joe's familiar tousled blonde hair, and she quickened her pace, eager to speak to them.

"Joe, it's really nice to see you." Her heart lifted as he broke into a wide smile. His twinkling blue eyes above a snub nose, with a smattering of freckles across his cheeks, were exactly as she remembered, and she realised with a pang that she had missed her friend who she had known all her life.

"Remember what Pa told us," Billy said in a low voice, giving Dolly a strange look. There were four years between the two boys. Joe was twelve, two years older than Dolly, and little Billy was eight. "We should go back to the canal and fetch Pa," he said more urgently, jabbing Joe with his elbow and jerking his head towards one of the narrowboats beyond them. Joe's smile faltered.

"How are you, Billy?" Gloria ran towards him and threw her arms around his waist, closely followed by Amy, who adored the two boys. "We've missed you so much, but we're proper narrowboat people now. We've got so much to tell you…Uncle Bert has broken his ankle, Sadie is teaching me to sew so I can become a dressmaker one day…and our Dolly looks after Jester over there. Uncle Bert says she can charm any horse she meets…" She chattered on brightly, oblivious to the way Billy's expression had hardened.

"Is…is everything alright?" Dolly asked Joe hesitantly. There had never been any awkwardness between them before, but it was as if the boys didn't want to be seen with them. She wondered whether it was because he thought she had forgotten about them and her old life. "We've been so busy working on the narrowboat to help my aunt and uncle that we haven't had a chance to come back to Middleyard since Pa's funeral." She gave him another smile, feeling suddenly shy. "We missed you, though. I've told Aunt Verity all about you."

A flash of something like guilt crossed Joe's face. "I'm sorry your pa died," he said gruffly. He put his hands in his pockets and dug the heel of his boot into the dirt. "I don't suppose you've heard… our ma has left."

"Left? What do you mean?" Dolly stepped closer

THE NARROWBOAT ORPHANS

to pat his arm, but Joe turned away coldly.

Before Dolly had the chance to ask anything else, an angry shout split the air. "Get away from those Hinton children!"

Dolly couldn't hide the shock on her face when she realised it was Evan Granger. He was walking briskly away from Arthur and Prudence's narrowboat, *The Skylark*, as though he had just finished a conversation with them. Two spots of colour stained his cheeks, and he scowled at Dolly. The venom in his expression made her stumble backwards.

"Don't talk to them, Joe and Billy; what did I tell you." He gripped both boys' arms and yanked them away, not caring that in doing so, he knocked Amy over, sending her sprawling face-first into the dust.

"Wh...what are you doing, Mr Granger?" Dolly stammered. "It's alright, lovey, he didn't mean to hurt you." She helped Amy up and brushed away the tears rolling down the little girl's cheeks with the corner of her apron, before looking up at her pa's oldest friend. Surely he would apologise for such a heartless act?

But if anything, he looked even angrier. His fists clenched at his side and he stepped towards her as though he wanted to make sure he had her full attention. "Your pa, Ruben, is the cause of all our troubles," he hissed. "I've lost everything because of him, so you needn't think you can come running up to my boys as though nothing has happened. Our families might have been friends in the past, but we're not now."

Dolly felt as though she'd been slapped, and her mouth gaped open. For a moment, she couldn't even speak. "But...I... I don't understand." Dolly gave Joe a searching look, but he wouldn't meet her eyes. "What did we do wrong?"

"I'm scared," Amy sobbed. She and Gloria scurried behind Dolly, clutching onto her skirt, scarcely daring to peek around her to see what was happening and why the man who had used to visit their cottage to call for their Pa to go to The Woolpack was behaving so strangely.

"Hush now." Dolly put her hand on Amy's shoulder and squeezed it. "You were Pa's friend," she said, turning back to Mr Granger. "Why are you being so mean? Isn't it enough that we had to bury our pa and now we're orphans?"

Evan's lip curled with scorn. "You hear that, boys? She says I was Ruben's friend." He laughed bitterly, without a shred of humour and shook his head. "Friends? I rue the day I ever met your pa, Dolly Hinton. Everything bad that's happened to us is his fault, and he's not even here anymore to make amends." He turned on his heel abruptly and stomped away. "Don't let me catch you speaking to them again, Joe," he yelled over his shoulder as a parting comment.

Joe sighed. "Come on, Billy, we'd better do as Pa says."

Shock gripped Dolly, and she started to tremble as Joe and Billy walked away. What had they done to deserve such a tirade from Mr Granger? *Why does he hate our Pa so much?* It didn't make sense. The last time she had seen Joe and Billy before their pa died, everything had been normal between them. They had played in the stream, looking for frogspawn, but now Joe would barely even look at her. The thought of parting on such bad terms felt like a shard of ice in her heart, filling her with a fresh sense of loss.

"Why was he so horrible to us?" Amy sobbed. More tears started rolling down her cheeks, splashing onto the front of her dress, and Dolly scooped her up into a hug trying to make it better, even though she had no answers. The truth was, she felt like crying as well. "Billy is my friend, and he doesn't like me anymore. What did I do wrong?" Amy hung her head, sounding bereft.

Dolly stood up again, suddenly determined to speak her mind. Even if her pa had fallen out with Mr Granger, it wasn't fair to take it out on them. "Stay here with Amy," she said to Gloria. She picked up her skirts and ran after Joe. Just as she came around the corner in the path she spotted the jauntily painted cart that Farmer Latham's son, Wilf, brought to the canal several times a week to sell their wares to the narrowboat families. She had all but forgotten she was meant to be buying milk and eggs.

"...I think there's summat wrong with the back wheel on your cart," Billy was saying, beckoning Wilf to walk around and have a look.

As quick as a flash, Dolly saw Joe's hand snake out as he snatched a loaf of bread from the bottom of the pile where it wouldn't be noticed and stuff it under his jacket. By the time Wilf got back, assuring Billy the wheel was fine, Joe had already sauntered away, whistling innocently.

"Joe! I saw what you just did. Put it back," she whispered, skidding to a halt next to him. "Do you know what might happen if the constable finds out you've been thieving? Did you forget about Percy

Higgs getting transported to Australia for stealing a cabbage?"

Joe grabbed her arm and bundled her further away from the cart before stopping and looking at her with an expression that was hard to read. "I don't have any choice. Not since Ma left. Pa isn't coping well, and I need to make sure that Billy doesn't go hungry."

"You only had to ask, and we would have helped you," Dolly said, feeling exasperated. "Aunt Verity is kind. She'll give anyone a meal rather than see them struggle, even though we haven't got much to spare." She placed her hand on his arm, wishing that everything could go back to normal. He was her oldest friend, but he seemed determined to forget that.

"We don't need help from the likes of you," he muttered, shaking her hand off. "Pa said your father encouraged Ma to leave us. She got an idea in her head to make her fortune on the stage in London and went off with some fancy man. Never gave us a second thought." His voice cracked with emotion, and he coughed to cover it up.

"I'm sorry." Her heart went out to him, and she racked her brains for a way to make it better, even though she still didn't understand why they were blaming her pa. "Why don't you come and visit us on *The River Maid* soon? It would be nice for you to meet my aunt and uncle."

For a tantalising moment, Joe's blue eyes brightened at her invitation, and she thought she had got through to him. But as Billy strolled over to join them again, Joe's mouth pinched into a thin line, and he tucked the loaf of bread more firmly under his jacket. "If you tell anyone about this, you'll be sorry," he whispered, leaning forward so only Dolly would hear.

"Come on, Joe," Billy said, grabbing his brother's sleeve. "We can't keep Pa waiting, or he'll be in a bad mood."

Joe jerked his head. "Go on ahead, I'll catch you up." He paused for a beat while Billy hurried away before turning back to Dolly. "We can't see you again," he said firmly. "That's just the way it has to be. Pa won't allow it, so we have to put the past behind us. It was just a silly childhood friendship, anyway," he added with an air of finality.

Dolly blinked back the hot tears that pricked at the back of her eyes. She would not let him know how much his words had hurt her. "Well, I wish you good luck, Joe. I hope one day we can be friends again in the future."

He shook his head. "It won't happen. Pa's right; it's for the best. Goodbye, Dolly."

He strode away, and Dolly noticed that even in the few months they had been apart, his shoulders had started to broaden, hinting at the young man he would soon become. She felt an ache of sadness in her heart. When she had been Gloria's age, she had hoped that she and Joe might get married and live in a little cottage in Middleyard village, just like her parents had. But now she realised it was just a foolish dream. She lifted her chin and took a deep breath. *My happiness doesn't depend on Joe Granger. Besides, we have new friends now on the canal.* The thought felt hollow, but she pushed the feeling away. Joe and his family might have turned against them, but it only made her more determined to make a success of their life on the narrowboat and to do everything they could to help Aunt Verity and Uncle Bert.

She walked away, trying to ignore the ache in her heart. At the last minute, she risked another look over her shoulder and was surprised to see that Joe had looked back towards her as well. Their eyes met, but there was no smile from Joe. Just a hint of regret. Or perhaps she had imagined it.

CHAPTER 9

The West Country - Four Years Later

JOE CUT the mouldy crust off his slice of bread and tipped his fried egg onto what was left before folding it in half to make a rough sandwich. With a flick of his wrist, the crust went sailing over the edge of *The Skylark*, landing in the water with a plop. He watched as two moorhens came scooting across the canal to peck eagerly at the unexpected treat. The tea had been brewing for several minutes, so he filled his battered tin mug and sat next to the narrowboat's tiller. It was a rare opportunity to enjoy some peace and quiet before his pa woke up and the workday began in earnest. The sun was just rising over the mellow rooftops of Thruppley village, and the morning was still milky and opaque, with a light mist hanging over the canal. Even though it was early summer, the nights were still chilly, but it promised to be another fine day once the mist had burnt off.

"Morning, Mr Jefferies," he mumbled around his mouthful of food, raising his hand to the stooped gentleman walking along the towpath. The man stared for a moment, then gave the briefest of nods in acknowledgement of Joe's greeting.

Four years we've been working on the canal...four years since we left Middleyard. Joe sighed and gulped down a mouthful of tea. He couldn't help but think that after that length of time, the man could have been friendlier.

"But that's the trouble, folks still think of us like outsiders, don't they, Patch?" The young black and white collie sitting at his feet nudged her nose against Joe's elbow. She wasn't scrounging for food, but Joe picked off a small piece of his bread and gave it to her anyway. She was a loyal dog, and he needed all the friends he could get.

The sound of clumping footsteps and clattering dishes told him that Billy had woken up. Sure enough, a moment later, his younger brother's tousled head appeared through the cabin doorway. Even though Billy was twelve years old now and Joe was almost sixteen, he still felt a wave of protectiveness towards his younger brother. He supposed it was because when their ma had left four years ago, and it felt as though their life had fallen apart, he had vowed to do whatever he could to look after the confused little boy, even though his own heart had ached with loss as well.

"Did you finish that last piece of bread?" Billy asked. He yawned widely and rubbed his knuckles over his eyes, struggling to wake up. "My stomach's been rumbling something terrible for the last hour." He eyed the remnants of Joe's sandwich hungrily.

"If you'd bothered to look in the bread bin, you'd see I left you a decent slice. And I cooked you the last egg; it's here in the frying pan." Joe rolled his eyes affectionately at the transformation in Billy's expression as his face lit up, and he turned back into the cabin to put a scrape of butter on his bread. The boy seemed to be permanently hungry, but at least he was easy to please.

A moment later, Billy came to join him on the outside deck, stretching his legs out and crossing his feet at the ankles as he devoured his breakfast. His socks were threadbare, with more holes than wool, and in desperate need of being darned, but Joe knew he would have to make do for the time being. Money was tight for them, and because it was just the two of them with their father on the narrowboat, luxuries like mended clothes and homely meals were something they had to do without. There were no such feminine touches in their lives since their ma had abandoned them, he thought, with a familiar sense of regret.

"I don't suppose Pa will be up for a while," Billy said. A drop of yellow egg yolk dripped onto the front of his shirt, and he absentmindedly scooped it up with his finger and licked it clean.

"Not after seeing the latest write-up of Ma in the newspaper yesterday," Joe said. He pulled a scrap of paper from his pocket and smoothed it open on his knee to read again in a low voice. It was a couple of weeks old, but at least it gave them some clue about what she was doing.

"Songbird Stella Delights With Her New Show

Stella Granger once again held the audience of The Adelphi Theatre entranced with her latest performance. After a successful tour in Paris, Stella has garnered a legion of new admirers.

"We are fortunate to have her back in London again," her manager, Mr Fred Portiscue, said at the close of last night's performance. "With a voice like hers, she deserves worldwide recognition, and I shall be doing my best to ensure she gets it."

Ever since being discovered at a country fair by Mr Portiscue four years ago, and whisked away from her humble beginnings, Miss Granger has been delighting theatre-goers with her remarkable repertoire of songs. She is in great demand, both on stage and at the soirées of London's high society.

It is rumoured that she and her manager will marry at the end of the season and spend the winter travelling in Italy to protect her voice from the perils of the city's cold weather."

"Why do you keep them when you know they only make Pa unhappy?" Billy glanced between the newspaper cutting and his brother, with a shadow of hurt in his eyes.

Joe hesitated for a moment, trying to find the right words. It was true that every time Ruben saw an article about his wife's success, it sent him into a black mood for weeks, accompanied by turning to the bottle for solace. He promised Joe and Billy each time that it wouldn't happen again, but they had given up expecting him to stick to those promises.

"She's still our ma, Billy," Joe said slightly defensively.

Billy pulled a face. "Is she, though?" His expression was guarded as he took a swig of tea. "What sort of woman just walks away from her family to follow her fancy man to London?"

"Maybe she wasn't happy being with Pa," Joe said quietly. He knew that Billy was only parroting what their father said. But Billy didn't remember the way his parents had argued. Joe didn't want to spell it out to him and ruin whatever happy childhood memories he still had from when they used to live on the Minsterley Estate before their father had been sacked.

Billy shrugged as though it was of no concern, but Joe knew their ma's betrayal still cut deep. It did for all of them, even after four years. They had gone from being a normal family, and Evan proud of his new job as Lord Longton's gamekeeper, to being abandoned by their ma and thrown off the estate in a matter of a few months. Joe didn't really understand why their pa had been sacked. He could still remember the whispered rumours.

He's frittered away that good job...turned poacher

himself, so I heard...got caught selling Lord Longton's salmon and pheasants just to buy more ale to drown his sorrows. I was shocked to hear it, I can tell you...

Well, can you blame him, with that flibbertigibbet Stella running away with a man of the theatre...it's them boys as will suffer...poor little things...

Joe thought they would be homeless and out on the street as the gamekeeper's cottage came with the job, as part of the Minsterley Estate. But much to their surprise, Evan had announced he had saved up a bit of money, and he was buying *The Skylark* from Arthur and Prudence. "It's goin' cheap, Joe," he'd said, with a beery hiccup, his eyes unfocussed from the ale and imagining better days ahead. "I bumped into Arthur a few weeks ago, and he told me he's getting too old to carry on working on the canal. Never mind Lord Longton and his hoity-toity ways...it'll be a narrowboat life on the canal for us from now on, my boy! And just you wait and see how I'll do a better job of things than those Hinton children and their aunt and uncle...I'll soon show them who's the best."

Joe had been relieved, thinking it would give them a new start away from all the swirling rumours in the village about Stella flouncing off to

London without so much as a second thought for her family.

But it hadn't really worked out that way. Joe soon discovered that even though they owned a narrowboat and it provided enough work for them to get by, it didn't mean that they actually belonged to the narrowboat community. If anything, they were still regarded with suspicion...as outsiders. It was as if they didn't belong anywhere anymore. They had turned their back on the village, but they hadn't yet managed to find a way into the tight-knit families of the narrowboat owners, many of whom had worked the canals for generations. And that was in no small part due to the ongoing simmering resentment Evan directed towards Dolly's family on *The River Maid*.

"Perhaps, if the newspaper is to be believed, Pa might finally let go of the idea that Ma will get fed up with everything and come home soon." Joe folded the paper up again and tucked it back in his pocket. "Maybe he'll meet another kind-hearted woman; we could do with a woman's touch on the boat, that's for sure," he added with a rueful smile.

Billy yawned loudly again. "So are we taking a load of coal today? There's barely any food left in the cupboards, and I may as well have bare feet, given the sorry state my boots are in." He held his hands up. "Don't worry, I know we can't afford to take 'em to the cobblers."

Joe grabbed the dirty plates and cups and swished them around in a bucket of water, before laying them out on the cabin roof to dry in the sun.

"You're not wrong, Billy. I counted out our money last night once Pa fell asleep. As per usual, our finances are in a perilous state." He sighed and ran a hand through his thick wavy hair. That was the trouble with still being regarded as outsiders on the canal; it meant that they were always bottom of the list when it came to new contracts being given out by the mill owners. And even though Joe did his best to let the other narrowboat owners know that they would be happy to work in tandem with anyone struggling, or unable to meet a deadline, they were seldom chosen. Evan's mercurial moods and general unreliability, when he'd stayed late at the tavern, were well known. Folks didn't want to risk trusting a newcomer. It was nothing personal, they said to Joe.

"Do we risk waking Pa up?"

This time it was Joe's turn to pull a face. "Better to let him sleep it off. We could do with another way to bring in a bit more money if you have any bright ideas."

Billy jumped up, suddenly full of enthusiasm. "Don't you think it would be more useful if I were doing another job?" His eyes had a hopeful gleam in them. Now that he had turned twelve, he was old enough to be considered for an apprenticeship, but Evan had been adamant that it needed the three of them to work on *The Skylark* until now.

"You know Pa won't agree," Joe said resignedly. Privately, he was fed up with how difficult their pa seemed to find it to face facts, but the truth was, they needed more money coming in. Especially if their pa was going to carry on drinking every time he was feeling morose about their ma leaving. Some days, he was spending more in the local tavern than they were earning. Maybe Billy had a point, and it was time for him to look elsewhere.

"He can hardly refuse if I actually tell him someone has agreed to take me on."

"You sound like you have something in mind already?"

"When I took Barnaby to Abe Wentworth, the blacksmith to be shod last week, he told me his apprentice was a useless good-for-nothing. He's upped and left. Said he could earn more at the mill."

"Are you suggesting asking Abe for the position?"

A guilty look flickered across Billy's face. "I asked him last week," he admitted. "He said, as long as Pa agrees, he'll happily take me on. He'll let me sleep in the hayloft of the barn and feed me, as well as pay me a few coins each week while I'm learning the trade."

A chuckle burst from Joe's mouth before he could stop it. "I should have known. You'd better run along and tell him we agree before he offers it to someone else, don't you think?" Joe was impressed at his little brother's initiative and wondered if he should stand up to his pa a bit more too. Billy would go far with his easy-going personality and good work ethic.

"I was hoping you would say that." Billy grinned and pulled his boots on. Then he spat on his hands and ran them over his hair, trying to tame it slightly so that it wouldn't look like he'd just got out of bed. "What about Pa? Are you sure I shouldn't ask him first?"

Joe shook his head. "We're not earning enough for the three of us to stay on *The Skylark*. Pa and I can manage between us, and it's a good opportunity for you. A chance for you to make something of yourself with a proper trade." He slapped his brother on his back and smiled. "I'll tell Pa that it might mean we can get Barnaby shod for a favourable rate. The might help sweeten the news."

As Billy hurried away along the towpath, Joe felt a pang of envy. He would miss his brother's presence on the boat if he moved out. Truth be told, it could be a lonely old business being on the canal with just his pa for company. He enjoyed the work, and he wanted to make more of *The Skylark* and what they did, but his pa's obsession with trying to get one up on Dolly and her family all the time was starting to leave a bad taste in his mouth.

The sound of Evans' deep, rumbling snores continued to come from the cabin, and Joe knew there was no point in hoping he would wake up anytime soon. He knelt down and pulled a small pouch of coins out from under the bench seat, where he kept them hidden so they wouldn't get frittered away on ale. It would probably be a few days before Billy would start with the blacksmith, so Joe decided to use the spare time he had to go and buy some more food so that they wouldn't have to stop again once they got going.

"Come on, Patch," he called. "We'll harness Barnaby when we get back." He whistled under his breath as he walked along the towpath. Even though he occasionally missed Middleyard and village life, and despite still feeling like an outsider, he liked the canal. Being on the move each day gave him a sense of freedom, and there was always something new to see. The winters were hard, but summer more than made up for it. He could understand why many of the narrowboat families couldn't imagine any other way of life.

In the distance, he caught sight of *The River Maid*, and his pace slowed. He hesitated in the shadow of an oak tree as the sound of laughter drifted towards him. It was Dolly. He would recognise her musical laugh anywhere, and he felt a strange sensation in his chest as he saw her climbing off the narrowboat, her raven-dark hair gleaming in the sunshine. Someone was waiting for her on the towpath, and he edged out of the shadows to see who it was.

"Horace Smallwood," Joe muttered, with a small shake of his head. "What does a wealthy man like him want with someone like Dolly Hinton?"

It wasn't the first time he had seen them together, and it made no sense. Horace's father was a man of great wealth if the rumours were to be believed. He owned Nailsbridge Mill, and the brewery on the other side of Thruppley, not to mention Chavenhope House, their grand country residence surrounded by hundreds of acres of prime farmland. It seemed strange that Horace would even notice a narrowboat family, let alone talk to Dolly like an old friend.

What's she up to? For a split second, he felt an emotion he couldn't quite describe as he saw Horace tuck Dolly's hand into the crook of his elbow. Was it anger? No, he thought with a sudden sense of surprise. It was jealousy.

CHAPTER 10

"I don't suppose I have much right to be envious that Horace is her friend, do I, Patch?" Joe said, ruffling the collie's soft ears. She whined, eager to get going again.

He knew he had to walk past *The River Maid* to reach Wilf Latham's cart, so he squared his shoulders and carried on. Part of him hoped that Dolly wouldn't notice him. But strangely, he also had the sudden urge to run after them and push in between her and Horace. He wanted to tell the well-do-do man who was not from their world that Dolly had been his friend first. *Stop being such a fool*, he chastised himself.

As it was, Dolly was deep in conversation and didn't look back in his direction, so as he followed them along the towpath, it gave him the chance to watch her. He noticed the way her dark curls framed her heart-shaped face under the battered straw bonnet she wore and how attentively Horace looked down at her every time she spoke. If it weren't for the fact that Dolly was still only fourteen years old, he would've said the man was sweet on her. What other reason could there be for him to seek out Dolly's company? The thought left a sour feeling in his chest.

He hung back a little, not wanting to catch them up. "Hello, Joe," Amy called as he drew level with *The River Maid*. "It's a lovely morning, isn't it." She was watering a tub with herbs growing in it on the cabin roof, and Bob was snuffling at her feet. He could see Gloria in the cabin cooking breakfast, and Verity and Bert were sitting at the table enjoying a cup of tea together before starting work.

"Aye, I suppose it is," he said gruffly. He had long ago stopped wondering how Amy knew it was him walking along the towpath when her sight was so limited. He could only assume it was something about the sound of his boots crunching on the gravel, or perhaps she had heard Patch barking excitedly at the ducks on the water. He hesitated for a second but then remembered that his pa would be cross if he found out he'd been fraternising with their rivals. Even though Evan was still asleep, he seemed to have an uncanny knack of sniffing out any hint of Joe weakening over their long-running animosity towards Dolly's family. "I can't stop to talk," he muttered.

"Come and visit our Dolly soon," she called after him, giving him a sweet smile. "She misses you...we all do."

Joe was glad Amy couldn't see the expression on his face at that moment. He felt guilty for the way his father had spoken so harshly to them on the common four years ago, and for the way he had so readily gone along with it. What made it worse was the way that Dolly and her siblings still tried to be friends with him whenever they saw him. They had never said a harsh word to him. In fact, Verity was one of the few people who had gone out of her way to welcome them to the canal, taking them an apple pie. But Evan had scowled and refused to accept her kindness, telling Verity he had no need of their charity.

I've left it too late. How can I ask for Dolly's forgiveness after all this time? He kicked a stone ahead of him on the path, reminding himself that it was

Ruben Hinton's fault that their ma had left. His father told him time and again that Ruben could have put a stop to it, but instead of doing that, he had practically encouraged her to leave.

But is that really true? Perhaps Pa is to blame? If anything, it sounds as though Fred Portiscue lured her away with promises of fame and fortune. The doubts flickered through his mind, as they had started to more often recently. Maybe his father had been too quick to point the finger of blame at everyone other than himself. The more his doubts multiplied, the more confused he felt. Had he really lost his friendship with Dolly for no good reason? But surely, he owed his loyalty to his pa.

As he approached Wilf Latham's cart, he noticed that Dolly had just purchased some eggs and vegetables. Horace was holding the basket for her, and she laughed at something he said. They continued walking slightly ahead of him, and their conversation drifted back towards him, making his ears prick up.

"...the trouble is, Uncle Bert is still suffering from a lot of pain in his foot since he broke it. Jonty and I manage to keep things going when it's too much for him, but Uncle Bert is trying to encourage Jonty to get work on one of the local farms."

"I'm surprised about that," Horace said, flicking some long grass out of their way with his silver-topped cane. "I thought your uncle would want Jonty to follow in his footsteps and take over *The River Maid* in the future."

Dolly laughed lightly. "I think he knows Jonty's heart isn't in it, not like mine. I couldn't imagine not working with Jester now."

"Perhaps he's hoping you will marry into another narrowboat family, and your husband will help? Or maybe you will marry someone wealthier and not have to worry about working on the canal anymore…"

Horace's suggestion sounded innocent enough, but it made the blood roar in Joe's ears. He remembered how long ago, when they were still children, Joe had been sure that he and Dolly would end up together; it seemed only natural. But everything had changed since then, and he felt a surge of anger as Dolly shrugged the suggestion away, giving her new wealthy friend another warm smile.

"I'm sure when I'm older I'll be far too busy to think about courting," she said easily. The distant hoot of the new steam train caught her attention for a moment, making her look away, and only Joe noticed the slight frown that crossed Horace's face.

"Did you hear the news about Nailsbridge Mill?" she said, changing the subject.

"I swear, you know more about it than me, even though my papa now owns the place," Horace chuckled. "Being in London took my attention to other things, but I'm back for good now, which means I'll be able to visit you more often. And get more involved with the business, hopefully."

"Uncle Bert found out that they have started milling grain instead of weaving cloth, so we're going there later this morning to ask if they will give us more work. Nobody else knows about it yet…Aunt Verity heard a rumour, so we're hoping they will agree to give us a good contract. It will certainly help put Uncle Bert's mind at ease because it won't be so hard on us compared to hauling coal."

Joe stopped in his tracks, feeling torn. Dolly hadn't even realised he was behind them, but this was his opportunity to get more work as well. If he mentioned it to his pa, perhaps they could go down to Nailsbridge later this afternoon. It wasn't that he wanted to take work out from under

Dolly's nose, but he needed to do something to bring more money in as well. They couldn't afford to be complacent, and it sounded as though there was only a small window of opportunity to get one of the coveted contracts at Nailsbridge Mill.

With a mixture of guilt and determination, Joe decided to seize the opportunity. He would talk to his pa about what he had overheard and hope that it might secure a better future for themselves and *The Skylark*. He had to put his confusing feelings towards Dolly aside. He hastily paid for a few eggs and some bread from the farmer's cart, and hurried away, hoping that his pa would be awake and in some semblance of readiness to work, in spite of being full of drink the previous night.

"Where has Billy got to?" Evan climbed slowly out of the cabin, pulling his braces over his shoulders and looked sourly around as he rasped his hand over his chin. "Don't tell me that boy's off up to mischief on the bank again?"

Joe bit back his sigh of irritation. His pa was always in a bad mood after he had spent the evening in the Black Lion Tavern drinking more than he should. He hoped it was out of guilt for spending money they could ill afford, but Evan looked unrepentant as he filled his mug with tea, not caring that it splashed over the sides onto the deck. Joe decided there was no point trying to skirt around the truth. Evan had to face up to the situation.

"We're short of money again, Pa," he began hesitantly.

Evan opened his mouth, as if to refute what Joe had just said, but then closed it again with a harrumph. "Yes, son, I'm well aware of that. Times are hard...especially when 'tis only me taking care of you two boys."

"There are a couple of pieces of good news," Joe said hastily. He didn't want to have to listen to another tirade about his ma's success on the stage in London and the terrible hand they had been dealt by her thoughtless actions.

"Good news? About time." Evan smiled, reminding Joe of the good-looking, kind-hearted man he had once been. "Are you going to tell me what it is then?" He went back down into the cabin and emerged a moment later, eating a wrinkled apple which had seen better days.

"Abe Wentworth's apprentice has gone to work at the mill. He's offered Billy the position instead."

"Huh? Are you telling me that Billy is considering leaving us to train to be a blacksmith?" Evan chewed thoughtfully, still looking half asleep as he considered this information.

"Well…yes…Abe Wentworth mentioned it to Billy last week, but Billy was worried that you might not agree, even though we do need the money."

Much to Joe's surprise, Evan nodded slowly a moment later. "I suppose that could help us out of a sticky situation. There ain't the work around that there used to be, not now the trains are carrying coal. I suppose it's one less mouth to feed, and Abe is a decent man. It might suit Billy well to learn a trade."

"Exactly," Joe said, inwardly heaving a sigh of relief. "I told him to get along and say yes before Abe offered it to someone else. And it's not far away, only on the edge of Thruppley, so we'll still see plenty of him. He'll have lodgings in the barn, and Abe's offered to pay him a fair wage while he's learning."

Evan gnawed the apple down to its core and then threw the remains into the water. "You've had a busy morning," he said dryly. "It could be useful for us as well, maybe he might charge us a bit less for shoeing Barnaby." His face brightened at the thought of saving a few pennies on one of their expenses.

There was a thrum of activity along the towpath as all the narrowboat families started going about their business, and Joe stood up to go and check Barnaby's harness so they could set offl.

"What about the other bit of good news? Or is that it?" Evan regarded the meagre pile of coal on the front of their boat. He didn't have to say out loud that their loads had been getting smaller and less frequent recently. It was etched in the frown of worry on his face.

Joe hesitated. Once he had shared his secret, there would be no going back.

"Come along, lad, spit it out," Evan lifted his cap and scratched his head, looking apologetic. "I know I haven't always been the best pa to you these last few years, but I'm going to do better. It's time to put what happened behind us and focus on making a better life for ourselves. I want to see you marry well, Joe. And Billy too, when the time comes. We're still a family, even without your ma, which means I need to earn more money to give you boys a bit more security."

It was the first time Joe had ever heard his pa speak like this, and it helped him make up his mind. "I overheard Dolly talking to Horace Smallwood this morning when I went to buy some food for us."

Evan's smile slipped a little at the mention of Dolly's name, but he nodded for Joe to go on.

"It's not common knowledge yet, but she said that Nailsbridge Mill is handing out contracts to some of the narrowboat owners to ferry grain and flour back and forth to Frampton Basin. She told Horace they're heading down there later today to try and get a contract ahead of everyone else, and he said it was a good idea."

A crafty look came into Evan's eyes, and he rubbed his hands together. "What are you waiting for? We need to leave immediately and get there before Verity and Bert." He looked puzzled for a moment. "What's Dolly Hinton doing chatting to Horace Smallwood?"

"I wondered the same thing. He seems to have befriended her, although I don't know why."

"Oh well, no matter. All I'm interested in is getting to Nailsbridge before them. Is Barnaby ready to go?"

Joe quickly checked the horse's harness and nodded. "What about delivering the coal? Should we do that first?"

"There's no time for that. Get that lazy horse going, and I'll think of an excuse to explain to Mr Tebbett why we're late with his delivery. We can go onward to Selsley afterwards, but we're not missing out on this, Joe. It's the best news I've heard all year."

Within a few short minutes, Barnaby had taken up the strain, and the narrowboat was travelling along the canal at a tidy pace. There was a gleam of excitement in Evan's eyes as he spotted *The River Maid* ahead. The fact that Verity and Bert were still moored up, and they would have to overtake, lifting their tow rope over the top of them, only added to his delight.

"Good morning, Mr Granger," Verity called a few minutes later, as *The Skylark* manoeuvred past them. "Where are you heading to in such a hurry?"

"Oh…nowhere special," he replied airily. He smiled even more broadly, unable to resist scoring a point against them. "Actually, Joe and I are going to Nailsbridge Mill to take care of some important business."

Joe's heart sank as he saw Dolly emerge from behind Jester, where she had been picking out his feet. He had to walk Barnaby straight past her, and there was no avoiding the look of surprise on her face.

"Hello, Joe. I couldn't help overhearing what your pa just said. I didn't know you did deliveries to Nailsbridge Mill?" She glanced towards the mound of coal on the front of *The Skylark*, looking puzzled.

"We're going to get one of those new contracts for carrying grain," Evan said loudly, making sure that everyone on *The River Maid* had heard. "Chances are, we'll get the best contract, what with turning up first while other folks are still supping their tea and dawdling."

Verity's expression darkened at the obvious dig at Bert, who was resting his bad foot and drinking the tea she had just made him. "How did you know about Naisbridge? They haven't told most of the narrowboat owners yet, and we need a decent contract from them, what with my Bert still struggling to walk properly." She put her hands on her hips and turned to stare at Joe and Dolly on the towpath. "Did you wheedle that information out of Dolly?" she demanded.

Joe felt his cheeks turning red and suddenly felt defensive. "I didn't need to wheedle it out of her. Besides, we're not friends. She was too busy chattering on about it to Mister High and Mighty Horace Smallwood. It's not my fault I overheard what they were talking about."

There was a burst of laughter from Evan as he slapped his thigh in amusement, standing at the tiller of *The Skylark*. "It's every family for themselves, Verity. Just like Ruben Hinton ruined my reputation as a gamekeeper with his poaching and sent my wife running up to London, now it's our turn to get one over you."

"Were you eavesdropping when I saw Horace this morning?" A shadow of hurt crossed Dolly's face as Joe squeezed past her and Jester with Barnaby. "Why are you still so set against us after all this time? Whatever happened between your pa and mine is their business. It doesn't mean that we should be enemies as well, Joe."

Her words hung between them, partly a challenge, but also an invitation that they could still be friends again. Before Joe had a chance to reply, another shout went up from Evan.

"Don't let her try and change our minds, son," he yelled. "We need the money just as much as them. She might think she can charm the birds from the trees, with Horace Smallwood as her friend, but we deserve a bit of luck."

Joe shrugged, feeling wretched and guilty, not quite able to look Dolly in the eye. "I expect there are more than enough contracts to go around for everyone," he mumbled. "I'm sorry that your uncle is still struggling from where his foot was broken."

Dolly looked torn but then suddenly crossed the towpath to his side and put her hand on his arm. "Thank you," she said. "Jonty told me he saw something in the newspaper about your ma being a great success on the stage now." Her expression softened, "It must be hard for your pa to accept that she left, and you and Billy. I know I struggled after my parents died. It's not quite the same, but perhaps we have more in common than you think."

Joe looked down at her hand and wished that he could return her kindness. There was something about being close to his old friend again, and the way her dark brown eyes held his gaze with warmth, instead of anger or resentment, even though his pa had spoken harshly, that made hope swell in his chest. He wanted to see her smile at him, the way she had at Horace, but he knew he had left it too late. "Perhaps we do…" he said quietly.

A rowdy family was walking towards them on the towpath, talking loudly about the upcoming summer fair, and Joe pulled Barnaby to one side so he wouldn't be in their way. It was on the tip of Joe's tongue to ask Dolly not to think badly of them, but when he turned around, she was already busy picking out Jester's feet again, and the moment was lost.

CHAPTER 11

Dolly brought Jester to a halt on the towpath at the yard of Nailsbridge Mill, waved forward by Mr Morton, the yard manager. No sooner had they stopped than Bob darted after a squirrel which was tantalisingly close before it ran up the trunk of a nearby hazel tree and danced mockingly along the branches until he gave up. "Come away, Bob, leave it be."

A breeze rippled the surface of the canal, providing a welcome relief from the midsummer heat, and Jester swished his tail to keep the flies away. She stroked his neck, enjoying the feel of his smooth summer coat under her hand. "Good lad, Jester." He turned his whiskery muzzle towards her, snickering softly. "Stand nicely for me, and as soon as we've finished unloading, I'll give you a handful of oats." She didn't care that one of the boys who worked in the yard was looking at her strangely for talking to her horse. Jester held an important place in her heart, and she patted his muscular neck again, smiling as he gave a mighty sigh, and his head started to droop. Jester knew that they would be here long enough for him to have a snooze, and made the most of the opportunity to rest before the next part of their journey started.

"Shall we start unloading, Mr Morton?" Jonty was already poised on the deck of the narrowboat, grasping a sack of grain on the top corners, ready to spring into action. It was a matter of pride to beat the other boys his age on the canal, he often said to Dolly, because he hadn't been born to narrowboat life.

"I reckon that sounds like a sensible idea, young Jonty," the jovial yard manager said, "otherwise what would be the point of you being here?" The man's plump face creased into a smile, accompanied by a wheezy laugh as he chuckled at his own joke. "Run and fetch that handcart for your brother, Miss Hinton," he said, jerking his thumb towards the large wooden warehouse at the side of the yard. "He's as eager as a lurcher chasin' a rabbit, which is a welcome sight." He laughed again, and his portly frame jiggled under the jacket, which strained across his belly.

Dolly enjoyed delivering to Nailsbridge Mill. Although they still took consignments of coal to Selsley Mill, they had also been given work with Nailsbridge over a month ago, and so far, it seemed to be turning out well. They travelled down to Frampton Basin to collect sacks of grain from the larger ships, which had sailed up from Bristol docks and brought them to the mill. Then they loaded up sacks of flour to take onwards up to Thruppley village, where one of the merchants took it over land to their various customers who needed the flour. Even though it was hard work, it didn't feel as backbreaking as manhandling coal. It was a good thing, too, she thought to herself as she saw Bert hobbling across the deck of *The River Maid*. His foot still twisted at a strange angle, making it hard for him to walk properly. Doctor Skelton said it would never come right again. There was too much damage to the ligaments even though the bones had eventually mended, but Bert was not one to complain. "Remember, love, I were lucky not to be killed, and we're doubly lucky to have Dolly and Jonty to help," was his usual comment when Verity made him a salt bath in a bucket to soak his foot in at the end of a particularly hard day.

Dolly hurried back to the side of the boat just as Bert reached the front, rolling up his sleeves. "Why don't you leave this to Jonty and me, Uncle Bert? We made it here in good time, so there's no need for us to rush. You know Doctor Skelton said that you'll have less pain in your foot if you keep it up and rest a bit more."

"Thank you, Dolly," Verity said, rolling her eyes slightly. "He doesn't listen when I tell him to rest, but he might pay more heed to you, ducky." She gave her husband an affectionate smile and held up a slice of moist fruitcake fresh out of the stove to try and entice him back to the seat by the tiller at the back of the boat.

"You women do make a fuss about nothing," Bert said with a harrumph, which was swiftly followed by a smile.

"You'm lucky they look after you so well, Bert," Mr Morton said from the bank. "Working on the boats is hard on a body, and you're not getting any younger, just like me."

"Some cake for you too, Mr Morton?" Verity asked. The yard manager was a pleasure to work with, and she wanted to keep it that way.

His face lit up as Verity cut an extra slice of cake and passed it across to him. "Aye, go on then. Jonty and Miss Hinton can take care of the unloading just fine, Bert. Leave 'em to it." He glanced over his shoulder before leaning closer to them. "Master Dominic is busy with work inside the mill today, so it won't matter if you take a little longer than usual to unload. I won't tell if you don't," he added, sinking his teeth into the cake and spraying a few crumbs onto the ground, much to Bob's delight.

Bert compromised by spending the next ten minutes sliding the sacks of grain across the narrowboat deck, allowing Jonty to lift them down onto the towpath, and Dolly to load up the handcart. "There, that worked out well," Verity said once he came to sit down with her again.

Dolly's shoulder muscles were soon aching from the exertion of wheeling the handcart back and forth to the warehouse, but she had the pleasing sense of a job well done by the time they had finished. She wiped her sleeve across her forehead and was looking forward to a mug of Verity's elderflower cordial when she suddenly saw Horace strolling across the yard towards her.

"Just the person I want to see," he said eagerly. "Have you finished loading up the flour?"

Dolly nodded, wondering whether she looked a frightful mess. She patted her hair hastily and wiped her hands down the front of her dress. "I wasn't expecting to see you here today," she said, suddenly feeling shy.

Over the last four years, since she had first met Horace, he had visited her and her family on *The River Maid* many times and now felt like an old friend. At first, Verity and Bert had been suspicious of his motives, until they realised he was just genuinely interested in their way of life. But not in a judgemental fashion, more because he wanted to put forward their ideas to people in positions of power who might be able to bring reform to the less well-off in society. But the meetings had always been him coming to visit Dolly and her family, wherever they were on the canal. She had never seen him at Nailsbridge Mill, even though his pa owned it.

"Good morning Mr and Mrs Webster," Horace

said, lifting his hat politely. "I hope you're both well."

"Can't complain, Mr Smallwood," Bert called cheerfully.

Dolly looked nervously around. She was worried that if any of the mill workers saw them talking, it would set tongues wagging. It was unusual for a man of Horace's class to mix with folks like them, and she didn't want to do anything which might jeopardise their precious contract.

Horace seemed blissfully unaware of such problems. "Seeing as you're here today, it would be a perfect opportunity for me to introduce you to Papa, Dolly. He's been away in London, but he's back here now. Travelling doesn't suit his health as much anymore."

Dolly noticed Mr Morton's eyebrows twitch up with curiosity, but he didn't say anything. "Meet your Papa?" she repeated in a low voice, feeling flustered. "I don't think that would be very wise, Horace. Why do you want me to meet him?"

"Don't worry," Horace said, waving her concerns away. "I've already suggested it to him, and he thought it would be a good idea. He's doing a lot to improve pay and housing conditions for his mill workers, but he doesn't have much understanding of the narrowboat families who also do so much work for us." Horace gave her a persuasive smile. "It's all well and good, me telling him the sort of things we talk about, but it would be better coming from you."

"I don't see any harm in it, Dolly," Verity said, tapping one finger thoughtfully on her chin. "It might be good for Mr Smallwood to understand our challenges, as long as you make sure to tell him that we're grateful for the work we have at Nailsbridge Mill."

"There's no need to thank us, Mrs Webster," Horace said kindly. "It's us who are grateful for all the hard work that you do for us."

"Go on, our Dolly." Bert gave her an encouraging smile. "Jonty will walk Jester forward and move the boat, so we're not in anybody's way. Take as long as you need." He lowered his voice slightly and beckoned Dolly a bit closer. "You're a sensible girl, and charming with it. It might work out well for us if you become acquainted with Horace's papa. He's a very influential man."

Even though Dolly's heart was already hammering in her chest at the thought of being introduced to such an important person, she nodded. She was willing to do anything which might help secure their future employment. "Will you be with me?" she asked Horace as they walked across the yard. She peeked up at the mill windows, hoping that nobody would be watching, but with the sun reflecting on the glass, it was hard to tell.

"Of course. I already know he's going to be very taken with you, and hopefully, it might even lead to a bit more work for your family if you want it."

Horace led her through a maze of corridors, and as they approached the mill office, Dolly felt a mixture of excitement and trepidation. She smoothed her dress one more time and took a deep breath. Horace opened the door for her, and they stepped inside.

Mr Smallwood, a distinguished-looking gentleman with silver hair and a kind expression, rose from his desk as they entered. "Ah, Horace, this must be Miss Hinton. It's a pleasure to meet you, my dear. My son has told me a lot about you."

Dolly curtsied, suddenly feeling very self-conscious. She wished she'd taken a moment to comb her hair and tie it up again, but it was too late now. "It's an honour to meet you, sir," she said, her voice barely above a whisper.

"Nonsense," Mr Smallwood replied, dismissing

her formality with a wave of his hand. "The pleasure is all mine. Horace has told me all about the hard work you and your family put into our business. Please, sit down. I'd like a moment of your time if that's alright?" He gestured towards two chairs on the opposite side of his desk, and she perched carefully on the edge of the shiny leather seat, hoping her dress wasn't too dirty.

As they sat down, Dolly was glad to have Horace's reassuring presence beside her. She looked curiously around the office, wanting to remember every detail to describe it to Gloria and Amy. Mr Smallwood's desk was imposing, with ornately carved drawers on one side, and he pushed aside a pile of thick vellum documents next to his fountain pen and inkwell. One wall was completely lined with leather-bound books which she thought would take a lifetime to read. There was a large window on her left which gave him a fine view across the mill and then towards the hills beyond, and she could see the church spire where Thruppley nestled in the valley.

"My son tells me he befriended you and your family a while ago," he began. "I used to have ambitions to be in Parliament, but alas, my health means I prefer to stay here in the West country now. But I have a lot of friends and acquaintances in high places, Miss Hinton. Perhaps you could tell me more about how we might be able to make your lives a bit easier? I can't promise reform, but I can mention your concerns and ideas to those who might be able to make changes for the better."

Dolly gulped, feeling rather overawed for a moment.

"I already told Papa that you're full of good ideas in spite of your young age," Horace said encouragingly.

Now that she looked more closely at Edward Smallwood, she could see there was a faint grey tinge to his skin, and he sounded rather breathless. Under his finely cut frockcoat, he seemed frailer than she first thought. He had the look of a man who was not much longer for this earth, and she wondered if that was why he wanted her opinion. To leave a legacy for the poverty-stricken people who had helped build his empire, before it was too late.

She took a deep breath. "Our biggest worry is that the new railway line will take work away from us, Mr Smallwood. This way of life…taking goods up and down the canal on our narrowboat, *The*

River Maid, is all my aunt and uncle have ever known."

"I'm afraid that the steam trains are the way ahead for transportation of goods, but it's in the name of progress. Could you not find work elsewhere?" The old man steepled his fingers, listening attentively.

"I think that's what people on the bank don't understand." Dolly felt her nerves fall away as she explained their situation, the words tumbling out of her. "...it's not just a job for us, you see, Mr Smallwood," she said finally. "The canal is a way of life. Moving grain and coal is hard work, but I hope to follow in Uncle Bert's footsteps. I can't imagine living back in a cottage again, like where I grew up. *The River Maid* and Jester, our horse... they're like family to us, not just the tools of our trade."

Mr Smallwood nodded and gave her an admiring smile. "I can see you're very passionate about this, Miss Hinton. In some ways, you remind me of myself, when I first started building my business. I wasn't born to wealth, you see. I got here through hard work, which is a philosophy I hope Dominic will continue."

"That's what Uncle Bert and Aunt Verity say,

Sir. Although I'm sure it has helped you having friends in high places."

Mr Smallwood chuckled and stood up to indicate that the meeting was over. "Indeed. I have been fortunate to know people of influence, and you're quite right, they have helped me on occasion. But you have friends in high places now, Miss Hinton. If you're ever in any trouble, Horace and I will gladly help you as a gesture of our thanks for your fascinating insights." He extended one arm and shook her hand. "I shall endeavour to continue using the narrowboats and families such as yours for as long as possible, so you don't need to worry about being out of work. I know some of us people 'on the bank,' as you call it, can seem uncaring about your way of life, but allow me to reassure you that I want to support you all and try and be more understanding of your hardships."

Dolly felt her cheeks flush at the kind words and bobbed a small curtsey to the old man as Horace ushered her back out again.

"Did I do alright?" She half skipped to keep up with Horace's long strides as they walked back through the corridors that led between the mill's cavernous rooms, which were all a hive of activity. The clattering machinery was loud, and their feet left footsteps on the flagstone floors, in the faint covering of flour dust, which drifted through the air covering everything.

"You certainly did," he exclaimed. "I knew Papa would be interested if he heard it from you, instead of me."

"I'm just glad I didn't make a fool of myself. I've never been anywhere as grand as your pa's office, nor met such a distinguished gentleman. Well, other than you, of course." Dolly couldn't wait to tell her family about everything she had just experienced. But more importantly, she wanted Bert and Verity to be proud of her being able to give a voice to the narrowboat families. She hoped more work might come out of it, to help secure her family's future if Bert needed to rest more.

"Far from it." Horace held the heavy outer door open for her, and they strolled across the yard.

"What are you doing with her?" The blunt question behind them was accompanied by the sound of heavy footsteps, and Dolly spun around to see who it was.

"Dominic, you remember Dolly Hinton?" A muscle in Horace's jaw twitched, and his smile faded as he eyed his older brother warily. "She's been telling Papa about what it's like for the narrowboat families who deliver to the mill. He wants to think of some ways to improve things for them."

Dolly felt her cheeks flush as Dominic turned his steely gaze on her before turning back to Horace again. "Why on earth would Papa want to bother himself with such a thing?" he drawled, sounding bored. "Everybody knows the future lies in using the steam trains, not those archaic narrowboats with the wretched families who constantly complain about how hard their lives are."

"Have you no manners, Dominic? That's no way to speak in front of Miss Hinton. You might not care about such matters, but Papa does, and you should remember that this is still very much his business."

Dolly tried to edge away a little, not wanting to be caught up in the obvious antagonism between the two men, but before she could beat a hasty retreat, Dominic turned on her again. "You might think you can wrap my younger brother around your little finger, Dolly, but your woe-is-us attitude won't work on me." The corner of his lip curled up in a sneer, and he pulled a handkerchief from his frock coat pocket and made a show of wiping his sleeve with it where her shawl had brushed against him.

She felt anger rising in her chest and, before she had a chance to think, blurted out a reply. "My aunt and uncle work very hard, Mr Smallwood. We've never asked for charity or expected special treatment, but folks who are better off should at least treat us fairly...or should I say, *decent* folks," she added under her breath.

Dominic's expression darkened, and he stepped closer, towering over her. It reminded her of his cruel taunts the first time she had encountered him on the towpath all those years ago. "People like you need to understand your place in society," he said scornfully. "You'll never drag yourselves out of poverty, no matter how much you want to. I called you a river rat back then, and I can see nothing has changed. It would be wise to remember that you and your family are here to serve our business." He gave her a thin smile. "Or perhaps I should just offer your contract to someone else. Your welfare is of no concern to me," he added carelessly.

Horace looked aghast. "Dominic! Don't speak to Dolly like that. Apologise immediately; there's no call for being so rude. And it's unkind to threaten her with losing their livelihood. What would Papa think if he knew you were doing this?"

"It's alright," Dolly said quietly. She gave Horace a quick glance of gratitude for sticking up for her. "We know our place very well, Mr Smallwood. We are grateful for the business that your Papa has given us, but if he asks for my help, I'm sure you would agree it would be rude of me not to offer it." She lifted her chin, looking defiantly into Dominic's cold blue eyes. "Your Papa is a very kind-hearted gentleman. I'm sure he hopes you might be the same…" She let her words hang in the air between them before turning on her heel and walking back towards the canal.

"Never mind getting your feet under the table with Papa," Dominic called angrily after her. "It will be me you're dealing with soon enough." With that, he stormed off, slamming the door behind him.

"I'm so dreadfully sorry about that," Horace said, running after her. Two spots of colour had appeared on his cheeks. "Dominic has a nasty streak when he thinks he can get away with it, but I'll be having words with him later. It's not right, talking down to you like that."

"He was always less well-mannered than you,"

she said with a grin, not wanting to see Horace looking so worried by his brother's behaviour. "I thought you said he was interested in helping reform the laws for poor people. Remember, when we first met...you said he hoped to go into Parliament like your Papa."

Horace fell into step next to her and sighed. "That was always the plan when Papa sent him away to study in London, except it didn't work out that way. Dominic took up with a bad crowd, who led him astray." He ran a hand through his hair and shook his head slightly as though it played on his mind often. "I don't think Papa knows half of what he got up to." He looked embarrassed and gave her a guilty smile. "Drinking and gambling, if the rumours are to be believed, although I did my best to make sure Papa didn't find out."

"I'm sorry to hear about that," Dolly replied. She didn't like to see Horace looking so troubled, especially when it seemed that their pa was in poor health. "Will you and Dominic take over from your father if the work becomes too much for him?" she asked hesitantly.

This time it was Horace's turn to look annoyed. "Unfortunately not. I love my Papa dearly, but he has always favoured Dominic, in spite of his unreliable behaviour. It's something of a blind spot he has, and I don't want to cause a division in the family by pointing out that Dominic doesn't care about the business the way Papa and I do."

"Won't you and Dominic work here as equals? Everyone on the canal says you'll make a good master to work for."

Horace looked startled and pleased by her comment but shook his head. "It's Papa's belief that the eldest son should take over the business. Dominic will become the owner of Nailsbridge Mill and the brewery."

Dolly's heart sank; this was not the news she had hoped for. "So what will you do?"

Horace put his hands in his pockets, and his shoulders drooped slightly. "Papa still wants me to work in the business, but I will very much be playing second fiddle to Dominic." He turned to look back at the imposing stone buildings and thrum of activity. "I only hope Dominic becomes more responsible, although I wouldn't put it past him to fritter away everything Papa has worked so hard for all these years and leave us in financial ruin."

Horace's unguarded words cast a sudden chill over Dolly, in spite of the warm sun. "I'm sure he wouldn't want to do that," she said, trying to sound reassuring. She chuckled, realising that she was letting herself get carried away. "I mean…I'm just a lowly canal girl, and I don't know about important business matters like you, but I can see your pa values your opinion. Perhaps you just need to tell him a bit more about what Dominic is really like."

Horace laughed but with little humour. "Forgive me, Dolly," he said. "It's just been a difficult few days, and I'm worried about Papa's health. I was probably speaking out of turn, and everything will be fine, so please don't repeat what I said to anyone. Dominic is not so bad; he just gets a bit bored with the responsibilities of business, that's all."

Dolly bade farewell to Horace and helped Jonty load up the last few sacks of flour, then roused Jester from his slumbers to set off on the long walk back to Thruppley. Her mind churned with everything that had happened at Nailsbridge Mill, fretting that she might have made an enemy in Dominic. Just when she had started to think there might be easier times ahead.

"He's a difficult man to like, Jester, that Dominic Smallwood," she murmured to the horse as they plodded along. She could only pray that

Horace was right and Dominic would become a more caring employer when he took up the mantle from Edward Smallwood. There were too many families' well-being at stake to contemplate what might happen if Dominic threw all of his father's hard work away.

CHAPTER 12

The West Country - Five Years Later

Gloria squeezed onto the seat next to Amy at the back of the narrowboat and shook out the dress that she was altering before folding it carefully onto her lap, taking care not to let it trail in any dirt on the deck. "I'm not sure how much longer I'll be able to work this way," she said, giving Dolly a worried glance as she threaded her needle and started sewing. Now that she was fifteen years old, Gloria was more than happy to speak her mind. "I know I'm making a few shillings each week doing these alterations for Mrs Jones, but there's not enough room on the narrowboat for me to work properly."

Dolly eyed her sister affectionately from the

towpath. Gloria had a point. She had been taking on bits and pieces of work from Betty Jones, one of the seamstresses in Thruppley village, for almost five years, but they all knew that Gloria was capable of more. Mrs Jones had already offered her full-time work and lodgings over her small shop, but Gloria was torn. She didn't want to leave Amy, even though she longed to work in Mrs Jones's quaint shop with the bowed windows, where she would be able to start doing proper dressmaking. She loved nothing more than to chatter to the family about what fashionable fripperies she would add to so-and-so's dress, and which colour fabric would suit the women she watched strolling past the canal.

"I think you should take up Mrs Jones's offer," Amy said. She leaned her head on Gloria's shoulder with her eyes closed, letting the soft cotton of the dress fall through her fingers. They were rarely apart, but Amy didn't like people feeling as though she was a burden. "Dolly will look after me for as long as we're on the boat, and it's not as if we won't see you. We're usually in Thruppley a couple of times a week at least."

Hope flitted across Gloria's face for a moment. "I know Dolly will take care of you, Amy, but we've always been together as a family since losing Pa. It will be a wrench to start going our separate ways."

"We can't all live on *The River Maid* forever," Amy said pragmatically. "You know Mrs Jones needs a full-time seamstress in her shop. You'd be perfect for it."

"You children will always have a place to lay your heads here," Verity said, appearing in the doorway from the cabin. The sunlight fell on her hair which was grey with age now, reminding Dolly how time was passing. "I promised you on the day your pa died, and no matter how far you travel to make your own way in life, this is always home. Even if it is a bit of a squeeze," she added, looking towards Jonty's broad-shouldered frame as he lugged sacks around on the front deck of the boat.

"You'll still see me when I come and pick up scraps of silk for my flower-making," Amy said, nudging Gloria. "Mrs Jones said her ladies are taking quite a fancy to them to decorate their hats and dresses. Perhaps we'll set up a little business together in the future."

"That was a lucky day when we realised how good you were at making things, Amy. I always said folks who thought you'd never work didn't know what nimble little fingers you have, ducky." Verity patted the wired silk flower on her bonnet which was hanging inside the doorway with pride. Amy was getting quite a name for her intricate silk creations, but Verity was adamant she wouldn't end up working in one of the sweatshops that so many of the city flower-makers toiled in.

Dolly felt a mixture of emotions as she halted Jester in the yard at Nailsbridge Mill. It was hard to believe that five years had flown by since they had first started making deliveries there, and since she had met Edward Smallwood.

Since then, in many ways, life had plodded along predictably in the same way. But Edward Smallwood's health was no better, which meant that Dominic had been taking on more responsibilities for almost two years. She still saw Horace when he wasn't busy visiting the brewery and the family's other businesses, but she was grateful that Edward Smallwood had been true to his word. He still insisted that Dominic should continue to employ the narrowboat families for bringing grain from Frampton Basin and to take the flour onwards to Thruppley. Money was always tight, but they were managing to make ends meet, in spite of Bert and Verity doing less on the narrowboat, now that they were both suffering more with aching joints.

"We're none of us getting any younger, are we, Jester?" she said softly. She felt a pang of wistfulness as she noticed that even he had a few grey hairs on his muzzle now. And Bob was no longer the spritely pup of her memory. Instead, he preferred to snooze on deck, unless he spotted a particularly enticing mouse rustling in the grass.

She thought about Gloria's comment as she walked over to the warehouse to fetch the handcart. She and her siblings were growing up. Jonty was sixteen years old, and Bert had recently started wondering whether he might prefer to find better-paid work as a farm labourer, even though it would be hard to manage the boat without him. And Gloria had the opportunity to become a proper dressmaker under Betty Jones's guidance. Times were a-changing, and Dolly couldn't help but feel a little nostalgic for when they had all been younger, and everything seemed simpler.

Or perhaps that's my memory playing tricks? I can't keep living in the past. It's only natural that the others might want to find different work.

She walked back towards the narrowboat with the handcart, pushing her thoughts aside. Jonty and Gloria would be able to take good care of themselves and would always be able to get work. As long as she could continue to care for Amy, that was what mattered. Even though Amy's sight hadn't worsened, it hadn't improved either. She was so young when they had first arrived on the narrowboat that canal life was all she knew. It would be hard for her to adapt to something different, especially without her family around her, and Dolly knew that if she ever married and left the canal, it would only be on the condition that Amy could come too.

"Are you going to stand there daydreaming, Miss Hinton, or get on and do the work we pay you for?" Dominic Smallwood didn't bother with any social niceties as he shouted his instructions across the yard.

Mr Morton rolled his eyes. "Better look lively, Dolly," he muttered. "The master has been in a foul mood all day."

Dolly didn't bother to acknowledge Dominic's comment, focusing on unloading the sacks of grain with Jonty instead. They had it down to a fine art and had unloaded and reloaded the narrowboat in less than an hour.

Mr Morton paced up and down the towpath

with his pocketwatch in his hand for the duration, before finally returning it to his waistcoat pocket just as the last sack of flour was loaded. He whipped a stub of pencil out of another pocket, licked the end, and wrote something on a chit of paper. "You need to take this into the office, Dolly," he said, holding it out for her to take.

"What is it?" Jonty took the piece of paper off him and looked at it curiously.

"Master Dominic is making efficiencies," Mr Morton said, wrinkling his nose. He made the word sound wearisome and gave a resigned shrug. It seemed that nothing stayed the same for more than five minutes since old Mr Smallwood had started handing over the reins to Dominic.

"I have to fill out this 'ere bit of paper, and you'm to take it into the office. He wants to know how fast the narrowboats are unloaded and loaded." He rolled his eyes slightly, making sure that nobody from the mill was watching. Clearly, it was not a popular idea.

"You'd better walk Jester on for me, Jonty," Dolly said. She paused to watch for a moment, making sure it was done to her liking so that whoever was coming behind them could start to unload.

"I'll make a cup of tea," Verity said. Mr Morton smiled. He knew it meant there might be cake, and there was no sign of Dominic anymore to tell him off if he took a breather for a few minutes.

"I won't be long." Dolly hurried across the yard. She didn't like the sound of Dominic trying to make more efficiencies. He was probably looking for an excuse to pay them less or start taking work away from them. Unlike his father, he treated the mill workers and narrowboat families with ill-disguised contempt. But anyone who complained was swiftly out of a job, with no reference, so the workers gritted their teeth and put up with his arrogant demeanour. It was a far cry from how things had been when they first started delivering to Nailsbridge when old Mr Smallwood still knew everything that went on and took the time to ask after folk as if he actually meant it.

When Dolly pushed the office door open, she was surprised to see Dominic Smallwood there, and no sign of the bespectacled clerk, who usually scurried out every few weeks to pay them. "Where's Mr Applewood?" she asked, hovering in the doorway. "Mr Morton told me I have to bring this piece of paper in for him on each visit now."

Dominic held his hand out. "I'll take it for him.

We have important visitors and he's busy putting together some financial documents for me at the moment." He put the piece of paper on the desk, not taking his eyes off her. "...so it seems we're all alone," he added, his voice silky smooth and laden with meaning.

Dolly felt the blood rise to her cheeks as Dominic's eyes lingered over her shapely figure. He didn't bother to disguise the fact that he was staring at her with a hungry look on his face, which filled her with dread. She had noticed on the last few occasions when she had been unloading *The River Maid* that Dominic always seemed to find an excuse to come outside and watch. Not only that, but she had heard the rumours amongst the mill workers about the way he liked to shower affection on some of the pretty young women before casting them aside without a care for besmirching their reputation.

"I'd better get going," Dolly said firmly. "The merchant at Thruppley doesn't like to be kept waiting. He'll be expecting the flour later this afternoon." She turned to leave, but Dominic was quicker than her, and he pushed past to shut the door, trapping her inside the dusty office with him.

"I pay the man, so he can wait." Dominic leaned one hand on the wall behind her and smiled down lazily at her. "You've blossomed into quite a beautiful young woman, Dolly, considering what a scrawny little thing you were when I first met you." He trailed his other hand over the tendrils of her hair which framed her face, and then down her arm. "You have a bit more spark about you than most of the dull young women your age. I've always enjoyed that about you. Tell me, how old are you now?"

"I'm nineteen." Dolly shrank back. She could smell alcohol on his breath and knew that his mood could change in an instant if he felt thwarted.

"Such a delightful age. Like a freshly unfurled rose, as yet unsullied by life."

"I'm sorry, Mr Smallwood, but I really must go. Uncle Bert will be waiting for me." She lowered her eyes, hoping that her reticence would be enough to make him change his mind.

"Oh, Dolly, my dear girl, don't you know I always get what I want? I've had my eye on you for a while, so you may as well just be grateful for my attention." He stroked her hair again, but there was no tenderness in his cold gaze, which held her rooted to the spot. "Don't forget that I'm in charge of giving out the contracts to the narrowboat families now," he continued with a low chuckle.

"How can I forget?" Dolly retorted. She was determined not to let Dominic have his wicked way with her, and she pressed her hands against his chest to push him away. All it seemed to do was inflame his passion, and he casually pinned her to the wall again, his hands holding her shoulders like a vice.

"Why are you always so friendly to that spineless brother of mine, yet you show me no respect?" Dominic's eyes, which had been full of lust, grew dark.

"Because I've heard the rumours about you," Dolly said, lifting her chin and glaring at him. "I won't let you ruin my reputation. Horace has always treated me kindly, but everyone knows you just take whatever you want." She could feel panic rising in her chest and wished that she hadn't agreed to come into the office. "I... I'm already courting," she cried, clutching at straws. It wasn't true, but she was prepared to say anything.

"I see." His grip on her shoulders tightened, but this time out of spite. "So you'll happily throw yourself away on some impoverished narrowboat lad over a man of influence and wealth like me?" His voice was scornful. "You don't know what's good for you, Dolly. But I'm about to teach you to show some respect...just you wait and see."

Before she could reply, the door suddenly flew open. It was Horace, and she felt relief sweep over her. "Are you all right, Dolly?" He took in the situation with one shocked glance. "I saw you coming to the office and not coming out again. Has my brother forced himself upon you?" His eyes glinted with anger, and he wrenched Dominic away from her.

"Aha, here comes dear Horace, galloping to your rescue," Dominic said nonchalantly. He shrugged his brother's hand off his arm and strolled around to the far side of the desk as if nothing had happened.

"I...it was just an unfortunate—" Words failed her, and she folded her arms across her chest protectively, still feeling shaken by the encounter.

"My brother's behaviour is despicable. I apologise on his behalf because I'm sure he won't say sorry." Horace shot Dominic a frustrated look, annoyed even more by Dominic's smirk of amusement. "What would Papa think if he found out about you dallying with the affections of our workers? This isn't the first time, and it needs to stop."

"Must you be so tediously judgemental of me, Horace? I don't care what you think, and some of the young ladies are very grateful for my attention. Besides, I've had enough of Papa clinging on to the business when he should retire and let me take over properly. It's time for things to change...in fact, it's long overdue."

"Let me escort you back to the canal," Horace said, offering Dolly his arm. "It's the least I can do."

As they walked across the yard together, Horace apologised several more times.

"It's fine, it really is," Dolly said. Now that she was away from Dominic, she knew she wouldn't make the same mistake again and get caught alone with him. "He just likes to show people like me that he is powerful, that's all. I'm glad you're not like him."

"That's very gracious of you to say so." The frown had not completely disappeared from Horace's face as they approached the narrowboat. "When are you next coming back to the mill?"

"We're taking this delivery of flour to Thruppley now, as we normally do, and then we probably won't be back here for another few days or more. It's the Midsummer Fair on the common tonight, and Aunt Verity has said that we can all go. The gypsies have gathered nearby, and there's a troupe of travelling performers, so it's sure to be a lively night."

"I hope you have a nice time." Horace smiled and lifted one eyebrow. "I'm sure the young men will be queuing up to ask you your sisters to dance. I'm leaving shortly. I have to travel to London for a few days to take care of some business matters related to the brewery."

"Perhaps the young ladies of high society in London will be hoping you'll take them out for dinner and dancing," Dolly quipped back at him, knowing that he would take her teasing in good jest.

"I doubt I'll have time. I rather wish I wasn't going because some wealthy business acquaintances are visiting Papa today. Dominic has been in a strange mood recently, so I only hope he won't spoil things. Papa is hoping that they might be interested in making some investments in Thruppley and some of the surrounding areas."

"That sounds promising. I didn't think your pa was still doing much work."

"He's making a special effort for these visitors.

The trouble is that Dominic's behaviour is getting worse. I think it's because he's bored by the daily work of running the mill."

"Hopefully, he'll be on his best behaviour if he knows how much it matters to your pa." Dolly paused as they got near the narrowboat and turned slightly so her family wouldn't hear what she had to say. "What happened with Dominic today… there's no need to tell Aunt Verity or Uncle Bert; it will only make them worry." She squared her shoulders. "If he tries anything again, I'll know to expect it. He'll soon get bored once he knows I'm not interested."

Horace scratched his chin and nodded slowly. "I couldn't help but overhear that you said you're already courting?" His words petered out, as though he was worried about prying. "Whoever it is, he's a lucky man."

Mr Morton bustled towards them, waving some documents for Horace's attention before Dolly could correct his mistake.

"You'd better look at these, Master Horace. Your brother doesn't want to bother with 'em, even though t'was his idea." His plump jowls quivered with indignation, and Horace was soon absorbed in the notes.

Joe was just manoeuvring *The Skylark* on the side of the canal, and Barnaby rattled his harness and whinnied, making Jester snap awake from his doze. Dolly's heart skipped a beat at the sight of Joe's muscular shoulders flexing under his shirt, and she allowed herself a moment to daydream about what it would be like to be swept into his arms before mentally giving herself a shake.

All this talk of courting is giving me fanciful ideas. The thought made her smile, but then she blushed as she realised Joe was looking at her with a strange expression on his face.

"Are you going to the Midsummer Fair tonight, Joe?" Amy called. Gloria nudged her, and the two girls dissolved into giggles, looking between Joe and Dolly.

"I expect so –"

"There's no time for us to stand around chatting," Evan said, rudely interrupting.

Not for the first time, Dolly noticed a flash of irritation cross Joe's face at the way his father had spoken to Amy. She met Joe's eyes and was surprised to see the corner of his mouth lift in a tentative smile that his father couldn't see because Joe's back was turned towards him.

"Well, it will be nice to see you there, Joe," Amy

said, unperturbed by Evan's brusque reply. "I fancy there will be lots of dancing…and who knows what might happen, with it being Midsummer and a full moon as well."

Gloria's eyes softened as she gazed wistfully into the distance, and Dolly smiled to herself. Her younger sister had reached the age where she entertained dreams of romance and falling in love, whereas Jonty was more interested in what food might be served at the stalls and the performances from the troupe of entertainers. She felt a ripple of excitement at the thought of doing something different from their normal, workaday lives, and found herself hoping very much that she and Joe might finally be able to put their rivalry behind them and become friends again if only his pa would allow it.

CHAPTER 13

"I've never seen three such lovely girls in all my life, don't you agree, Bert?" Verity's eyes misted with tears of pride as Dolly, Gloria, and Amy stepped off the narrowboat onto the towpath. She clasped her hands to her chest and sighed happily with an approving nod, not only for their natural beauty but for their resilient spirit. "You deserve a lovely evening out. You've all been working very hard recently, so mind you enjoy yourselves."

Bert hobbled up the steps behind her, but he had a small frown of worry on his face. "Be sure to look after your sisters, Jonty," he warned. "Three beautiful maids like them are sure to attract attention. I trust the travelling community, but there are plenty of men who would take advantage of your sisters if they had the chance."

"Don't worry," Jonty said with an amused smile. "I won't drink any ale, and I'll be keeping a close eye on them. I won't let any ruffians or ne'er-do-wells steal their hearts, Uncle Bert."

As the four of them walked across the common, the sun was already sinking in the west, casting long mauve shadows on the ground. The three girls were unmistakably sisters, with their dark beauty. Dolly's hair was pinned up in loose curls, with tendrils framing her face. Gloria had twisted her hair into an elegant chignon at the nape of her neck. And Amy's curls tumbled down her back, held in place with a green ribbon which matched her dress. Several young men turned to watch their progress, even though the sisters paid no heed as they were too busy chattering about the evening ahead.

Verity had surprised them all a month earlier, offering to buy each of them a new gown for the event from the cramped shop called Second Hand Rose in Frampton. Since then, Gloria had worked wonders, turning up hems, sewing invisible tucks to take them in, mending tears, and then adorning them with artfully fashioned remnants of lace until they looked as good as new.

"It looks like it's going to be a good turnout. The gypsy vardos are so pretty." In the distance, the highly-decorated horse-drawn wagons were spread in a large circle near the spinney at the edge of the common, and she could see young children darting between the wagons, playing tag amidst squeals of laughter. Their two communities had an affectionate respect for each other, and she was looking forward to catching up with some of her travelling friends who she hadn't seen for a year. Dolly couldn't remember feeling this excited for a long time, and the air of anticipation carried them over the undulating common faster than usual, all their weariness from the day's work forgotten.

The fair itself was being held in a flat area at the centre of the common, and there was a pyramid of wood in the middle, already starting to crackle as the flames took hold. "They've lit the bonfire already. I swear it's the tallest one I've ever seen." Gloria clapped her hands and did a little skip of delight.

There were gaily decorated stalls around the edge of the western side, offering anything from sprigs of lucky heather, decorated tin mugs and plates to adorn dressers, posies of flowers, and an array of food. The rich aroma of a roasting pig on a spit jostled with the scent of hot chocolate and ginger cake. A little further along, there was a wooden stand with casks of ale, and the clink of bottles of gin and rum carried towards them, where a crowd of men had already gathered. Judging by the raucous laughter, they had already been drinking for most of the afternoon, and Dolly steered her family in the opposite direction.

"Can we have a go at hoopla?" Gloria asked eagerly.

"Will there be a dancing dog, do you think?" Amy pondered, trying to make sense of the hazy shapes she could see. She looked less certain of herself than usual, with all the competing noise and hubbub of the crowds, and Jonty tucked her hand firmly in the crook of his arm.

"I reckon so, Amy," he said. "Don't worry, we'll walk around everything, and you won't miss out on a thing, I promise."

By the time they had strolled between the stalls and stopped to chat with friends and acquaintances who they didn't see very often, darkness was starting to fall.

"You go on without me," Dolly said. She knew

they didn't have too much money to spend, and poor Jonty kept eyeing the roasting pig as though he hadn't eaten for a month. "Go and buy some food, and I'll catch you up. I'm happy just to stand and watch the bonfire for a moment." She pulled some coins out of her dress pocket and handed them over to Jonty, laughing as his face broke into a broad smile.

On the far side of the bonfire, the musicians started to tune up their instruments, and there was a palpable sense of excitement. Some of the gypsy girls were already linking arms and twirling in lively dances, which made their exotically colourful skirts swirl around them, reminding Dolly of butterflies rising and dipping over nectar-laden flowers. It was going to be a wonderful night, and she sighed happily.

"We meet again, Dolly. I trust you will dance with me once the music starts properly." The deep well-spoken voice behind her was slightly slurred by drink, and she spun around to see Dominic clutching a tankard of cider in his hand.

"What are you doing here?" she blurted out without thinking. "The Midsummer Fair isn't for the likes of you, Mr Smallwood. It's for the gypsies, narrowboat families, and villagers. Can we not enjoy one evening of simple pleasures without you trying to interfere?"

Dominic took a long drink of his cider, watching her closely over the rim of his tankard before answering. "I go where I please, Dolly. The roughness of a gathering like this with folk who are free to travel where they like is too alluring to resist."

Dolly noticed that he was wearing his usual smart frock coat and elegantly cut trousers. His obvious wealth was in sharp contrast to everyone else, but he didn't care.

He noticed her appraising look and grinned wolfishly. "Every now and again, I like to step outside the tedious boundaries of my life as the eldest son of Mr Edward Smallwood. I enjoy throwing off the expectations of being a respected businessman and upright pillar of society." A sardonic smile lifted the corner of his mouth as his foot started tapping in time to the music.

She felt cross that he had rudely inserted himself into their evening and stolen some of the pleasure she had been enjoying. "I meant what I said earlier today. Other women might be flattered by your attention, but it's not something I want."

This time, Dominic threw his head back and

laughed out loud. "You might say that now, but once we've spent the night dancing together…and hopefully more…I'm sure your mind will be changed." He spoke with the arrogant certainty of a man who was never denied. He expected her to bend to his will, and as far as he was concerned, what she wanted was irrelevant.

The approaching darkness and hum of energy around the bonfire emboldened Dolly enough to put a stop to whatever he was planning. She turned to face him squarely, with her hands on her hips. "I won't dance with you, Dominic. Not tonight…not ever."

Just as Dominic was about to reach for her, a shadow fell over them. "I'm sorry I'm late, Dolly; it took me longer than expected to unharness Barnaby."

Dolly hid her shock as Joe appeared by her side as if from nowhere and placed his arm protectively around her shoulders. He gave Dominic a cool stare, and Dolly was gratified to see the man stumble backwards several steps, looking at Joe with annoyance.

"This boy is who you're courting?" Dominic snorted with feigned amusement and took another swig of cider, carelessly splashing it down the front of his shirt.

"It's none of your business," Dolly snapped. "Now, if you'll excuse us, my family and I want to enjoy the rest of our evening."

Dominic laughed again, but this time there was a cruel tone to it. "Don't worry, I'll get my adventures elsewhere…not with the likes of you," he said scornfully. With that, he turned on his heel and hurried away, slamming his half-empty tankard angrily on the wooden counter of the ale stall on his way.

"Sorry," Joe said, hastily withdrawing his arm from Dolly's shoulder. "At the mill earlier today, I overheard Horace telling Mr Morton that Dominic was bothering you, and then when I saw him trying it on again this evening, I couldn't just stand by and let him get away with it. I hope you didn't mind…about me putting my arm around you. It was all I could think of in a hurry." He ran a hand through his tousled blonde hair, suddenly looking embarrassed.

"I'm very glad you were so quick-thinking," Dolly said. She felt the corner of her mouth twitching up into a smile now that her shock had subsided. "Anyway, it's not the first time you've put your arm around me," she added. "There were many times when we were climbing trees and scrambling through streams when we were nippers in the Middleyard, if you remember."

Joe exhaled loudly and chuckled. "I remember only too well. You always wanted to climb higher than me or get into the stream first, which is why I had to rescue you so often." His blue eyes twinkled at the memory, and suddenly it felt as though all the awkwardness and animosity of the last nine years had never happened.

"Dominic really is an odious man," Dolly said, shaking her head. "He rides roughshod over everybody. I just hope he won't hold what just happened against us." This time, it was her turn to give Joe an apologetic smile. "I'm sorry; he might have got the impression that we are courting. I had to say something earlier to try and get him away from me. Not that it worked. Horace had to intervene. It seems I owe you and Horace a debt of thanks today."

"Courting, eh? I'm sure Bert and Verity might have something to say about that, so it's a good thing it's not true!" Joe chuckled again and tipped his head back to look at the first stars, which were faintly visible. "Anyway, there's no need to thank me, Dolly. It's what any friend would do. I'm glad I could be there for you when you needed me."

"I'm sure Aunt Verity and Uncle Bert would think you're a fine young man...even if you did used to put frogs in my boots when we were little."

They both looked towards the bonfire for a moment, letting this new change wrap around their hearts, taking them back to their easy childhood camaraderie, which had been lost for so long.

"I SEE you managed to shake him off," Jonty said jovially as he walked towards them with Gloria and Amy a few minutes later. "I was just about to come over, but Joe beat me to it."

"What's going on? Did I miss something?" Billy asked, running up to them. He seemed to have forgotten about the animosity between the two families as well, and it felt like old times with the six of them together.

"Oh, it's just Dominic Smallwood living up to the rumours about him," Joe said with a twitch of his eyebrow. "Dolly gave him what for, and he soon left with his tail between his legs."

"How are you, Billy?" Amy asked. A faint pink flush coloured her cheeks as she smiled up at him.

"Oh...you know, everything is just fine." He cleared his throat awkwardly and shuffled his feet in the grass. "I'm a blacksmith now, learning a trade from Abe Wentworth." He couldn't keep the hint of pride from his voice.

"A very good one, too," Amy said.

"How...how do you know?" Billy looked puzzled.

"Did you forget? Our Amy knows everything." Jonty slapped Billy on the back with a chuckle.

"I can tell by the sound of Jester's hooves on the towpath," Amy explained, as though it was obvious. "And I hear other folk singing your praises. Tell me everything about your new job, Billy. I've been wondering how you are, and it's so lovely to see you and Joe tonight."

Billy jingled some coins in his pocket. "Mr Wentworth paid me today. Can I buy you a hot chocolate while we talk? You always liked it... when you were a little girl, I mean," he added, stumbling over his words.

Gloria and Dolly exchanged a knowing glance, both thinking how well-suited Billy and Amy were. Amy had always held a special place in Billy's affections when they were children, and Dolly was heartened to see that he still cared for her, in spite of Evan's best attempts to try and turn the two families against each other.

No sooner had the thought entered her mind than she suddenly spotted Evan striding towards them, and her heart sank.

"Come away, boys; what have I told you?" His brow was drawn down in its usual frown, but Dolly noticed that he looked tired. Age was catching up on him, and she wished for Joe and Billy's sake that he could find a kindhearted woman to care for him and help him get over Stella leaving.

Dolly expected Joe and Billy to walk away from them immediately as they always had done before, but this time something felt different.

Joe shook his head stubbornly. "No, Pa, it's time to draw a line under everything that happened in the past. Dolly and the others never did anything to harm us. Even if you still believe their pa is to blame for ma leaving, we shouldn't take it out on them."

Evan's expression darkened at Joe's refusal to do what he wanted, and she knew she had to speak now, or any chance of friendship might be lost forever.

She walked towards Evan and placed her hand lightly on his arm. " Please, Mr Granger," she said quietly, "we miss having Joe and Billy as our friends. Especially Amy. Things might not always be easy for her in the future, what with struggling to see. She'll always do her best to find her way in the world, but she looks up to Billy. You've raised a wonderful boy who Amy adores…can't you allow them to be friends again?" She let her heartfelt words hang in the air between them, holding her breath and desperately hoping he would finally relent on the rivalry, which he had held onto so determinedly for all these years.

For a moment, there was a frosty silence, and Dolly wished she had walked away, regretting her rash attempt to mend things between them.

Evan looked down at her hand on his arm, and then across at Amy and Gloria, who were standing nearby, not quite meeting his eye. "You remind me of Anne, your ma," he said, hesitantly. He took a deep breath and blew out his cheeks before rereleasing it, and Dolly could feel some of the tension draining out of him. "I saw that scoundrel Dominic Smallwood bothering you earlier," he continued, seemingly changing the subject. "It's not right...the likes of him preying on us narrowboat families. Someone with his wealth and standing should know better. I suppose...we should stick together...those of us with the same background."

Dolly smiled, feeling tears prick the back of her eyes. She knew that this was probably as much of an apology, and a tentative step towards friendship again, as Evan could manage. But it was enough. It felt like a door opening, and a chink of light, coming back into a darkened room again, and her heart squeezed with happiness.

"Shall we go and get that hot chocolate, Amy? And how about you two," Billy said, looking at Jonty and Gloria.

The air was suddenly filled with the sound of lively music as the fiddlers struck up a tune, and Joe grinned at Dolly as Evan wandered off to speak to some other families from the canal. "Well, it seems as though Pa has finally mellowed." He shook his head in amazement. The music got louder. "Do you remember the gypsies played this song when they came to Middleyard one year?"

"Yes, it was when I was eight years old, and they came for the horse fair." As the music picked up to an even faster rhythm, some of the gypsy girls started spinning and twirling in the shimmering shadows and orange glow of the bonfire. A moment later, some of the young men and children ran to join them, and then the more formal dancing began as they lined up to do a reel.

"Shall we dance, Dolly?" Joe's eyes were alight with enthusiasm that she found infectious. The music, the dancing, and the laughter were intoxicating, and Dolly suddenly felt a surge of joy.

"I'd like nothing better." She picked up her skirts and ran ahead of him towards the group, grinning at Joe over her shoulder. "Come on then, I think I can still remember the steps."

The next couple of hours passed in a blur of colour and laughter, as the couples spun around each other, separating and coming back together, joining hands, and weaving in circles and figures of eight. As she and Joe whirled, her feet barely touching the ground, Dolly felt a new sense of connection with him. The firelight was reflected in his blue eyes, and sparks floated from the bonfire up into the velvety, soft night sky. For one magical evening, the weight of worrying about earning enough money and having enough work to keep them fed and clothed seemed to fade away. Jonty and Gloria came to join in, and before long, Billy shyly asked Amy to dance as well.

I hope I remember this night forever, Dolly thought. As the golden moon slowly rose over the hilltops, she couldn't help but think that this had been the most wonderful evening of her life.

As the night wore on, the music slowly changed, and at the end of a lively 'excuse me' waltz, Dolly found herself in Joe's arms, in the darkness at the edge of the dancing area. In the blink of an eye, she knew that her feelings towards Joe had changed. She had longed for their friendship to blossom again, and it seemed that it had. But the way her heart beat faster as she looked up into his eyes felt unfamiliar. It was as if she was seeing Joe as the burly, kindhearted man he had become for the first time, instead of the snub-nosed boy of her childhood memories. And as the last strains of the fiddle died, she hastily stepped away from him, not sure why she felt suddenly so flustered in his company.

"I'm glad Papa didn't stop us from spending time together this evening," Joe said. He sounded slightly breathless from all the dancing as he let go of her, and his expression was hard to read. "Shall we get a glass of lemonade? It will be time to go back to the boat soon, we have an early start in the morning."

As they strolled across the grass towards the stalls again, Dolly felt as though she had a hundred questions on the tip of her tongue; it had been so long since they could talk properly. "Do you…do you still hear from your ma?" She could have kicked herself for starting with that one. Joe probably didn't want to talk about it at all.

"I still see articles written about her in the newspaper," Joe admitted. He shrugged, and Dolly was relieved to see that he didn't look hurt talking about it anymore. "She has made a great success of herself on the stage. I think she and Mr Portiscue are living together as husband and wife. There's never any mention of us anymore. She must have put her time in Middleyard behind her, and I think Pa has finally accepted that she won't be coming back." He handed over a sixpence and passed her the lemonade.

"Is your Pa lonely, do you think?" She thought about how her own father had seemed quieter after her mother had died.

"He keeps himself busy, although with Billy working for Abe Wentworth at the forge now, and it just being him and me on the boat, I do worry about what might happen in the future…if I were to leave."

Before Dolly had a chance to think about what Joe meant by leaving, there was a sudden commotion just past the hoopla stall. It was Wilf Latham, the farmer's son, and for some reason, he seemed to be making a beeline for them, running as if his life depended on it.

"Dolly…" He coughed, doubling over to catch his breath. "Your aunt Verity sent me to come and get you. It's your uncle…he's had a bad turn."

It took a second for his words to sink in. "What do you mean, a turn?" She looked around hastily, wondering if she should gather Jonty and the others.

"I don't know, Dolly," Wilf said, looking anguished. "All Verity said was that you were to get back to the narrowboat as quickly as possible… something about that old cough knocking him for six…"

"I have to go immediately," Dolly said to Joe. "Will you walk back with the others and tell them what's happened?"

"Of course. Go back with Wilf now. Don't worry about the others, Dolly, and try not to worry about Bert. He's stronger than he looks. I'm sure Doctor Skelton will have him better again in no time."

Dolly was grateful for Joe's reassurances, and she picked up her skirts and ran over the tussocky grass by the light of the moon, chasing after Wilf, who had already set off again. As she got to the edge of the common, she paused to catch her breath and glanced back over her shoulder. Joe was already rounding up Jonty and Gloria, and Billy was carefully helping Amy, trying not to hurry her. Joe suddenly looked up and met her eyes. He lifted his hand in a gesture of friendship, and she knew that no matter what might happen, at last she had someone she could rely on, someone to share her hopes and fears for the future with.

CHAPTER 14

Verity was already waiting on the towpath, wringing her hands and pacing back and forth, as Dolly rounded the corner.

"What's happened to Uncle Bert?" Dolly's chest was burning from running all the way back from the common. She had overtaken Wilf, driven by fear, and his footsteps crunched behind her a moment later.

"He hasn't been feeling well all day, but I didn't want to say anything. You know that he doesn't like anyone to make a fuss, and he was worried it might spoil your evening at the fair. I knew something was wrong when he didn't eat the cake I gave him after you left. He stood up from the table and collapsed. I managed to get him onto the bed, but I don't like the look of him."

Dolly clambered onto the boat and clattered down the stairs. In the flickering light of the oil lamp, she could see a faint sheen of sweat on Bert's brow, and his complexion was a strange greyish colour. His eyes were tightly closed, but not in a restful way, more with pain, and he gave a faint groan as she put her hand on his shoulder.

"Can you hear me, Uncle?" Dolly felt a fresh wave of fear as his eyes flickered open briefly. His gaze was unfocused, and he groaned again.

"I can't get much sense out of him." The shadowy light of the oil lamp made Verity's face look old, etched deep with lines of worry.

"I think I should go and get Doctor Skelton." Dolly could see that Verity had made him a herbal tincture, but she nodded in agreement.

Dolly hurried back outside to find Wilf again. He was waiting patiently, eager to help. "Have you seen the doctor around this evening?"

Wilf shook his head. "I ain't seen him for a few days, Dolly. I'm sorry. Do you want me to go into Thruppley and ask around?"

The bobbing light of a lantern approached, and Dolly saw it was Sadie. She quickly explained what had happened, and Sadie hurried to Verity's side. "I can't believe it. Bert never gets ill, apart from that bad cough he couldn't shake off last winter." She pulled her shawl tighter around her shoulders. "I overheard one of the Lawson nippers saying that Doctor Skelton was on his way to Middleyard to visit a woman struggling with having her baby. The midwife would have helped, but she's contagious with pox, so he had to be fetched instead."

"I'm going to ride up there on Jester," Dolly said decisively. "It won't take long, and the quicker we can get the doctor back to see Uncle Bert, the better."

"Bless you, Dolly. I knew you would know what to do." Verity sounded shaken, and at that moment, she seemed to have aged almost ten years in Dolly's eyes. It was inconceivable to think that Bert might not recover, and Verity would be left alone. The thought spurred Dolly into action, and she was grateful to have something to do.

"Help me get Jester ready, will you, Wilf?" Dolly retrieved the bridle she used for normal riding from beneath the seat next to the tiller. She had no saddle because Jester was mainly used for pulling *The River Maid*, but it didn't matter; she was a confident, bareback rider.

Within a few minutes, Dolly had put Jester's bridle on, and Wilf manoeuvred him to stand next to a grassy bank to make it easier for Dolly to spring up onto his back. She gathered up the reins and kicked him into a canter, giving them a quick backward wave. "Keep an eye out for the others, Wilf. They're on their way back from the fair. And look out for the doctor, too, in case the Lawsons were mistaken, and he's still in Thruppley."

Ragged clouds had started to drift across the sky since she had left the Midsummer Fair. It meant the moonlight was not as bright, but she knew the route well enough. She decided to take the most direct way, along the old cattle droving track, which skirted around the edge of the common before descending into Woodford Valley and then up the other side to Middleyard village. It would be quicker than following the lanes from Thruppley, even if it was overgrown with billowing cow parsley in places.

Under any other circumstances, Dolly would have enjoyed riding on such a warm summer night. The heady scent of honeysuckle and wild roses hung heavy in the air, and every now and again, she heard the squeak of a bat swooping over her head. The thrum of Jester's hoofbeats told her that they were covering the ground quickly, and the faint sounds of the fair were soon left behind. Before long, she saw the dark outline of the uneven rooftops of cottages and the once-familiar sight of Middleyard's church spire with its cross on the top.

She trotted through the dusty lanes, deciding to head straight to the Woolpack Inn. If anyone knew where Doctor Skelton was, it would be someone there, and she didn't want to start knocking the villagers up from their beds.

She slipped down from Jester, throwing his reins over the hitching post outside the Inn, then took a deep breath and strode into the pub.

"Well, if it ain't a visitor from the past." George Lloyd, the landlord, looked startled as he caught sight of her. He rubbed his eyes in a display of surprise, and two men hunched over a game of cards in the corner laughed. "I haven't seen you for nigh on ten years, but I'd bet a shilling that you are Ruben and Anne's daughter? You're the spit of your ma. Dolly Hinton…I'll be blowed. What do you want, maid?"

Dolly ignored her discomfort as the room fell silent, and the drinkers turned to stare. She had forgotten her bonnet in her haste, and her hair hung down her back. The sight of a dishevelled young woman bursting through the door in the middle of the night was not something they were accustomed to.

"You're quite right, Mr Llloyd," she said hastily. "I'm sorry for disturbing you...I know this is no place for a single woman, but I must find Doctor Skelton. It's my Uncle Bert, he's taken ill, and we need help." A couple of rough-shaven labourers looked at her with hungry interest, nudging each other, but she ignored them. There was no time to worry about that.

"Doctor Skelton?" George sucked on his teeth and paused in the middle of pouring out a tankard of ale for a ruddy-cheeked man who was leaning on the bar. "I'm not rightly sure where he is. What makes you think he's in Middleyard? You've come a long way from the canal."

His plump wife, Ruby, bustled in from the taproom. Her sleeves were rolled up to reveal brawny arms, and she was carrying a small cask of brandy as if it weighed nothing. She balanced it on a shelf behind the bar and pushed back a lock of hair which had fallen into her eyes. "Goodness me, if it ain't Dolly Hinton. What brings you up here, my love? Last we heard, you and the nippers were down Frampton Basin way."

"She's lookin' for the doctor," a wizened man with a broad burr of an accent explained from the rickety chair next to the fire where he was sitting. Pipe smoke curled around his head. "Her uncle's took bad."

"I'm sorry, my love," Ruby said, with a shake of her head. "He was tending to Mrs Roberts an hour ago, but she's had the baby, and he went on his way again." She gave Dolly a sympathetic smile. "I saw him riding past, as it happens. I was outside because our dog was barking. It turned out to be nothing, though. The doctor told me he was going back to Thruppley, which is no good for you."

Dolly exhaled the breath she hadn't even known she was holding, feeling a wash of relief. "Thruppley? That's perfect, Mrs Lloyd. That's where we are moored up at the moment, not Frampton Basin. If he set off an hour ago, I expect my brother or Wilf will have spotted him already."

"Will you stay for something to drink and eat, for old times' sake?" George asked kindly. "It was a shame when you all left the village after your pa died. He was a good man, Ruben...he used to look after us with the odd rabbit for the pot, not as you'd probably remember."

Dolly hesitated for a moment. A cup of tea would have been welcome, plus it would give Jester a chance to rest, but she couldn't linger until she knew that Bert was going to be alright. "Another time," she said gratefully. "I'll bring Jonty, Gloria, and Amy with me. They're all grown up now, but it would be good to remind Amy and Gloria what the village is like. They've all but forgotten about when we lived here."

"Well, mind how you go, riding back," Ruby said. She crossed the smokey room and opened the heavy door, peering out at the dark night beyond. "Is it safe for you to ride back alone?"

"I'll be fine," Dolly said firmly. She didn't want to put anyone to the trouble of escorting her. "I came on the drovers' route on the way here, which is why I must have missed seeing Doctor Skelton on the lanes. But I'll ride back via Tom Long's Post. It's a clear, moonlit night, and Jester will look after me, don't worry."

George came to join his wife as Dolly hurried back outside and got back onto Jester's broad back. "Remember us to your family, and to Joe's family as well." He lifted his hand to wave goodbye. "Mind how you go, Dolly. It ain't so long ago that there were highway robberies around here, so keep your wits about you."

THE MOON WAS high in the sky by the time Jester had carried Dolly along the lane from Middleyard, down to the valley bottom, and up the steep hill onto the common land at the top. Ragged clouds still drifted across the sky, and the moon had changed from a rich buttery colour to a silvery white, casting deep shadows on either side of her in the undergrowth. She tried not to think about the folklore of Tom Long's Post. The story of how the highway robber had been hanged from a gibbet was still muttered under people's breath on dark winter nights, but she pushed the thoughts away. She already felt jumpy enough as the occasional fox screamed, sounding almost human-like, and other night creatures rustled, going about their business. Jester's solid bulk beneath her was comforting, and she held the reins lightly, knowing that he wouldn't spook, no matter what might cross their path.

As they crested the hill, hugging the tall stone wall which surrounded one of the grand country estates on top of the common, a prickle of apprehension ran down Dolly's back as she heard gruff voices ahead. It was the first sign of anyone since leaving Middleyard, and worryingly it sounded like the two men were arguing.

"Whoa, boy," she said softly. The sound of Jester's trotting was muffled by the dusty road, and the light breeze was blowing into her face, from the men's direction. She knew they probably hadn't heard her, and as Jester slowed to a walk and then stopped with gentle pressure from her heels, she wondered what to do. The last thing she wanted was to become embroiled in a drunken brawl. *Perhaps we should retrace our steps and go across the common another way.* The thought was tempting. It would take longer, but help her avoid meeting them.

The breeze carried the conversation towards her, piquing her interest.

"...I ain't so sure about this, Mr Smallwood." The voice sounded nasal and disgruntled, and Dolly froze at the mention of the name.

She edged Jester forward, making sure that they remained in the deepest part of the shadows, well away from where the silvery moonlight might reveal their presence. By leaning forward over

Jester's neck, she was able to see two figures, standing near two horses, which were grazing quietly. She gasped as the moon slipped out from behind a cloud, and she realised that the taller of the two men was none other than Dominic Smallwood.

What's he doing here? And who is he talking to? The questions poured into her mind, as the second man walked away from Dominic a few steps before turning around to face him. He was shorter than Dominic by half a head, wearing ill-fitting clothes, and his face looked lined with poverty and the stresses of a hard life.

"Why the sudden change of heart?" The rough-looking man said. He crossed his arms and looked up at Dominic. His tone was not as deferential as Dolly would have expected. In fact, there was almost a hint of rudeness to it, as if he was doing Dominic a favour by being there.

Dominic slapped his riding crop against the side of his leather boots, clearly feeling irritated. "Papa refuses to sell, even though they offered a price that most sensible men would have jumped at the chance of accepting."

"...he ain't like you...lives to a different sort of morals..." The breeze had changed direction slightly, and Dolly couldn't quite hear the other man's full reply.

"There's only one thing left for it. We'll have to go ahead with my plan." Dominic had raised his voice slightly, confident that nobody could overhear what he was talking about.

"It's risky...for me, at least." The man coughed and then hawked up some phlegm, which he spat in the dirt, making Dominic step back slightly in distaste. "I ain't so sure I want to go ahead anymore. My wife is nagging me to get back home and get a job in the docks, and especially since she had the baby...another hungry mouth to feed."

Dolly saw the gleam of Dominic's smile in the moonlight. The other man had just played right into his hands; even Dolly knew that. "All the more reason to take up my offer," he said, slapping the man on his shoulder, as though it had all been already agreed. "I'll pay you handsomely once everything is settled."

Jester fidgeted slightly under Dolly, and his bridle clinked, filling her with fear that they might see her.

"Hush a moment, will you." Dominic held up his riding crop and tilted his head to one side, straining to listen. Dolly stroked Jester's neck, praying that he wouldn't fidget again.

The air was suddenly split by the sharp barking and yelping of two foxes fighting, and Dominic's head snapped around to stare in the direction it came from. "It's alright…just animals. We can't risk anyone finding out."

"So, this thing you want me to take care of… how will it be explained once they find out? It ain't an everyday occurrence, and in my experience, when things is out of the ordinary, them in charge start getting suspicious. Your pa will want to know." The man lifted his grimy cap, giving Dolly a glimpse of reddish hair that lay unevenly because of a scar on his hairline. He scratched his head thoughtfully before putting his cap on again, not yet willing to agree to what Dominic wanted, which surprised Dolly even more. Dominic was rich and powerful, whereas the other man looked as though he barely had two shillings to rub together. It seemed like a strange sort of relationship, and all the more odd because he wasn't pandering to Dominic like most people did.

Dominic snorted contemptuously. "Papa? Don't you worry about that doddery old fool. You can leave him to me; just make sure you're careful, and nobody can trace it back to us."

The two men turned and started walking back towards their horses, making it harder for Dolly to hear them.

"...when...want it done by?" The smaller man swung himself up onto his scruffy piebald horse and pulled his cap lower over his face.

Just as Dominic was about to answer, she heard a new sound. It was the rhythmic clopping of another horse, and she saw Dominic glance nervously across the common as a man driving a rickety cart approached. It looked as though they were heading towards Middleyard.

"Evening, gentlemen...got anything for a hard-working rag-and-bone man?" The fellow hiccupped and swayed slightly on his seat, giving them an amiable grin, and Dolly realised he was probably on his way home from the pub.

"No," Dominic snapped. He turned back to his acquaintance, needing to conclude their meeting. "I'll let you know when. It won't be much longer."

As the rag-and-bone man drew closer, Dolly knew she had to move. He had already spotted her, and she could tell that in his drunken state, he was probably going to strike up a conversation or ask whether she had any rags to add to the meagre pile in the back of his cart.

"Come on, Jester." She clicked her tongue against her teeth and pulled lightly on the right rein, turning Jester around and kicking him into a trot in the opposite direction from Dominic. Hopefully, he wouldn't suspect she had heard their conversation, and she would be far enough away for him not to realise who it was. Five lanes over the common intersected at Tom Long's Post, so it could be feasible that she was just a traveller passing through, minding her own business.

She kicked her heels, and Jester broke into a steady canter, quickly putting some distance between her and Dominic. As another cloud slid over the moon, she risked a backward glance, but Dominic was nowhere to be seen. All she could hear was a tuneless song from the drunken rag-and-bone man, and if she hadn't witnessed Dominic's strange meeting with her own eyes, it would have been as if it had never happened.

* * *

"Dolly! Is everything all right?"

A shadow loomed in front of her, startling her.

But then she realised at the same moment that it was just Joe on Barnaby.

"You gave me a fright," she gasped. Jester slowed to a walk, as Joe wheeled Barnaby around to come alongside her.

"By the time we got back to the narrowboat, Doctor Skelton was already there. I didn't like the thought of you being out alone at night." He looked bashful. "I didn't mean to frighten you, though."

"Do you know how Uncle Bert is?"

"Not exactly, but I did hear the doctor telling Verity that it's probably not as bad as she thinks."

They rode on in silence for a few minutes, and Dolly felt some of her worries start to ease. "You'll never guess who I saw on my way back from Middleyard. It was quite the strangest thing."

Joe looked at her curiously. "I'm surprised you would meet anyone at this time of night. Especially up here. Everyone from the fair has gone back to the village, and the gypsies are sitting around their own campfire by their vardos by now, I should imagine."

"When I was up near Tom Long's Post, I heard two men talking…arguing more like. It was Dominic Smallwood, and he was with a scruffy-looking man I haven't seen before."

"What were they arguing about? I know Smallwood has a short temper on him, but it seems rather mysterious to be meeting someone in such a remote place as that in the middle of the night."

"I couldn't make out everything they were saying. It sounded like he wants his pa to sell the mill, and he's annoyed that he won't. The other man looks like a shifty sort of fellow. Dominic was trying to persuade him to do something...I don't know what, but he seemed quite insistent that it mustn't be traced back to them, whatever it is."

Joe shot Dolly a worried look. "Sell Nailsbridge Mill? That doesn't sound like something that Edward Smallwood would agree to at all. He likes it to be known how proud he is of what he's done with the mill and that he'll always keep it going because it supports so many folks on the canal, not to mention all the villagers who work there."

"That's the problem," Dolly said, with a rueful smile. "Over these last few months, I've learnt from Horace that Dominic doesn't care about whatever promises his father has made in the past. And Horace can't stop Dominic from doing whatever he likes because he's the younger brother. For all his shrewdness in business, it seems as though

Edward Smallwood is blind to what Dominic is really like."

"Maybe we should try and find out more about what he's planning? It's up to the two of us, don't you think?" Joe said slowly. A ghostly white barn owl glided across the grassland in front of them on silent wings, hunting for its next meal.

Dolly felt a warm glow in her chest at the way Joe had casually assumed they would tackle this together and was glad it was too dark for him to see the blush on her cheeks. "I agree, but I have no idea how. Horace told me he's away in London for a few days. I could talk to him about it when he gets back when we're next at Nailsbridge."

"That's a good start. He seems very fond of you —" Joe looked away for a moment, not finishing his sentence. When he glanced at Dolly again, his expression was hard to read in the moonlight, and Dolly sensed that perhaps he saw Horace as a rival, now that their friendship had blossomed again.

"It's a friendship which goes back a long time," she said lightly. "He's like his pa, kind-hearted with good intentions towards the canal families who work for them. Look, we're almost back in Thruppley," she added, trying to change the subject.

Dolly didn't want to embarrass herself by

saying more about it. She knew that with their different social standings, it was an unlikely friendship sort of friendship between her and Horace. There was nothing more to it, but if she said so, it might betray the confusing emotions she felt towards Joe now that they were older. She still didn't quite understand the sense of attraction she felt towards him, as though a tiny seed of love had taken root and started to unfurl in her heart. It would be too hurtful if he didn't feel the same way, and for now, she didn't want to do anything to risk their newfound friendship.

"We need to work together. Dominic Smallwood is as slippery as an eel, and he has money and connections at his disposal to do as he wishes. But if he's planning to sell the mill and put us all out of work, we need to know, Dolly."

"I agree. But I don't want to mention anything to Aunt Verity and Uncle Bert. They have enough to worry about at the moment."

"I don't want to tell my pa yet either," Joe said. "He can be a bit hotheaded at times, and I wouldn't put it past him to march straight up to Dominic and demand to know what's happening."

Dolly and Joe exchanged a conspiratorial smile. "We can ask a few discreet questions, and keep a lookout for anything that seems unusual," Dolly said. She felt a shiver of intrigue and excitement, knowing that they were bound together now by this mystery that needed to be solved.

By the time they got back to the canal, the sky was starting to lighten in the east, and sunrise wasn't far away.

Dolly jumped down from Jester and ran towards *The River Maid*, while Joe took care of the two horses. "What did the doctor say?" she asked as Verity climbed wearily up the steps out of the cabin. Her heart went out to her aunt, who looked exhausted.

"Good news and bad," Verity said, sinking slowly onto the bench as if she was too tired to stand up. She gave Dolly a tentative smile. "Doctor Skelton thinks his heart is weak after he had that cough in the winter. It could have been pneumonia, and we didn't realise. He'll recover, thank goodness, but the bad news is that he won't be able to work for a while."

Dolly threw her arms around Verity's shoulders, before sitting down next to her, all thoughts of Dominic and the strange meeting gone from her mind. "As long as Uncle Bert gets well again, that's all that matters, Aunt Verity. Jonty and I can do the work now perfectly fine. We won't be beaten by this, even if it means we have to work night and day. I won't let everything Uncle Bert has built up over so many years go to nothing, I promise."

Verity finally allowed her tears to fall, partly out of relief and partly out of worry. "Thank you, our Dolly. You're a kind girl. What would we do without you?" She sniffed and dried her tears. "Thank goodness we'll never be short of work. I think if we lost the contract at Nailsbridge, it would finish poor Bert off, but he'll be happy knowing that you and Jonty are keeping Mr Smallwood happy, that's for sure."

Dolly nodded and patted her aunt's hand. As she watched Joe putting a nosebag of oats on Jester, ready for another hard day's work ahead, she was more determined than ever to find out what Dominic was up to. Their livelihood depended on Nailsbridge Mill staying open, and she doubted that old Mr Smallbridge would approve of Dominic's scheming. She had to find a way to tell the old man that his eldest son was going to ruin his life's work...without Dominic finding out. But how? That was the troubling question swirling through her mind.

CHAPTER 15

"Are you sure I can't get up and work just a little bit?" Bert asked.

Verity rolled her eyes. "No, Bert Webster. For once, you'll do exactly what Doctor Skelton has told you. Otherwise, you'll have me to answer to."

"And me to answer to as well," Dolly added with a smile. She poured out two mugs of tea, handing one to Jonty. It had been a long day, getting down to Frampton Basin and loading up with sacks of grain. She was glad to take the weight off her feet for a few minutes and quench her thirst.

"He didn't say how long I had to rest for," Bert said, trying again. "I've been lying on this bed for practically two weeks already, no use to man or beast."

"There will be plenty of time for you to get back to work again, but only once Doctor Skelton says it's alright." Verity leaned forward and smacked a kiss on Bert's cheek, laughing at his stubbornness. "Dolly and Jonty are doing a grand job, so there's no need for you to worry."

"Are we staying here for the evening, or heading back to Nailsbridge?" Amy looked up from the silk flowers she was making. The little table was covered in scraps of brightly coloured fabric, and she had a basket by her side, which she was slowly filling up. "I only ask because I promised Betty Jones I would get this to her as soon as possible. So many of the well-to-do ladies want them to go with their dresses, I can scarcely keep up."

"And might it be to spend some time with Billy Granger, as well?" Gloria asked, arching one eyebrow mischievously.

"Get away with you," Amy said, turning pink.

Dolly smiled inwardly at the exchange, noticing that Amy hadn't denied what Gloria asked. Now that she was almost fifteen, with her figure looking more womanly by the day, plenty of the village lads were paying her youngest sister more attention. But Dolly suspected that Amy only had thoughts of one person who held the keys to her heart, and that was Billy. At least, she hoped that might be the case in the future when Amy was old enough to start courting.

"I reckon we should leave now, even if it means travelling in the dark for a few hours," Jonty said. He stuffed a mouthful of fruit cake into his mouth and hastily chewed it, looking at Dolly to see if she would agree.

"Good idea," Dolly said, with a nod. "Jester's had a rest, and there's no point waiting here if we don't need to. We can moor up outside Nailsbridge Mill and be ready to unload at first light, as soon as Mr Morton gets in."

"That should keep Dominic Smallwood happy," Bert muttered from his bed.

"Chance would be a fine thing," Verity said. "He's been giving me some very strange looks the last two times we were there, as though we've done something wrong. I can't imagine what it must be, though. Do you have any idea, Dolly?"

Dolly thought back to the night she had seen Dominic talking to the scruffy stranger on the common, feeling slightly guilty that she hadn't mentioned it to her aunt.

"No…although it doesn't take much for him to be in a bad mood," Dolly mumbled. She sipped her tea again, hoping Verity wouldn't press her. Dominic hadn't said anything directly to her since that night, but she had a sneaking suspicion that perhaps he had seen her riding away on Jester. The fact that he hadn't said anything about it since made her nervous. He was the sort of man to harbour a grudge and use things against people, and she wondered when he might choose to confront her with it. Knowing him, he was bound to want to keep some sort of threat dangling over her head.

The sun was already starting to go down by the time they had finished eating, and she had checked Jester's harness. Her shoulders ached from handling the heavy sacks of grain with Jonty, but she hummed quietly as she worked, not wanting her aunt and uncle to know how tired she felt.

"Ready to go?" Jonty called from the back of the narrowboat, his hand already on the tiller.

"Yes." She turned towards Mr Ferguson, the new yard manager at Frampton Basin. He was an unfriendly sort of man, unlike the jolly Mr Howard, who had recently retired, but she wanted to keep on his good side. "See you next time," she called.

"I suppose so." He watched her disapprovingly

with folded arms, before putting his cap on. "Don't make a habit of working through the night. It messes up my routine, and I don't like it." He jangled the keys to lock up behind them, impatient to head home for a mug of cider and the lamb and dumpling stew his wife had promised.

"Come on then, Jester," Dolly said, giving the horse's neck an encouraging pat. She slipped him a couple of slices of apple, and he munched happily as he leaned into the harness, and started plodding along the towpath, with her at his side.

After they had gone a little way, Dolly's heart lifted as she saw *The Skylark* in the gathering dusk up ahead. Joe and his pa had stopped for the evening, and Barnaby was contentedly grazing on the rough grass beyond the towpath. "We're going on ahead," she called to Joe as they got closer.

"Are you sure you can manage?" He paused from coiling the ropes on the top of the cabin, looking happy to see her. They hadn't had a chance to find out much about Dominic's plans since the night of the fair, as *The Skylark* had had to go to Selsley Mill. "Can you stop for a cup of tea?" he asked. It might give them time to talk and make a plan.

The smell of sizzling bacon wafted from the

cabin, and a moment later, Evan appeared, hearing the voices. "We'll be leaving before dawn, Verity, so if Dolly and Jonty need help, we won't be far behind."

"That's very kind of you," Verity said, looking touched. Nothing had pleased her more than the thawing of Evan's attitude towards Dolly and her siblings. As Dolly and Jonty carefully lifted the towline of their narrowboat over the top of *The Skylark*, so they could get past, she handed over a wedge of fruitcake, giving Evan a broad smile. "There's too much for us, so you two had better have it."

Evan thanked her gruffly, knowing full well that she couldn't really spare the cake, but it was a gesture of friendship that he was grateful for.

Dolly allowed Jester to walk on without her for a moment and hurried back to speak to Joe. "I haven't had a chance to ask Horace if he knows what Dominic might be up to yet," she whispered.

"Perhaps tomorrow would be a good time? I can help Jonty, and hopefully, it will be too early for Dominic to be in." They both knew that Horace was usually at the mill bright and early, unlike his brother.

"Do you think I should say something to Mr Morton?"

Joe gave her question some consideration. "Only if Horace isn't there." He put one foot up on the side of the narrowboat and leaned his elbow on it, thinking about their situation. "It's been a couple of weeks, and nothing has happened. Perhaps Dominic has changed his mind."

"I hope so." Dolly stepped away as she saw Jonty giving her an inquisitive look. "We'll see you in the morning." She hurried after Jester, with a renewed sense of energy. Spending time with Joe always made everything feel easier, and she found it hard to believe that they had spent so many years not speaking to each other. She couldn't imagine her life without him in it again…nor did she want to.

The night air was soft and velvety as Dolly guided Jester onwards. Fat, fluffy moths bumped against the glass windows of the cabin, drawn by the flickering light of the oil lamps inside, and the air was filled with squeaks as bats flew overhead. Every now and again, there was a rustle in the reeds or a plop in the water, from roosting moorhens or a fish breaking the surface of the canal, hoping to catch a fly before it was completely dark.

As she trudged along the towpath, and the moon started to rise, Dolly thought back to what Joe had said. It hadn't occurred to her that Dominic Smallwood might not go through with whatever it was he was planning. But it wasn't strictly true that she hadn't spoken to Horace at all; she just hadn't been able to pluck up the courage to ask him outright about his brother.

"My family and I owe Horace a debt of gratitude for taking an interest in our lives," she had explained to Joe when he suggested telling him about what she had seen on the common. "I have to find the right words. I don't want to go to him with unfounded suspicions."

Even though she and Horace had been friends for so many years, she was still conscious of the fact that he was the son of a wealthy businessman, and their livelihood depended on the Smallwood family to a very great extent. She had always sensed that Horace didn't like his brother, but that didn't mean he would relish being pitted against him.

Blood is thicker than water, Dolly...always remember that. Bert often said this about the narrowboat families, but she supposed it might apply to the Smallwoods as well.

If she had barged in and suggested that Dominic was up to no good, Horace might feel that the business was threatened and that the good name of the Smallwood family would be dragged through the mud, or brought into disrepute. She couldn't just assume that Horace would take her side. She was worried that he might close ranks with his brother and that it would be her and her family who would find themselves with no work.

What exactly should I tell him tomorrow morning? Her mind whirled with concerns as she tried to figure out the best way to move forward without putting her family in jeopardy. Part of her desperately wanted to hope that perhaps Dominic had given up whatever he was planning, but her intuition told her it was probably a foolish wish. Even from the few dealings she'd had with Dominic, she had the impression that he couldn't care less about the pride his pa took in the business. It seemed as though he only saw the business as a means to an end...a way to feather his own nest, rather than continue the legacy that his father had started.

By the time they reached Nailsbridge Mill, Verity and Bert, and the girls had already gone to bed, at Dolly's encouragement. "It's best that you all get some rest," she said when Gloria asked if Dolly wanted her to stay up to help.

"I reckon that's as much as we can do for tonight," Jonty said, stifling an enormous yawn. His dark hair stuck up in all directions, and he rubbed the back of his hand across his eyes, struggling to stay awake.

In the distance, the village lay in darkness. It would come to life again in about three hours, as the millworkers got up to eat some porridge and then walk the dusty track down to the mill, but for now, the night felt silent and empty.

"We should get a couple of hours of sleep as well," Dolly said from the towpath. "It will be a busy day tomorrow, by the time we unload the grain and then get the flour to take onwards to Thruppley."

Jonty needed no second telling. He took his jacket off and retreated into his narrow bunk at the front of the cabin. Dolly knew that he would be snoring within minutes, but strangely, even though she was tired, she didn't feel ready to go to sleep. Whether it was the talk of Dominic with Joe or the fact that it seemed too good to be true that Dominic might have put his plan aside, there was a trickle of unease in her stomach that made it hard for her to settle.

"I'll make sure you have a nice rest once we get to Thruppley," she murmured to Jester, loosening his harness. The horse exhaled loudly with a groan. He shifted his weight and crooked his back leg, standing with his foot tilted forward, which showed that he, too, would be dozing very soon. She gave him one last pat on his muscular neck and climbed back aboard the narrowboat.

Dolly quietly emptied the last of the lukewarm tea from the teapot into her mug and sat down by the tiller where Jonty had been a few minutes earlier. She let her thoughts drift, wondering idly what the future might hold for her family, and if she dared to hope that one day Joe might think of her as more than a friend.

She smiled to herself as an image of Joe's tousled, blonde hair and broad shoulders came into her head. She had so many memories of them together as children when times had been better... making dens in the woods, tramping through the snowy lanes in the middle of winter to see the candlelit Christmas tree at Minsterly Grange. And then the more ordinary memories, tinged with sadness, like when he came to help chop wood and look after the little 'uns after her ma had died. His comforting presence was like a golden thread through her early life, and she sighed with happiness that they had managed to put the past behind them and pick up where they had left off.

That's enough reminiscing. I don't have time to daydream about falling in love when there's so much work to be done. Her eyelids were starting to feel heavy, but she couldn't be bothered to go back down into the cabin. The thought of getting undressed and squeezing into bed next to Gloria and Amy made it tempting to stay where she was, so she tightened her shawl around her shoulders instead.

Just a few more minutes where I am...it's comfortable enough. Her head lolled forwards as sleep finally claimed her in the cool night air.

* * *

DOLLY'S EYES suddenly flew open as she jerked awake again. For a moment, she felt disoriented. Why wasn't she lying in the narrow bed next to Gloria and Amy? She could feel a slight dampness on her dress from being outside as a faint mist shrouded the watery surface of the canal. Her shoulders were stiff, and she shivered with a mixture of tiredness and cold. Judging by the position of the half-moon overhead, dawn was still some way off, and she hastily rubbed her eyes and stood up. If she didn't have at least a couple of hours in bed, she would be good for nothing the following day, which would be no help to the family.

Bob had been curled up by her feet, but as she stood up, he suddenly jumped onto her seat and growled. His hackles went up, and he growled again, turning to look up at her with worried brown eyes.

"What is it, Bob? It's time to go below now." Dolly yawned and shushed him. She didn't want Bob barking and waking everyone up, especially not Bert and Verity.

But instead of stopping, Bob whined and jumped over the edge of the boat onto the towpath, his hackles still up.

A sense of foreboding gripped Dolly, and she glanced down into the cabin, wondering whether she should wake Jonty up. But the steady sound of his snores made her hesitate. It was probably nothing, and he wouldn't thank her for being dragged from his bed for no good reason.

Dolly picked up the lantern and came to a decision. Something had clearly upset Bob, and she wanted to know what it was. She stepped off *The River Maid* onto the towpath, following the terrier who was snuffling ahead of her, zigzagging across the mill yard with a determination that meant he was onto something and not about to give up.

Her heart jumped as two pigeons suddenly clattered noisily out of the nearby trees in alarm. Holding her lantern aloft, she crept across the yard.

You won't do anything silly, will you? She recalled Joe's warning when she had suggested snooping around the yard, and realised that the light of the lantern would give her away if anyone was watching.

Looking around, she changed direction, heading to the shed where the handcarts were kept. "Bob, come here," she called in a low voice. The little dog scampered over, joining her where she was hiding in the shadow of the shed wall, and she turned the lamp down low and placed it carefully just around the corner.

"Don't go ahead of me, Bob," she whispered,

stroking his soft head. She paused to give her eyes a moment to adjust to the darkness before continuing.

Everything looked different in the faint moonlight. Shadows loomed unexpectedly, making her feel jumpy, and every rustle sounded magnified in the quietness of the night. Suddenly, Bob stopped in front of her and cocked his head with one ear up. Dolly stopped as well and held her breath. For a moment, all she could hear was the sound of her own pulse pounding in her ears, but then a new noise reached her. It was the sound of stealthy footsteps, given away by the slight scuff of shoes on the gravelled ground. She shrank back against the side of the shed and edged along it, trying to stay in the shadows.

When she got to the end, she peered slowly around the corner, and her hand flew to her mouth to stifle a gasp of shock at the sight that greeted her.

Flickering flames were taking hold inside the mill. Even from where she was standing, she could see that the fire had only just started, but it would soon become unstoppable if she didn't do something.

"Come away, Bob!" she shouted as the dog

darted ahead of her and started yapping and growling. She had to know how bad it was, so without thinking, she ran towards the mill, wondering if her eyes were deceiving her.

But no…as she reached the window, there was no hiding from the truth. There was a fire in the mill, and she was the only person who knew.

"We have to raise the alarm…but that will take too long…wake the others and start putting the fire out first…send Gloria into the village to rouse the men with the fire engine.…" Her panicked words tumbled out in gasps as she stood rooted to the spot for a few seconds, trying to decide what she should do.

The flames crept higher.

"Water…we'll try and douse the flames first."

She spun around and sprinted towards the narrowboat, but out of the shadows, a swarthy figure barrelled towards her, slamming into her and sending her sprawling face-first onto the ground.

"Wh…what…who…?" Dolly's chest heaved as she tried to drag air into her lungs. She was winded, and for a terrifying moment, as she shakily pulled herself up onto her hands and knees again, all she could think was that she might never see her family again.

She turned around as Bob growled and yapped, trying to bite the legs of whoever had knocked her over.

"You have to help me put out the fire," she cried. Her head was spinning, and she felt dazed.

"What are you doin' creeping around the mill at this time of night?" The voice was gruff and deep, and Dolly gasped in shock again as she looked up into the lined, craggy face of the man she had seen on the common talking to Dominic. He leaned over her, making her edge backwards to try and get away from him.

"You...you started the fire?" she croaked.

"Nothin' to do with me," he snarled. "I keeps meself to meself, and you should too." His dark gaze bored into her as if he was as shocked to see her as she was to see him. "Best you keep quiet about seeing me...or you'll pay the price."

The orange glow of the flames grew stronger, and he seemed to come to his senses. He stood up, looked around to make sure they weren't being watched and then ran away into the night.

CHAPTER 16

Dolly scrambled to her feet, knowing that she had to act fast if they were to have a hope of stopping the fire from sweeping through the entire mill and reducing it to ashes. She picked up her skirts and ran across the yard. Behind her, the sound of glass breaking made her run even faster. The heat from the fire had shattered the window, and she knew there wasn't a moment to lose.

"Jonty, wake up!" she screamed. "The mill is on fire. We have to send for help."

Jonty shot out of the cabin, stumbling as he tried to lace his boots up at the same time. "Crikey, Dolly, I feel like I've barely been asleep for an hour. What on earth is happening?"

"I think someone is trying to burn the place down," she said. A moment later, Gloria came scrambling up the steps, following Jonty, with Verity right behind her. "There are buckets in the shed, Jonty. Go and fetch them, so we can start hauling water from the canal."

"Should I go and get help?" Gloria asked.

"Yes. Run into the village and wake everyone up. I don't even know if there will be time for the men to fetch the fire engine, but we have to try."

As Gloria hurried away, Dolly felt a wave of relief when Joe appeared a little way further down the towpath leading Barnaby. In all the terror of the fire, she had forgotten that Evan had said they would be at Nailsbridge before daybreak to help them unload. Joe threw Barnaby's reins over a post and sprinted towards her.

"I thought I could smell smoke. This must be what Dominic planned." Horror, and then anger filled Joe's eyes as he skidded to a halt next to her.

"We need everybody to start passing buckets of water along," Dolly cried. Evan had followed Joe, and he nodded wordlessly, running after Jonty to fetch more buckets from the shed.

Dolly didn't know how long they carried water from the canal, passing it between themselves like a human chain, because it felt as though time had stood still. The fire had taken hold in the area of the mill where the grain was received, and it licked up the timbers of the old building like a ravenous creature devouring everything in its path. The pall of smoke that filled the air was making it difficult to breathe, and she pulled her shawl up to cover her mouth as she stumbled back and forth with each bucket of water.

"It's getting worse," Evan shouted. "If it goes beyond the intake area, it could sweep through the whole mill."

An idea suddenly took shape in Dolly's mind. "There are some big double doors at the back of the intake area. If I can just shut them, it might stop the fire from spreading."

"You can't go in there," Jonty said firmly. His eyes were red-rimmed from the smoke, and he coughed as it drifted across the yard.

"It's the only way," Dolly cried. The distant clang of the fire engine bell showed that it was still some way away, and even though they were doing their best with the buckets of water, she could see they were fighting a losing battle. "We have to do something more than this. And we can't wait for the fire engine."

"If you're going in, I'm coming with you," Joe said. He grabbed her hand, and they ran together towards the flames.

Dolly pulled him towards the side of the building. "I remember when I went into the office; if you can open this door, we can go through the back corridors and come to the intake area from inside. If we shut the doors from there, it should confine the fire to just that area of the mill."

Joe tried the side door, but it was locked. "Stand back, Dolly, I'll see if I can force it open." He lowered his shoulder and rammed his body against the door. It resisted, and he tried again, taking more of a run-up. His shoulder thumped against the wood with a sickening crunch, but this time he was successful. It flew open, scattering splinters of wood everywhere, and they charged through it into the mill, knowing that every minute counted.

"It's this way," Dolly said, as Joe grasped her hand again. They groped their way along the smoke-filled corridors together, going as fast as they could. Every so often, Dolly paused, racking her brains to try and remember the layout of the mill. With the darkness and her heightened emotions, it would have been easy to make a mistake, which might be the end of them.

Just when it seemed as though their attempt might be futile, they turned a corner, and a pair of heavy wooden doors lay ahead of them. As she had suspected, they were wide open, and the fire raged in the area beyond.

"Quick, Joe, we need to shut them!" They grabbed a door each, and it took all their strength to swing them closed together, and then shoot the bolts across. "The man must have opened them deliberately, hoping that the fire would run throughout the whole mill."

"We have to get out," Joe shouted. "It could have gone up and be over our heads. We can't risk the floor above us collapsing on top of us." Hand-in-hand, they ran back through the corridors and burst out of the side door, just in time to see four cantering horses pulling the fire engine into the yard.

"Good Lord, I had given you up for dead." Verity stumbled towards them, grabbing Dolly in a hearty embrace, quickly followed by Joe. "My heart was in my mouth from the moment you two disappeared inside."

"Stand aside, everyone," a man said, leaping from the still-moving fire engine. He wore a brass helmet and fire tunic, and there were six more men hanging off the fire engine as it came to a halt. They jumped down, quickly swarming around the wagon to unravel the hose and start manning the pump.

"It's time to leave it to the professionals now," Evan said. "I've never been as glad to see both of you as now. I reckon you've both saved the mill, practically single-handed." His face was covered in soot, making his teeth look whiter than usual when he smiled. "Don't ever frighten me like that again, Joe. I couldn't bear the thought of losing you and Dolly." His voice was rough with emotion, and he dragged his arm wearily across his brow, leaving a streak of black soot on his sleeve.

"You two need to go and wait over there," the man in charge of the fire engine said, hurrying over to Dolly and Joe. "I've sent one of the villagers to fetch Doctor Skelton. It was very brave of you to go into the building, but it's more dangerous than you think, breathing in smoke. I won't be able to rest until the fire is out, and I know the doctor has given you a clean bill of health.

"I quite agree," Verity said. "Take yourselves away to sit on the bank. I'll send our Gloria over with a mug of tea and something to eat in a minute. I don't want you fainting from the shock of it all."

It was only now they were back outside again, that it started to sink in for Dolly, what exactly had happened. She hadn't even had time to get over the terror of being attacked by Dominic's shady acquaintance before all her thoughts had been consumed by putting out the fire. She started to tremble, and her legs suddenly felt weak under her.

"We'd better do as they say," Joe said quietly. He put his arm around Dolly and gently guided her towards the grassy bank at the edge of the towpath. "I think we've seen quite enough for tonight," he said, with a wry smile. He took his jacket off and laid it on the ground under the sturdy trunk of an oak tree so that it was facing away from the mill. "A nice seat with a view of the canal for you, Miss Hinton," he said with a chuckle.

Dolly sank gratefully onto the ground, with a deep sigh. "I couldn't have done any of that without you by my side," she said, giving Joe a weary smile.

They sat quietly, in companionable silence for a while, looking out over the water and beyond to the common, where the first hint of dawn and sunrise was colouring the eastern sky faintly pink.

"Dolly…can I ask you something?" Joe said hesitantly after a few minutes had passed. "When I saw you running ahead of me towards the fire, I was terrified that you might get injured."

Dolly's heartbeat quickened, as she wondered what Joe wanted to ask.

"Do you remember when we were children, and our parents used to joke that you and I would end up living together in a little cottage in Middleyard? We were that inseparable."

"How could I forget it?" Dolly said. She plucked a piece of grass and twisted it between her fingers, feeling suddenly shy. "Our families were as close as any until everything changed."

"Well, the thing is…" Joe continued.

"Dolly!" Gloria suddenly appeared on the towpath, beckoning them urgently. "Mr Smallwood and Horace have just arrived," she called up to them. "I think they want to speak to you both, and I expect the doctor won't be far behind. News of the fire has spread through the village." She turned on her heel and ran back towards *The River Maid*, without waiting for a reply.

Dolly felt a tinge of disappointment that the moment had been lost between her and Joe.

I was probably reading too much into things. It was just the shock of discovering the fire that brought Joe and me closer to each other than before. For a moment, she had hoped Joe might declare that he loved her, but then she told herself it was a ridiculous notion.

Joe jumped up and held his hand out towards her, grabbing her and pulling her upright. She stumbled slightly, and he put his hands on her shoulders to steady her. Soft dawn sunbeams filtered through the oak tree as the sun crested the horizon, bathing them in golden light for a moment.

"Sorry, I'm still a bit shaky," Dolly muttered. She looked up into Joe's blue eyes and wondered why she was finding it difficult to catch her breath. There was something about the way he held her gaze and the heat of his hands on her shoulders that made her want to stay close to him forever.

"I'm glad we went through this together." He suddenly leaned forward and brushed the lightest of kisses on her cheek, so fleeting that it was over as quickly as it had happened. "We'd better go and speak to Mr Smallwood," he said, quickly pulling away again. "Are you going to tell him about the stranger you saw in the yard?"

The blood pounded in Dolly's ears, and she touched her fingers to her cheek, where he had kissed her a moment before. Joe was bending down to pick up his jacket, so he didn't see her doing it, which she thought was probably for the best. "I...I don't know," she stammered. "I expect Dominic would just deny everything. And I still don't know who the man running away from the fire is. I don't recognise him from the village, and I don't want to sound foolish. They might not even believe me."

"Perhaps we should just see what Mr Smallwood and Horace have to say first?" Joe tucked Dolly's hand into the crook of his elbow, and they walked down the bank and along the towpath back towards the mill. The firemen had finally managed to extinguish the flames so that all that remained was a steaming, sodden pile of ash. The nightmare was over.

CHAPTER 17

"You must come into my office," Edward Smallwood said. Horace strode ahead of them to open the door and ushered them all into the room that Dolly remembered from all those years ago when she had first met Edward. "I can scarcely believe what's happened. We're always so careful to make sure that there's no chance of anything catching fire. I can't understand how the nightwatchman didn't see anything."

Dolly and Joe sat down at Horace's invitation. It was a while since she had seen Edward, and he looked frail and vexed by the turn of events.

"Perhaps he was keeping watch on the other side of the mill at that time," Dolly said. She clasped her hands together in her lap, not wanting to get the nightwatchman into any trouble. They had never spent the night moored up outside Nailsbridge Mill before, so she didn't know how often the fellow walked around the grounds, but it was a large plot to patrol, and she didn't doubt for one second that the scoundrel who had started the fire would have known exactly when to do it to avoid the night watchman seeing him.

Horace poured a tot of brandy into a cut-glass tumbler and handed it to his father. "It's been a terrible shock for you, Papa. I don't want you to upset yourself about it. The men have managed to extinguish the fire, and Dominic and I can assess the damage once all the ash has been cleared out."

"What about all the deliveries of grain we're expecting today?" Edward asked querulously. He turned to Horace, wanting his son to take control of the situation.

"I think the worst of the fire was contained to a small area." Joe looked at Dolly, and she nodded in agreement.

"We can't just shut the place down, and as long as the mill is in working order, I don't see why we should. The villagers and the narrowboat families rely on us to be paid at the end of the month, so I don't want to let them down." Old Mr Smallwood sipped the brandy, and some colour returned to his cheeks.

"I think we can arrange to unload the grain through the side entrance, for now," Horace said. He drummed his fingers on the desk as he tried to figure out how they could work around the damage.

"I don't even want to think about how this might have ended if it hadn't been for your quick thinking, Miss Hinton." Edward Smallwood sat up straighter in his chair, revived by the brandy, and looking more like his usual self. "Did you see anything out of the ordinary? Horace tells me it was probably an accident, but you never know. You don't get to own as many businesses as me without a few people being jealous of our success."

"Or ruffling feathers and making a few enemies along the way," Horace added with a rueful smile. "Papa has always tried his best to be honest and hard-working, but being in business can be cutthroat. Not everyone has the same morals, although I would hate to think that somebody did this deliberately. People could have got badly hurt putting the fire out."

Dolly exchanged a glance with Joe, and he

twitched one eyebrow and gave her a tiny nod of encouragement as if to say that now was the time to tell them what she knew. Her heart started thumping in her chest, and she took a deep breath to begin.

"The worst thing is," Edward Smallwood continued before she had a chance to speak, "I was planning on signing over everything to Dominic in the next few weeks. But now that we've had this fire, I'm sure there will be all sorts of delays with the bank."

"Papa only recently took out a policy with the Albion Fire Insurance Association in London," Horace murmured. He had a thoughtful look on his face.

"Exactly…and it's a good thing I had the foresight to do so." Edwards took another sip of brandy. "But even so, the bank doesn't like to see incidents like this, and it makes them nervous about the value of a business. Poor Dominic will have to wait a little longer for everything to settle down, but I know he only has the best interests of the place at heart. It will be an inconvenience for him, but I'm very proud of the businessman he is becoming, so I'm sure he won't mind."

The words Dolly had been about to speak died

in her throat. Horace had been right when he said that his papa was blind to Dominic's true nature. And now, if she made wild accusations about the old man's favourite son, with no evidence of who had started the fire, it would only make things worse. The last thing she wanted was to turn Edward Smallwood against her family. She nodded slowly, knowing now was not the time to share her suspicions. "I certainly hope everything is sorted out in a timely manner for you, Mr Smallwood. And Joe and I are just grateful that we could play a small part in making sure things didn't turn out worse."

Edward Smallwood gave her a direct look from under his bushy eyebrows for a beat and then smiled. "I owe you both a debt of gratitude, and the Smallwood family will make sure that your loyalty and brave actions are never forgotten. I promise that you will always have work with us...for both of your families." He sat back in his chair and sighed. In the pale morning light, his face looked gaunt, and there was a slight tremor in his hands. He didn't look like a well man, and Dolly's heart went out to him.

"I think we'd better leave you to rest, Papa. There's a lot to consider, but you must let me take care of as much as possible." Horace stood up and opened the door to usher Dolly and Joe out again.

"And Dominic..." The old man's eyes closed, and the lids looked practically translucent. "We can rely on your brother to do what's right, I'm sure. Especially as this is soon to be his business."

"I'll be on my way, Mr Smallwood," Joe said diplomatically to Horace once they returned to the corridor. He locked eyes with Dolly for a brief moment, and she realised that he was leaving them alone so that she could speak to Horace about her suspicions without anyone else hearing. "I expect Mr Morton will be here by now, so Jonty and I can start unloading *The River Maid*. It's best to get back to normal as quickly as possible and keep the mill open like your pa said."

"He's a fine young man," Horace said, giving Dolly a smile as he watched Joe walk away. "I didn't want to say too much in front of Papa, but we are truly very grateful for everything you did to stop the fire from spreading. It was very brave of you. Papa doesn't like to show it, but he hasn't been very well recently, and this will take a lot out of him."

"I'm glad he has you to care for him and to look out for the interests of the business..." Dolly let her words hang in the air, hoping that Horace might read between the lines.

A faint frown appeared on his forehead. "Is there more to this than you told Papa? If so, I need to know."

"I didn't know whether I should say anything," Dolly began.

No sooner were the words out of her mouth than the sound of running footsteps stopped her mid-sentence.

"Dolly, my dear," Dominic exclaimed loudly. He strode towards her, covering the distance between them with a sense of great urgency. "I just found out about this terrifying fire and your plucky role in stopping it from taking hold and destroying the whole mill."

"Where have you been?" Horace asked, looking at his brother with exasperation. "We've been here an hour already, but nobody knew where you'd got to."

"I was out with a work acquaintance last night, and I stayed at his house as we had a late supper. Not that it's any of your business."

Dominic turned back to Dolly and took hold of

her arm. "I must give you some sort of reward to thank you for what you've done. Words are not enough, so you must come with me to my office so I can give you something more meaningful. Perhaps a small sum of money will help make things a little easier for your family, Miss Hinton?"

Dolly tried not to flinch as he steered her away from Horace. His moods were so mercurial, and he made such a good show of being kind and friendly in front of Horace that, for a moment, Dolly wondered whether she had completely misjudged him.

Dominic whisked her into the office, where the clerk was just settling at his desk, about to start writing in a leather-bound ledger. "I'd like you to go and check that all the villagers have turned up for work today," he said briskly to Mr Applewood. He tapped his foot impatiently as the timid man jumped up and scurried away. As soon as they were alone, Dominic closed the door firmly and then rounded on her. "It's time for you and me to get a few things straight," he snapped. All pretence at friendliness and gratitude had vanished, and Dolly realised that Dominic hadn't changed in the slightest.

"I don't know what you mean," she said defiantly. She folded her arms across her chest and took a step backwards to put some distance between them. She was not going to make that mistake again.

"Stop treating me like a fool, Dolly Hinton. I saw you eavesdropping on the common the other night, and then riding away on that cart horse of yours. Do you think I'm blind?"

Her mouth went dry. It was exactly what she had feared. "I wasn't eavesdropping…my Uncle Bert took ill, and I had to ride to Middleyard to fetch the doctor. That's all there was to it."

A bark of laughter came from Dominic's lips, and he didn't bother to hide his disbelief. "The time for pretending I like you has come to an end," he said harshly.

Dolly hesitated momentarily, wondering whether to try and deny it again, but it seemed futile. Dominic had the power and wealth to outwit her at every turn. "I know this fire is down to you," she said, lifting her chin to glare at him. "I saw the man you were talking to on the common running away just after the fire started. He attacked me and would have probably done worse. What do you think your pa will say about that when I tell him?"

Dominic's eyes widened with surprise, but then he quickly hid his emotions from her. His mouth pinched into a thin line, and he drew himself up to his full height. "If you tell anyone about this, or even so much as hint that this was anything to do with me, I will make sure that you and your family…and Evan Granger and his son never get to work again on the canal. I will personally make sure that you are ruined, Miss Hinton. Do you understand?"

Dolly's heart sank. He hadn't even bothered to deny it, but that was because he held all the cards. Who would possibly believe an impoverished narrowboat girl compared to a wealthy businessman like Dominic?

"I… I understand. I won't tell anyone." Tears of frustration at the injustice of it all pricked at the back of her eyes, but she blinked them away. She would not give Dominic Smallwood the satisfaction of seeing how upset she felt. He had got away with a terrible crime, and he would continue to ride roughshod over poor people like her. It was just the way of the world, she had come to realise.

"I'm glad we've reached an understanding," Dominic said with a thin smile. "I expect you'd like to think this is the end of it, but I may have a few favours to ask of you in the future. I'm sure you will be more than happy to oblige," he added with a humourless chuckle. "You can see yourself out." He threw the door open again and gave her a cold look of dismissal.

Dolly stumbled away, suddenly feeling as though she barely had the strength to walk, she was so exhausted. All she wanted to do was finish unloading the grain, load up the flour, and get away from Nailsbridge Mill, so she could try and sort out her tumultuous thoughts as far away from the Smallwood family as possible.

"Dolly! Wait a moment." Horace hurried after her, following her across the yard. "What were you about to tell me before my brother interrupted?" His expression was troubled, but kind.

"I...I'm sorry...but I can't say anything," she said, choking on her words.

"I thought you trusted me. What has Dominic said to you that you can't tell me?"

Dolly felt wretched, torn between needing to protect her family and wanting to tell Horace the devastating truth about his brother.

"I won't let anything bad happen," Horace said gently. "We've been friends for so long, you have my word."

"I saw your brother talking to a disreputable-looking man on the common recently in the middle of the night," Dolly blurted out. She wanted to tell Horace everything and trust that he would protect them from Dominic's scheming ways.

"Who was the man? What did he want with my brother?" Horace looked puzzled.

Just as she was about to continue, she saw a shadow appear at one of the windows of the mill. It was Dominic, and even from that distance, she could see his icy expression.

"I don't know. I can't tell you anything other than that." She picked at the edge of her shawl, full of anxiety. "I'm sure if Dominic is up to no good, you would know about it."

She glanced up at the window again and saw Dominic shaking his head and putting a finger to his lips to silence her. "I have to go now...I'm sorry." She turned on her heel and walked away from Horace, even though it was the last thing she wanted to do.

"I think there's more to it," he called after her. "I think you're scared of something, and I want you to know that, even if you feel you can't tell me now, I will always listen to you, Dolly."

She glanced over her shoulder and gave him a

small smile, hoping that one day, somehow, she would be able to make him understand the impossible dilemma that Dominic had put her in. But it couldn't happen yet. Not when Dominic Smallwood's threats of ruining her family, and Joe's as well, were still hanging over her.

CHAPTER 18

Dolly tucked a loaf of bread under her arm and deftly cut some slices, then scraped butter onto them before laying them on a plate. "When are you next going to work at Betty's dressmaking shop, Gloria?" She turned to stir the ham and vegetables, which were simmering on top of the potbelly stove. There was barely enough to go around, but it would be payday at the mill soon, and the bread would help fill them up.

"I was about to ask the same thing," Amy said, looking up from the silk flower she was working on. The tip of her tongue poked out of the corner of her mouth as she went back to her task, deep in concentration. She took great care not to waste a single scrap of fabric, to earn the most money that she could, and her basket of completed flowers was almost full. "I have these ready for Mrs Jones to sell."

"Whenever you can spare me." Gloria looked guilty as she tidied her sewing away. "As it happens, Betty did ask if I could go and spend more time at her shop."

"Why didn't you say something sooner? That's wonderful news, and I know it's what you wanted." Dolly was pleased to see Gloria's eyes light up.

"Are you sure? Things have been such a struggle since last year; I thought you would prefer me to stay on *The River Maid* a bit longer so that I could help out."

Dolly leaned over and gave her sister a hug. "You always think of others first, but it's time for you to do something for your own future. Besides, things aren't that bad. I know Uncle Bert still has to take it easy, but Jonty and I are managing just fine, and the extra money that Amy's flowers bring in is always a great help."

"So can I tell Betty it's alright for me to spend more time at her dressmaking shop?"

"I thought you'd never ask, ducky," Verity said, joining the conversation halfway through. "Mind she treats you well, though; I don't want anything but the best for our family."

Dolly lifted the lid on the stew and peered into it. She could have done with a few more potatoes and carrots in there, but it would have to do for tonight. "I'll serve up dinner now."

"Thank goodness for that," Jonty said eagerly from outside. He rubbed his hands together, permanently hungry as always.

An appreciative silence fell over the narrowboat as everyone tucked into their food. "I hear Edward Smallwood is looking much better these days," Bert said. "Much like myself, thanks to Verity and you girls," he added. He mopped up some of the gravy from the stew with his last crust of bread and chewed it happily.

"I was surprised to see how well he looked last time we were at Nailsbridge Mill," Dolly said, nodding. "It's hard to believe a year has passed since the fire. I didn't think he would see out the winter, he looked so poorly on that day, but I'm very happy for Horace that his pa seems to have rallied."

"I doubt if Dominic is quite so happy," Jonty said with a snort of laughter. "If ever there was a man impatient to take over a business, it's him. He probably thought he would have got his hands on everything by now, although I dread to think what sort of changes he will introduce when he's in charge."

"Nothing in our favour, I'm sure." Verity sniffed with disapproval. "'It won't be like the old days when old Mr Smallwood was a man of honour. I'll warrant that son of his only cares about making his fortune, never mind who he uses to get his own way."

Dolly gathered up the dirty plates and climbed up the steps to leave the cabin and wash them in a bucket of water outside. Hearing Jonty and her aunt's comments brought all her memories of Dominic's threat flooding back. For the first few weeks after the fire, her heart had been in her mouth every time they went to Nailsbridge Mill. He had hinted at wanting her to do some favours for him, but as the days turned to weeks, and then the weeks turned to months, nothing seemed to come of it. If anything, she rarely saw him at the mill when they were unloading. That suited her just fine, and she had gradually managed to push his threats to the back of her mind so that they could concentrate on just surviving the winter and looking forward to the easier days of summer.

"Good evening, Dolly. It looks like the rain is holding off for a few days."

A lock of her dark hair had fallen into her eyes, and she pushed it back with a soapy hand as she looked up. She smiled as she saw Billy striding along the towpath. His work as a blacksmith had given him the same broad shoulders and strong physique as Joe, but he still had the smattering of freckles across his nose, which reminded her of when he had been a mischievous young boy. "It's nice to see you, Billy. What brings you this way?"

"Oh…you know…I just thought I would stretch my legs on such a pleasant evening." He put his hands in his pockets and kicked a pebble along the towpath with a nonchalant air. "I don't suppose Amy is here this evening, is she? I don't want to disturb anyone, but seeing as I'm passing…"

"Amy?" Dolly looked up into the sky. "Let me think."

"Oh, don't tell me she's out?" Billy looked deflated.

"Of course, she's here, I'm just teasing you. And you know you're welcome here any time."

Billy grinned and jumped onto the deck. "Joe said he might be along a bit later. If you're not too busy to see him, of course," he added, teasing her in return.

"You're just in time for a cup of tea," Gloria called. She poured an extra mug for Billy, and they all squeezed into the small space around the tiller, enjoying the warm evening. The conversation ebbed and flowed about the latest news and gossip from up and down the canal; who was working where, who'd had a baby, and which mills were being affected the most by goods being taken by the new steam train.

Billy sometimes mentioned that he missed out on the variety of gossip the narrowboat families heard because of living in one place, in his lodgings over the forge, but Verity and Bert's garrulous family soon made him feel part of canal life again.

"What news from Thruppley?" Amy asked when there was a lull in the conversation. "Do you have any new customers bringing their horses in for you to shoe?"

"Well, it's funny you should mention it. There was a proper palaver when the new owners of Dudbridge Manor came calling. They're recently down from London, and some scoundrel has done 'em a wrong turn by selling them horses they can barely control. I fair thought Mr Shaw…or should

I say, Lord Shaw, was going to be bucked off into the water trough by his stallion. And then Miss Shaw was almost unseated by her mare."

"I'm sure you soon got everything back under control," Amy said, with an admiring note in her voice.

"Abe and I have come up with a plan. The Shaws could be good customers, and Abe said there's a marvellous set-up in their stables. He's asked me to ride up there with the wagon once every couple of weeks to shoe their horses at the manor instead of them coming into Thruppley."

"They'll be fortunate to have you, ducky," Verity said.

"I'm being paid a few more shillings each month for it, too, and Abe said if I work hard, I might get the cottage next to the forge…if I get wed…in the future." Billy took a slurp of his tea, to cover his bashfulness as Verity and Dolly exchanged a happy glance.

"Amy will be able to visit you more often, because I might be living in Thruppley soon as well, over Mrs Jones's shop," Gloria said.

"I brought you something, Bert." Billy rummaged in his jacket pocket and pulled a crumpled newspaper out. "It's a few days old, but I thought it would help while away a few hours for you while you're getting better."

Bert rolled his eyes. "I've been telling that doctor that I'm well enough to work for months, but he and Verity are colluding to make me rest for longer."

"It's just because we love you," Verity said fondly, patting him on his arm. "You've put many years into providing for us all, so it's about time you took things a little easier so I don't have to worry about you having another bad turn."

Jonty picked up the newspaper and idly flicked through the pages. "It looks like your ma is doing well in Paris, Billy." He paused to look at an article about Stella's latest sensational reviews.

Billy nodded, with no hint of sadness. "She sent us a letter not so long ago, apologising for leaving. She and Mr Portiscue are going to remain in Paris. She said it's better for her singing career."

"How did your pa take that?" Amy asked softly. She reached for her mug of tea, and their fingers brushed together, which made Billy's cheeks turn red.

"He took it surprisingly well. I think we've known for a long time that Ma wouldn't be coming back here, and I'm glad he's finally accepted it."

"Maybe he'll meet a nice local woman instead to have as a companion?" Gloria said. The corner of her mouth twitched up in a smile, and her eyes sparkled with mischief. "Perhaps he should bring his jacket to be mended at Mrs Jones's dressmaking shop. I could do it for a very reasonable price."

Billy scratched his head, looking puzzled. "Why would he want to do that?"

Amy's musical laugh rang out. "Betty Jones has been widowed these last five years. She would be perfect for your pa if we could find a way for them to spend some time together...like waiting for a jacket to be mended, perhaps?"

Billy looked shocked for a moment and then laughed. "I'll see what I can do. I expect he'll say no to start with, but I'm sure between us, we'll find a way to get him into that shop. I don't like to think of poor Pa being lonely if Joe ever decides to marry."

This time it was Dolly's turn for her cheeks to go pink, as Gloria gave her a sly look under the guise of pouring out another cup of tea.

Jonty folded the paper up again and handed it

to Bert. "That'll keep you happy for a few days, Uncle Bert. Plenty of news to read about."

"I almost forgot to tell you something else," Billy said, suddenly sitting up straighter. "The constables have been questioning folks in Thruppley and beyond about the burglary at Felton Hall on the other side of the Middleyard. There are rumours that the burglars made off with the family's jewellery. It's worth a fortune, apparently."

"You don't have to tell us," Jonty said. His eyes darkened. "I'm sure it's only a matter of time until they start questioning the narrowboat families. We heard about the burglary, alright, and everyone is on edge. You know how they like to blame the gypsy travellers and us for crimes like that, just because it's easy to point the finger at folks who live differently."

"Look, there's Joe, come to join us." Gloria reached for another mug and got ready to add an extra pinch of tea leaves to the teapot.

"Would you like a few vegetables?" Joe stood on the towpath, holding up a hessian sack. "I managed to get these from the costermongers at the market just as they were about to go home for the evening. I figured you have so many people to feed, it might be helpful."

"That's very kind of you, ducky," Verity said. "You boys will have to come and eat dinner with us tomorrow to say thank you, and bring your pa too."

"I'm sure we would enjoy that," Joe said, climbing aboard.

"Are you staying for a cup of tea?" Gloria asked.

"Not this time, but thank you for offering. We've got an early start in the morning, to make a delivery at Selsley Mill, before heading onwards to Frampton Basin."

"We're going to Frampton tomorrow as well," Dolly said. "In fact, I think I'd better walk up to the common now and fetch Jester. He's had a good day of grazing, and I want him near us to get him harnessed up bright and early tomorrow."

"I'll walk with you," Joe said quickly. "If that's alright, Mrs Webster?"

Verity chuckled and nodded, her grey curls bobbing. "Why so formal all of a sudden? I know you'll take good care of our Dolly, so there's no need to ask."

"Perhaps it's because she's getting to an age where some of the young men in Thruppley might be interested in courting her?" Bert said, giving Verity an innocent look.

Before they could say anymore, Dolly jumped up. "We'll go now before it gets dark."

"I didn't just come to bring you the vegetables," Joe confessed after they had been walking in companionable silence for a while. "I wanted to check that you were feeling alright today. You do know what day it is, don't you?"

Dolly shot him a grateful glance and nodded. "A year exactly since the fire. The others were talking about it during dinner." She sighed and absent-mindedly tucked a stray curl behind her ear. "I still feel bad that I didn't tell Horace everything I knew, but with hindsight, perhaps it was for the best. Old Mr Smallwood is better, and nothing more has happened at the mill to make me suspect that Dominic is up to his old ways."

Joe pulled a hazel stick from the hedge and whittled it as they walked. Dolly knew he only did this when he was trying to think something through. "Do you really believe that's all there is to it?" His blue eyes darkened, and he looked troubled. "I didn't say anything before, but the last few times I've been into Thruppley to buy supplies, I saw Dominic coming out of the Black Lion Tavern, looking very much the worse for wear. It doesn't bode well for the mill if he's drinking too much."

"Horace said it's just the way he is. I don't suppose it matters, as long as it doesn't affect our livelihood."

Jester's ears pricked forward, and he whinnied softly when he caught sight of Dolly. "I hope you're right," Joe said. "I'd better get back to *The Skylark* now. Will you be alright walking Jester back to the canal?"

Bob darted around their feet, wagging his tail and dancing on his back legs, making Dolly laugh. Even though the terrier was getting on a bit, he still had plenty of energy. "I'll be fine, I have Bob to look after me. He makes a good little guard dog, so there's no need to worry."

Dolly slipped a rope around Jester's neck, enjoying the peace and quiet as she retraced her steps across the common. With all the family living on the narrowboat, it was rare for her to have any time alone, let alone to daydream, and she enjoyed the chance to let her thoughts wander and think about the future. She and Joe had grown closer than ever during the last year since the fire, but she still hadn't been brave enough to tell him her true feelings about him, in spite of Gloria's best attempts to mention courting whenever she could.

Darkness was falling fast, and just as Dolly

approached a spinney of silver birch trees, Bob started growling. "Come back, Bob. There's nobody there." She quickened her pace, feeling a shiver of foreboding.

'Tis just all this talk of the fire. We'll be back at the canal in a minute.

Suddenly a broad-shouldered figure stepped from the dense shade under the trees.

"Tell that wretched dog to stay away from me," Dominic Smallwood grumbled. He smiled at Dolly, as though their meeting was the most normal thing in the world. "How have you been, Miss Hinton? I thought it would be a good time to resume our acquaintance on this auspicious day…a year after that dreadful unexplained fire at the mill." He sniggered to himself, then pulled a hip flask from his pocket, unscrewed it and gulped down a mouthful of brandy, gasping as it burnt a path down his throat.

"Bob only growls at people he doesn't like," Dolly said crisply. She didn't break her stride and tightened her grip on Jester's rope. "I don't have time to stop and talk. I need to get back to the narrowboat. Jonty is waiting for me."

"Oh, don't worry, I won't take up much of your time." Dominic took another swig of the strong liquor, then wiped his mouth with the back of his hand before closing the hip flask again.

Dolly eyed him warily. She couldn't help but think that the ornately engraved silver hip flask was probably worth more than a month's wages to the likes of her, yet it was just a small trinket of pleasure for Dominic.

"You may recall during our delightful chat after the fire that I said I might ask you to do me a favour now and again." Dominic raised his eyebrows, waiting for her nod of agreement.

"I have a faint recollection, yes," Dolly said. She tried to carry on walking along the track, but Dominic blocked her way and glanced furtively over his shoulder to make sure they weren't being watched.

"I have a parcel that I need you to deliver for me."

"A parcel?" Dolly couldn't keep the surprise from her voice. This was not the sort of favour she had expected Dominic to ask of her, and she wondered why he needed her help. "What is it?"

Dominic tapped the side of his nose. "This little arrangement will only work if you put your curiosity aside, Dolly. I think you'll find that being nosy is not a good trait for a young woman in your position…who needs to put food on the table for her family." His veiled threat was clear to understand, and Dolly realised that he still had all the power in his hands.

"Who do you want me to deliver it to?" She sighed with weary resignation.

"You're to give this to Mr Ferguson, the yard manager at Frampton Basin." Dominic reached inside his coat and pulled out a parcel, not much bigger than his fist. It was a padded brown cloth pouch, tied tightly around the neck, and he held it in his palm with an expression that was hard to read.

Ferguson? The bad-tempered man had still not become any friendlier in the year he had been working at Frampton Basin.

"Don't you already have dealings with Mr Ferguson?" Dolly blurted out, forgetting that she wasn't supposed to be asking any questions. "Surely you see him when you discuss matters to do with Nailsbridge Mill, seeing as so much grain comes to you from Frampton Basin?"

Dominic scowled. "Of course, I have dealings with him," he snapped. "This is a different matter altogether, and it suits me to have you as our go-between. I trust I can rely on your discretion to keep your mouth shut."

He stepped closer, and Dolly sensed his pent-up anger and sense of entitlement. It was the same as she had felt that time when he had tried to corner her in his office. The nature of his demands might have changed, but she was under no illusion. Dominic was determined to use her for his own benefit, and he expected her to comply. Otherwise, he would find a way to ruin her life.

"Is it just this once?" She hoped he wouldn't notice the slight tremor in her voice. Darkness was falling quickly, and she was very aware that there was nobody else around.

Dominic gave her a long look, then shook his head. "If everything goes to plan, this will be the first of many deliveries." The brandy seemed to be taking effect, and he turned away and paced back and forth on the track, muttering to himself. "Papa might think he has me on a tight rein, but I'll make my fortune one way or another…" He stumbled slightly and gulped down some more drink, weighing the package in his hand as though he didn't want to let it go. "A few more of these, and the mill won't matter…neither will that old fool…

I'll forge my own future, without having to live up to his ridiculous expectations..."

"Are you going to give it to me then?" Dolly's question snapped him back to the present, and his grip tightened around the pouch momentarily before he handed it over.

"There's one thing I want to make very clear," he said, breathing heavily. "You are never, under any circumstances, to look at what is in these parcels. All you have to do is give them to Mr Ferguson, but only do it when you're sure nobody is watching. D'you understand?"

Dolly's heart sank. It sounded as though Dominic was asking her to do something which would get her into a lot of trouble if anyone found out. She shivered, and her mind churned with fear at the thought of what might happen if she was dragged off to jail. How would the family manage without her?

"I...I suppose so." She took a deep breath, hoping one last time that she could appeal to his better nature. *If he has a better nature.* She had to try, even if it made her sound desperate. "Mr Smallwood...I've never told anyone about what really happened on the night of the fire. That I suspect you were behind it. Isn't that enough? It's not fair that you're making me do something which could turn out badly for me and my family."

Dominic's eyes narrowed, and his expression hardened. "What makes you think I care about you and your family, Miss Hinton? Just because my spineless brother shows an interest in you doesn't mean anything, at least not to me." In another alarming change of mood, he suddenly gave her a lazy smile. "Now that you come to mention the fire...it wouldn't take much for me to speak to a few people in power and point out that your family were the only ones there when the fire first started." His lip curled with scorn. "Everybody knows that you narrowboat people pay scant regard to the laws of the land. Who's to say you didn't start the fire and then pretend to be the saviour of the day, just to curry favour with my papa?"

Her mouth gaped open. *How could he sink so low?* With a regretful sigh, she slipped the parcel into her dress pocket, knowing she was beaten. Dominic was blackmailing her, and it sounded as though he would continue to do so for a while. "I'll do as you say. Just keep my family out of it. They don't deserve to be sucked into your scheming ways."

"I knew you'd come around to my way of thinking." Dominic sniggered again. "See you soon, Dolly. And remember, this is just between you, me, and Mr Ferguson. Don't let me down."

With her heart in her mouth, Dolly squared her shoulders, and marched off, with Bob scampering ahead of her. She was back in Dominic's clutches again, and there was nothing she could do about it.

CHAPTER 19

A buttery-coloured harvest moon hung low in the sky as Joe finished his evening chores on *The Skylark*, a little way up the canal from Frampton Basin. He had washed down the deck and fed Barnaby, and now he had a little time to rest before it would be time to go to bed. His pa had left a pot of bitter coffee on top of the small stove in the cabin, and he poured some out for himself. Verity had delivered some poppyseed cake when she'd passed the boat a few days earlier, and although it was a little stale, it would go down a treat with the coffee. He sat on the bench next to the tiller, glad to take the weight off his feet. Even though he was used to hard work, there was rarely any time to relax.

Or perhaps, I just prefer it that way, to stop myself from thinking about things I can't seem to fathom. A rueful smile tugged at his mouth as he realised that was more like it. Patch nudged his elbow, with a hopeful look in her soft, brown eyes, and Joe broke a piece of cake off to give her. "There you are, girl. Don't tell Pa I'm giving you good food."

A fish plopped in the canal nearby, catching his eye with a flash of silver. It was a mild evening, and a few flies danced over the top of the water. He wondered idly whether it might be worth dropping a fishing line in to see if he could catch something, but most of the fish that lived in the canals were far too wily to be caught. If he had a day off soon, he would walk to the river and go fishing there instead. "That would be a nice way to spend an afternoon with Dolly," he murmured to his dog. It was swiftly followed with a heartfelt sigh. *Not much chance of that happening*, he thought to himself. Summer would be coming to an end soon, and he had noticed a new hint of crispness in the morning air the last few days, which told him that autumn would soon be on its way.

"Have you heard any more about that to-do at Dudbridge Manor?" Evan called from the cabin below.

"Nothing more than what Billy told us."

"I don't know what the world is coming to," Evan continued, sounding disgruntled. "Three burglaries in as many weeks, and the constables have no idea who is doing it. I just hope they don't start making life difficult for us folks on the canal. Any excuse to paint us as criminals, and they'll be happy to take it." He yawned loudly, settling down with a frayed rope that needed mending.

Joe thought back to Billy's visit to the boat a few days before. He had ridden down to Selsley Mill with news that Thruppley was swirling with gossip and rumours because there had been another burglary.

"I can't believe it happened at Dudbridge Manor," he had exclaimed. "I went up there to shoe the horses, and Lord Shaw is furious about it. I could hear him shouting at the constables from the end of the drive, and he was none too impressed with the reassurance that they are looking into it."

"What was taken this time?" Evan asked.

"I overheard him saying that it was silver and jewellery. Poor Miss Shaw was in floods of tears because they took the ruby necklace her pa gave her for her coming-out ball in London. I bet it was worth a pretty penny. He dotes on her."

"Whoever is doing it seems to be getting bolder," Evan mused. "Targeting grand country houses, as if they don't care about what might happen if they get caught. They could be transported to Australia."

"Lord Shaw has certainly got the constables jumping to his every request. He told them that he's no country bumpkin to be fobbed off with feeble excuses. Poor Constable Redfern didn't know where to put himself when Lord Shaw told him he has plenty of well-connected acquaintances in London, and he won't hesitate to invite them down to look into matters if the local bobbies aren't doing a proper job of catching the burglars."

"I bet he did. Folk like him expect everyone to do as they're told."

"All the horses were prancing around, as skittish as they get on a stormy day, with all his shouting. It took me twice as long as usual to shoe them because he was marching around the farm buildings, seeing what else might have been stolen, roaring about what a lawless place the West Country is."

. . .

EVAN APPEARED in the hatch from the cabin, snapping Joe out of his thoughts about the burglary. "...did you hear what I said?"

"No, sorry, Pa. What was it?"

Evan shook his head. "If I didn't know better, I'd say you've got something on your mind. Care to tell me what it is?"

Joe shifted uneasily on the wooden bench and gave a small shrug. He had hoped his pa hadn't noticed because he didn't really know how to explain what was troubling him. He barely understood it himself.

"I haven't seen young Dolly talking to you lately," his pa said casually, not wanting to let the matter drop. "Is it something to do with that?"

Joe paused, draining his coffee before replying. "I reckon she's just been a bit busy lately, that's all."

Evan grunted, seemingly satisfied by his explanation, and clattered back down the steps again. "I'm going to turn in for the night soon, son. We'll set off early in the morning and get loaded up with grain before it gets too busy."

Joe stood up and fetched another rope from the deck at the front that needed mending. The repetitive task of weaving in the frayed ends would stop him from worrying about what his pa had just brought up. At least, he hoped so.

"It's no good," he muttered to Patch a few minutes later, as he realised he had been gazing into the distance instead of doing the task at hand.

His pa was right when he said Dolly hadn't been around much lately. Joe had noticed that they barely spent any time together anymore. He couldn't quite pinpoint when it started, but her demeanour had changed at about the same time as when Gloria had started spending more time working at Betty Jones's dressmaking shop. To start with, he wondered whether it was because Dolly wished she could work somewhere away from the canal, but then he dismissed the idea. She loved working on *The River Maid* and everything that went with canal life, so it couldn't be that.

He had asked her several times if something was wrong, but she always denied it with a bright smile, changing the subject, and never really giving him a proper answer.

"It's as if she's avoiding me, Patch," he said, stroking the collie's soft ears. "Perhaps it's because I haven't told her how I feel about her." The palms of his hands suddenly felt slightly clammy. He knew deep down that he had loved Dolly for as long as he could remember, but he could never quite find the right words or the right moment to make his feelings known.

But somehow, he sensed it wasn't just that. He felt as though something was troubling her. It reminded him of how she had been those first few weeks after the fire at Nailsbridge Mill. *But what could it be? Dominic is lying low, not causing any trouble. Mr Smallwood is still grateful for how we helped save the mill from worse damage.*

Evan suddenly appeared at the cabin entrance again with a determined look in his eye, making Joe jump

"I thought you were going to bed?"

"I know things have been difficult for you at times without having a ma, and there are things which a woman might be better at explaining than me, but I need to speak my mind."

Joe stared at his pa, wondering what was so urgent that had brought him back on deck again. "Have I done something wrong? Did I make a mistake?"

"No, son, it's nothing to do with work." Evan scratched his beard and shook his head firmly. "I'm not good with words…just a simple labourer, as you know." He looked up at the moon, and the moment stretched out between them. "I want you to be happy, and I've noticed that the time when you are most content is when you're with Dolly."

"It's like I said, Pa, I think she's just very busy at the moment." Joe coiled up the rope he was working on and stowed it under the bench, thinking that was the end of the conversation.

"You probably might think I'm not the right person to be giving you advice about courting and marriage." For a moment, there was a hint of bitterness in Evan's voice as he remembered the way that Stella had waltzed off with Mr Portiscue, tempted by the lure of a career on the stage. He coughed and rubbed his hand over his eyes to banish the past. "Your ma and I were happy once, Joe. And all I will say is that if you love Dolly, you need to tell the girl. Do whatever it takes to win her heart. Don't let her get away from you and then regret it…not like I did."

Before Joe could reply, Evan slapped him on his shoulder and vanished back into the cabin again. "I noticed *The River Maid* is just up yonder ahead of us. No time like the present," he added with a chuckle as he closed the cabin doors firmly behind him and left Joe alone again outside.

Joe sat there in stunned silence for a couple of

minutes, too surprised by his pa's unexpected advice to move. But then, the more he thought about it, the more he realised his pa was right. Something was bothering Dolly, and he had to find out what it was. Perhaps she would tell him to go away, but if he didn't try, what sort of friend did that make him?

As THE MOON EDGED HIGHER, Joe waited for his pa to go to bed before leaving *The Skylark*. He had spotted *The River Maid* moored up further along the canal earlier that evening, closer to Frampton Basin, no doubt so that Dolly would be able to get a head start on everyone in the morning. He only hoped she hadn't already gone to bed herself. Otherwise, he might not see her again for a few days. It was a quiet night, with barely a sound other than the occasional rustle of nocturnal animals out hunting for food. Patch trotted along silently behind him, but as they approached Dolly's boat, her tail started to wag.

Joe was just about to call out a greeting, but there was something about the way Dolly tiptoed off her narrowboat which made him hesitate and stay in the shadows. He watched as she double-checked that her family were asleep and set off towards Frampton Basin at a brisk pace.

In a spur-of-the-moment decision, Joe decided to follow her, partly out of curiosity but also out of concern for her safety. The way she kept glancing around made him think that whatever she was doing, she didn't want to be seen.

It was only as they got closer to the yard, and Dolly stopped to catch her breath, that Joe realised she was upset about something. She sat on a fallen tree trunk, with her head bowed, and then he saw her pressing her handkerchief to her eyes. He couldn't stay quiet for a moment longer, not when the woman he cared about more than anyone in the world was in tears over something.

"Dolly, what's wrong?"

She gasped and shrank back.

"Don't be frightened; it's just me." He ran the last few yards between them, and Patch bounded ahead, nuzzling against Dolly's side and whining as she sensed her distress.

"Joe, what are you doing here? Were you following me?" She sounded defensive, and Joe could have kicked himself as he realised that perhaps she was waiting to meet a young man.

"I...I'm sorry. I was walking towards *The River*

Maid to come and visit you, and I saw you hurrying away. I guess my curiosity got the better of me, and...yes, I followed." Joe sat down next to her and gave her an apologetic smile. "I wanted to make sure you were safe, as well. There are plenty of unscrupulous men hanging around at night, walking home from the tavern after too much ale, and I'd hate for you to come to any harm."

Dolly hastily tucked her handkerchief back in her sleeve, and then rested her hands protectively over her apron pocket, as if she had something to hide. "I was just stretching my legs. I haven't been sleeping very well lately."

Joe didn't reply for a moment, wondering whether he dared speak to her about what was really on his mind. He decided he had nothing to lose. If Dolly didn't like him anymore, it would be better to know now and not hold out false hope. And if she was in some sort of trouble, he wanted to offer his help.

"Is something bothering you?" he asked quietly. "We've known each other all our lives, and I think something has been upsetting you these last few weeks." He took a deep breath, and then turned towards her, to take her slim hands in his own. He looked into her brown eyes he knew so well.

"Whatever is wrong, I'll always be here for you, Dolly. I want you to know that."

Her eyes suddenly filled with tears, and Joe thought he had made a terrible mistake. But she blinked the tears back with a juddering sigh and then smiled at him. "I needed to hear that, Joe. I've been feeling so alone, with a terrible secret. I haven't told anyone, but I'm scared for the safety of my family and our future...because of what I've been doing." She bit her lip, looking worried.

"What have you been doing?"

She pulled her hands away and laid them back on her lap. "I'm almost too ashamed to say. The thing is, I had no choice. I'm just terrified that it will all end very badly."

Joe noticed she was gripping something through the fabric of her apron. "Do you have something that you shouldn't?" An owl hooted, gliding over the canal, and a sudden gust of wind rippled the surface of the water, making Dolly shiver. He was filled with a sense of foreboding. The Dolly he knew was as honest as the day is long, but guilt was written all over her face.

She gave a small nod, not quite meeting his eyes.

"You can tell me anything. I just want to help

you, Dolly," he took a steadying breath, then plunged on, "because I think you've been forced into something through no fault of your own. Am I right?"

Dolly sniffed and then nodded again, but this time Joe could see relief in her eyes. "Dominic was on the common that night a few weeks ago when you walked to get to Jester with me."

A knot of dislike formed in his chest towards the arrogant man who seemed intent on hounding Dolly, even though his attentions were unwelcome. "Again? Wait until I see him…"

She shook her head. "No, it's nothing like that. He asked me to deliver a parcel to Mr Ferguson."

"You mean the yard manager at Frampton Basin? Why would he ask you to do such a thing? Surely he sees the fellow often enough himself without needing to ask you to do it for him?"

"You know Dominic," Dolly muttered. "Clearly, it was something he didn't want to do the normal way, for reasons known only to himself. I have to do the deliveries at night when nobody will see me meeting Ferguson."

Joe couldn't keep the surprise from his face. "How many times has this happened?"

"This is the fourth time." Dolly glanced down at

her lap, and then reluctantly put her hand into her apron pocket and pulled a pouch out, which was tied tightly around the neck.

"Do you know what's in there?" Joe held his hand out, and Dolly handed it to him. One look at her face told him everything he needed to know. "He told you not to look, didn't he? And I'm sure he threatened you as well." Anger burned through his veins again at the burden which Dominic had so cruelly thrust upon Dolly to further his own interests.

"Of course, but this time it wasn't just the threat of missing out on work. He said that because my family and I were the only people at Nailsbridge Mill that night the fire broke out, it would be easy enough to sow some seeds of doubt and point the finger of blame at us." Dolly sounded bitter but also defiant. "I'll find a way out of this, Joe, I must. But I haven't thought of the best way to do it yet so my family is protected from his despicable ways."

"I think the first thing we have to do is understand exactly what he's up to, don't you agree?" Joe weighed the parcel in his hand and tried to feel what might be inside, but it was impossible to tell.

"If we open it, there's no going back," Dolly whispered, suddenly looking scared again. "Mr

Ferguson will know if it has been tampered with, I'm sure. He never says anything to me when I hand it over, but if he's an associate of Dominic's, he's probably just as dangerous to us."

"I never liked the man." Joe squeezed the pouch again. "It's the only way. We have to find out what Dominic is doing, and then tell someone. Perhaps Constable Redfern. Or Edward Smallwood and Horace. I'm sure they're not part of this. It's all down to Dominic. We've always known that he had no morals." He gave Dolly a searching look, hoping that she would agree.

"I'm meant to be giving this to Mr Ferguson tonight. If I don't turn up, who knows what might happen?"

"Dominic goes out drinking at the Black Lion almost every night," Joe said firmly. "He won't find out that you didn't make the delivery until tomorrow morning. He never rises early, not after a heavy night at the tavern, so that gives us until then to get help."

"Are you sure?"

Joe knew he had to tell Dolly everything, to make her understand. "I love you, Dolly, and I couldn't bear it if you got caught. Whatever he's asking you to do, it must be against the law. But we both know he'll find a way to wriggle out of it. You would get the blame for everything…and you would spend the rest of your days in prison. I can't just stand by and let that happen, not for you, or your family." His voice cracked with emotion, and, without thinking, he leaned forwards, and their lips met in a tender kiss, which promised more in the fullness of time.

Dolly gasped and looked slightly stunned as he pulled away a moment later, but then her generous lips curved into a smile. "I love you, too, Joe," she said simply.

His heart jumped. "You do?"

Her soft laugh sounded like music to his ears. "Of course. We're best friends." She picked up the pouch from his hand. "I'm fed up with dancing to Dominic's tune. Let's open it, and see what we're dealing with."

A moment later, they stared down at the exquisite jewellery spread out on Dolly's lap. Diamonds glittered in the moonlight, and Joe gave a low whistle. He picked up one of the necklaces and laid it on his palm, turning it this way and that. The gold chain was heavy, and a sumptuous teardrop-shaped ruby hung from it.

"I think I know what Dominic has been up to,"

he said in hushed tones. "Billy was at Dudbridge Manor shoeing the horses the other day when the constables were meeting Lord Shaw about the burglary there. It was a proper to-do, he said. Miss Shaw was inconsolable because her ruby necklace was taken. The one her pa gave her to wear for her coming out ball. And they got away with other silver and jewellery, apparently."

Dolly's eyes widened, with fear and shock as a dawning realisation came over her face.

"This can't be a coincidence, Dolly. I have a terrible feeling that Dominic is behind all these burglaries in the area. First, Felton Hall. Then there was another one over Cirencester way. And now Dudbridge Manor...and maybe others that we haven't heard about."

Dolly's hands shook as she returned the jewels to the pouch and tied it up tightly again. "If I'm found with these, I'll be thrown into prison for sure." She stood up abruptly, looking horrified. "What are we going to do?"

Joe took the pouch from her and tucked it safely inside his jacket. He walked up and down in front of the fallen log for a moment, his thoughts churning. "We can't just take these to the police. It's too risky because they'll be only too willing to try and pin it on the likes of us."

Patch snuffled in the grass, her tail wagging, and then started trotting off in the direction that they had just come from. Joe watched her and then came to a decision. "I think we have to tell Edward Smallwood and Horace. They know you well enough to believe that you would never do such a thing as being responsible for stealing these jewels. We just have to hope that our honesty will pay off."

Dolly glanced anxiously in the opposite direction, towards Frampton Basin. Mr Ferguson would be waiting in the darkness for her, expecting the delivery. But then she turned back towards him and slipped her hand in the crook of his elbow. "You're right. I've been a fool thinking that if I just do what Dominic wants, he'll eventually stop. It's time to tell Edward and Horace the truth, and there's not a moment to lose."

CHAPTER 20

The drumming of Jester's hooves beneath them matched the pounding of Dolly's heart as they rode through the night towards Chavenhope House, the grand country home of the Smallwood family. Dolly and Joe had run back along the towpath, waking Evan and Jonty, to tell them that they were going to be away for a few hours on a matter of great urgency to try and secure their future. She had been grateful that both of them had accepted the explanation without demanding more information. She knew she could trust Evan to help her family in the morning if they weren't yet back on the canal, which gave her one less thing to worry about.

"What happens if Dominic is at Chavenhope?"

Dolly asked as Jester slowed to a trot. The long sweeping drive leading towards the imposing house stretched away from them, and she felt her nerve starting to fail.

"I doubt he will be," Joe said from behind her. He had remained a respectful distance from her as they sat together on Jester, but Dolly found his solid presence and the warmth of his broad chest against her back comforting nonetheless. "He's too fond of the taverns in Thruppley, and last I heard, his pa has given him the use of one of the houses he owns there for the evenings he's too drunk to ride back to Chavenhope."

By the time Dolly and Joe had managed to wake one of the housemaids, who was dozing by the range in the cavernous kitchen, Dolly's courage had returned.

"Wait here and don't touch anything," the maid said, eyeing them suspiciously as she listened to their urgent request. "I can't say the master will be very happy to be woken up, so you'd better not be causing a rumpus for nothing. You'm narrowboat folk, ain't you?" She adjusted her mob cap and sniffed. "Hammering on the door as if 'tis the devil himself come callin'...I ain't heard anything so strange in all my days," she muttered.

"I promise Mr Smallwood will be very grateful that you're waking him up," Joe called after her reassuringly. "Just remember to tell him that Dolly Hinton has important news about the fire at Nailsbridge Mill."

The sound of striding footsteps ten minutes later reached Dolly's ears, and Horace appeared in the doorway of the kitchen looking remarkably wide awake. "Please come through to Papa's study. Miriam has gone to wake Cook up, and she'll bring a pot of tea and something for you to eat as soon as it's ready. I'm sure you must be hungry and thirsty, riding all the way here from the canal at this time of night."

Dolly felt a surge of gratitude for her old friend. He would have been quite within his rights to throw them out, and most men of his social standing would not have entertained the thought of being dragged from their beds by two narrowboat folk. But Horace was different.

Joe whipped his cap off and turned it in his hands. "We probably should have waited until the morning, but when you hear what we have to tell you, I hope you'll understand. Time is of the essence, which is why Dolly and I came as quickly as we could."

They barely had time to take in the splendid interior of the house as Horace led them along the back corridors, through the echoing entrance hallway with its wide staircase that led upstairs, and onwards to Edward's study. She was vaguely aware of ornate oil paintings hanging on the walls, a vast marble fireplace, polished wooden floors, and the occasional glint of silver in the dim lamp-light. She had never seen anything like it in all her life, and she wished she had time to stop and admire everything so she could describe it to Gloria and Amy when she got home.

No sooner had Horace pulled up two chairs for them in front of the large desk than the door creaked open behind them again, and Edward Smallwood hobbled in. He leaned heavily on his silver-topped walking stick, and he was wearing a burgundy smoking jacket instead of the usual smart frock coat, which Dolly had only ever seen him in before.

"I do hope you don't mind my casual appearance, Miss Hinton, and Mr Granger. I didn't want to disturb the servant who usually helps me dress, and I didn't want to keep you waiting either." Horace helped his father sit down and then pulled up a seat for himself.

"It's me who should be apologising, Mr Smallwood," Dolly said hastily. "I know it's probably rude of us to come knocking you up in the middle of the night, but there's something very important that we have to tell you. And to show you."

Edward Smallwood leaned his elbows on his desk and steepled his fingers, giving Dolly an encouraging nod. "The housemaid said it's something to do with the fire. Believe me, I don't mind being woken up at any hour of the night to hear more about that. We never did get to the bottom of why the fire started, and I had the devil's own job dealing with the insurance company. We are still very grateful for your quick thinking. If the mill had been razed to the ground, I could have been made bankrupt."

"So you found out something new?" Horace asked. "And after this length of time as well? Papa and I had given up on thinking that we might ever hold anyone to account."

The housemaid tapped lightly on the door, and then entered, carrying a tray with four cups and saucers and a pot of tea. "Do you take milk, ma'am?" She asked, raising one eyebrow in Dolly's direction. She still wasn't convinced they deserved such hospitality. "Cook has made buttered crumpets as well. Would you like one?"

Joe's stomach rumbled, and the maid giggled, breaking the tension in the room.

"Thank you, Miriam," Horace said, once the cups of tea had been given out, and Dolly and Joe had food in front of them. "I'll ring the bell if we need anything else," he added, dismissing her.

The maid sidled out again, her eyes wide with curiosity. Dolly knew that every member of the household would know about their unexpected visit by the time the morning fires were lit and that speculation about why they were there would be swirling through the village within a few hours as well. She nibbled some of the crumpet out of politeness, but even though it had been hours since dinner on the boat, as she thought about what she had to say, her appetite deserted her. She felt too nervous for anything other than a quick sip of tea to ease the dryness of her throat.

"We haven't just come about the fire," she said, replying to Horace. "Before I continue, I want to tell you that I'm an honest person. Times have been hard for me and my family since we were orphaned, but I've never done anything bad…leastways, not until now." She took a shaky breath, as she saw a faint frown appear on Horace's face, and Edward Smallwood's expression became slightly disappointed.

What if this is a terrible mistake, and my trust in Horace is misplaced?

"You have to believe her, Mr Smallwood," Joe said, sitting up straighter so they would see he was serious. "Dolly got caught up in something, but only because…the person behind it…gave her no choice. My Dolly is kindhearted and honest. That's why we are putting ourselves at your mercy tonight."

"All we ask is that you listen to everything before rushing to accuse us. It's almost too shocking to believe, but I promise it's true."

"Just tell us what you know, my dear," Edward Smallwood said, giving her a kind smile. "I've heard plenty of strange and shocking things in my time, believe me."

Joe handed Dolly the pouch, and she pushed her cup and saucer and plate aside. "Your son, Dominic, has been giving me parcels. The arrangement is that I am to deliver them to Mr Ferguson, the yard manager at Frampton Basin." Her fingers shook slightly, and she put them in her lap for a moment, so that Edward wouldn't see.

"Go on."

Dolly had half expected Edward to look shocked at the mention of his eldest son, but his face remained impassive.

"This parcel is the fourth one Dominic has asked me to take to Mr Ferguson. He was very insistent that I must not look at what is in them, but tonight, Joe persuaded me."

"Would you allow me to open it?" Horace asked. At Dolly's agreement, he pulled a pearl-handled pocket knife from his jacket and cut the cord tying the pouch up. He tipped the jewellery out onto Edward's desk, and it lay in a tangle of glittering gemstones. In the soft light of Edward's study, the diamonds and rubies looked even more spectacular than they had when she had first seen them, and Dolly couldn't even begin to imagine how much they must be worth.

"Well, I'll be—" Edward croaked. He slumped back in his chair and blew out his cheeks in disbelief.

"You say Dominic gave you this package?" Horace's face had turned white, other than two red spots on his cheeks.

She nodded, feeling miserable. "I didn't want to, I promise. But Dominic told me that if I didn't…"

Edward held up his hand sharply, stopping her mid-sentence. "I thought you came here to tell me about the fire, Miss Hinton? Is that something to do with my son as well?"

Dolly felt even more miserable as she saw the pain in his eyes. Part of her wanted to jump up and run away as if nothing had happened, but it was too late for that.

"Dolly saw Dominic talking to a rough-looking fellow on the common, not long before the fire," Joe said, taking up the story. "She overheard them making some sort of plan and talking about Nailsbridg Mill. It sounded as though Dominic was angry because you hadn't just handed over the business to him, Mr Smallwood."

Dolly's mouth was as dry as dust, and she took a sip of tea. "I tried to put it to the back of my mind, but what I didn't tell you is that when I discovered the fire that night, I saw the same man running away from the mill. He knocked me over and said if I ever told anyone I'd seen him, my family would pay for it."

"I knew there was more to that fire than met the eye," Horace said with a grim smile. "I could tell there was something you were afraid of saying,

Dolly. I should have given you more encouragement."

"It's not your fault. It's kept me awake many a night, but when you said that the damage hadn't been too bad, and the insurance would pay up, I thought it was best to keep quiet."

"I can't believe Dominic had something to do with the fire," Edward said under his breath. He shook his head sorrowfully. "I was too soft on the boy after my wife died. I always knew he had a wild streak in him, but I thought he would grow out of it. I hoped that giving him the business would make a man of him. What a fool I've been."

"Nothing happened for a year after that night, and I thought that would be the end of it," Dolly said slowly.

"I don't understand why he has got involved with these burglaries if what you say is true."

Horace shifted uneasily in his chair. "I'm afraid I have something to tell you as well, Papa. Dominic fell in with a bad crowd when he was up in London. I found out he had run up gambling debts with some very unsavoury characters, but rather than pay them off, it seems he just carried on gambling, hoping to win back enough money to get himself out of trouble." He gestured at the jewels on the table. "This must be his desperate attempt to pay back his debtors."

Joe pointed at the ruby necklace. "My brother, Billy, described a ruby necklace just like this that he overheard Lord Shaw and the constable talking about at Dudbridge Manor. Lord Shaw gave it to his daughter, and we think these were stolen from there."

Edward groaned and put his head in his hands for a moment, his shoulders slumped.

"Are you all right, sir?" Dolly cried. "Please don't say that what I've told you is making you feel ill." She had a terrifying image of Edward collapsing and dying because of her shocking revelation.

The old man lifted his head again, but this time there was a steely glint of determination in his eyes. "Dominic has gone too far this time. I'm sure it hasn't actually been him breaking into people's houses to steal jewellery, but if he's involved, it might as well be."

"I reckon it's more likely to be the other man I saw. He thought nothing of setting the mill on fire. Dominic probably tells him what to do, if you don't mind me saying, Mr Smallwood. If that's any comfort to you?"

"Hardly," Edward harrumphed. "I've discovered

that Dominic can be lazy, and if he can get others to do his bidding, he will. But if he's telling this scoundrel what to do, the law won't look favourably on that, I can tell you."

"We wondered if Mr Ferguson is well placed at Frampton Basin to pass the jewels onto ships that might cross to France from Bristol. I expect they can sell the jewels over there without raising any suspicions about where they've come from."

Horace gave her a surprised look with a wry smile. "Perhaps you're wasted on the narrowboat, Dolly. It seems you could give Constable Redfern some ideas on how to solve crimes." He took a sip of his tea and looked at his father. "I believe Dolly and Joe, Papa. I think they have been very brave telling us everything tonight, and I hope you are of the same mind."

Dolly held her breath as Edward hesitated for a second. He was powerful enough to sweep Dominic's wrongdoings under the carpet if he chose, and she wasn't quite sure what his decision would be.

Edward nodded wearily. "Will you trust us to deal with this appropriately, Miss Hinton? I give you my word that everything will be all right. I will not allow Dominic to continue on this path of self-destruction, or to bring the Smallwood family name into any more disrepute. We will speak to the constables at first light."

"And we'll tell the police that you were forced to be the go-between," Horace added. "You've never been anything but loyal to our family…more loyal than Dominic, as it turns out. Papa knows all the local judges, so your name will be kept out of things. We just have to hope that Constable Redfern can catch the scoundrel who started the fire, although once the servants start gossiping, I fear he'll be long gone."

By the time Dolly and Joe got back onto Jester's broad back, her head was spinning from the events of the night. They rode in silence, each hoping that finally, life could return to normal, and they could look forward to the future. *Perhaps a future together.* She shivered, not sure whether it was from shock, the chilly night air, or Joe's arms wrapped around her as Jester carried them back towards the canal.

CHAPTER 21

Dolly tightened her shawl around her shoulders and waved her aunt and uncle goodbye as they strolled away to visit Sadie and Isaac, who were moored further up the canal. "Are you sure you don't want to come with us, Amy?" Jonty and Gloria were already standing on the towpath, and she could see that Jonty was itching to get going.

"I think I'd rather stay here for the evening and finish making these flowers," Amy said, frowning with concentration. "I'll see Gloria in a few days, and I don't want to give her any excuse to change her mind."

Dolly swallowed the lump in her throat, knowing exactly what Amy meant. This was a big day for all of them. Gloria was finally leaving *The River Maid* to live above Betty Jones's dressmaking shop as her full-time assistant. Even though they would no doubt see her any time they were moored up in Thruppley, it would still feel strange to know that Gloria no longer lived with them on the narrowboat. She squeezed Amy's shoulder, hoping that her youngest sister wouldn't feel too upset.

"I'll be fine," Amy said, patting Dolly's hand. She looked up at her and nodded with a tremulous smile. "Go on, you and Jonty get her settled in, while I carry on working and look after the boat."

It was a week since she and Joe had ridden up to Chavenhope House to tell Edward and Horace their suspicions, and Dolly still felt on edge. Jonty and Evan had loaded up the narrowboats with grain while they were gone, but the yard at Frampton had been in disarray all morning because Mr Ferguson was nowhere to be found. Once Dolly and Joe had explained to their families about her terrible dilemma and what Dominic had forced her to do, everything made sense.

"It seems that Mr Ferguson must have taken fright when you failed to show up," Constable Redfern reported with a grave expression later that morning when he visited them. "I've had reports of him spotted on a ship at Bristol port headed to the East Indies…and someone else reckoned they saw him on that there steam train on the way to London."

"So it's safe to say he's scarpered," Jonty concluded. "Good riddance. He never had a good word to say about us narrowboat folk, and if I'd known he was making poor Dolly be part of their crimes, I'd have given him a black eye or worse…"

"Are you two still nattering? Come on, Dolly." Jonty's shout snapped Dolly out of her worries and back to the present. "Betty Jones will be wondering where we've got to." He picked up Gloria's carpet bag and swung it over his shoulder.

"Bob can stay here with you, Amy."

"I'll be perfectly fine."

Dolly hesitated again. "I won't be away for too long, but Constable Redfern says nobody will bother us. Mr Ferguson is probably at sea by now, and Dominic and that other fellow won't dare show their faces around here again." She ruffled the dog's ears. He was stretched out on the bench next to Amy in a sunny spot, quite happy to rest with her, rather than walking all the way into Thruppley and back. Dolly tried not to feel sad at the sight of his greying muzzle. His joints were stiff in the mornings now, and she wondered how much longer he would be with them.

"Go on." Amy shooed her away with a chuckle. "Gloria needs you."

Gloria chatted brightly as they walked into Thruppley, keeping up a steady stream of conversation about the new clients that Betty Jones already had lined up for her. "She's going to let me start making dresses from scratch." She did a little skip to keep up with Jonty's long stride. "She's got some very well-to-do ladies on her books now. Even Miss Shaw said she would favour using us instead of her London dressmaker for some of her winter gowns."

"You'll be too grand for the likes of us soon," Jonty teased as the bow windows of the dressmaking shop came into view.

"Don't be so silly," Gloria said, nudging him with her elbow good-naturedly. "I'm a narrowboat girl and always will be. I'll never forget my humble beginnings."

Widow Jones was already standing in the doorway of her shop as they crossed the cobbled street, and the tempting smell of baking wafted from the pie shop next door, catching Jonty's attention.

"Come in, Gloria. I've made up your room under the eaves, and you already have two ladies booked in for dress fittings tomorrow morning."

"Why don't I treat us all to a ham pie, Mrs Jones," Jonty said cheerfully. "We can eat together, and then Gloria will be all settled in and ready to start work."

"I don't like to leave Amy alone for too long," Dolly murmured, "not with everything that's been happening." She pulled Gloria into a hug and promised to visit the next time they were in Thruppley.

"You get back to *The River Maid*." Gloria sniffed, determined not to cry. "There will be more pie for us. Also, you could call at *The Skylark* and see if Joe might walk you home," she added with a mischievous wink.

DOLLY LET her thoughts meander as she walked back through the village towards the towpath. She had expected Constable Redfern and his colleagues to swoop in and round up Mr Ferguson and

Dominic's mysterious partner in crime, and the fact that they all seemed to have vanished felt like something of an anticlimax. When she had first told her family what Dominic had been making her do, Bert and Jonty had been all for charging up to Chavenhope House to demand some sort of retribution, until Dolly had pointed out that Edward Smallwood could have made her situation very tricky if he'd chosen to.

"It ain't right; Dominic has taken advantage of your good nature so many times," Verity grumbled.

"I suppose we must be grateful that Horace and his pa are honourable people, even if Dominic's behaviour has been despicable," Burt had said, trying to calm everyone down.

There was a hint of autumn in the air as Dolly walked along the track through the fields towards the canal. It wouldn't be long until the swallows left to head to warmer climes, and it made her feel a little nostalgic for the long summer evenings they wouldn't get for another year. She hoped they would not be in for a hard winter. Bert's health had never fully recovered since his bad turn, and she knew that the damp, cold conditions of working on the canal played havoc with his weak chest, not to mention Verity's poor hands, gnarled with arthritis, getting worse each winter as well. It was a hard enough life on the narrowboat, and she didn't like to see her aunt and uncle struggling, even though it was all they had ever known. Some of the more fortunate narrowboat families managed to find lodgings off the canal in their old age, but she knew in her heart that Bert and Verity would never turn their back on the canal. Living on the water was in their blood, much as it was for her and Joe now, she had come to realise.

Just as her thoughts turned towards Joe, she was pleased to see him on the towpath ahead.

"I'm just back from taking Barnaby up to the common to graze," he called. His bright blue eyes crinkled with an affectionate smile that made her heart skip a beat. "I'll walk back with you to *The River Maid* if you like?"

Patch was already gambolling towards her, her tail wagging, and Dolly nodded eagerly. "Amy's been working hard, making her silk flowers all day. Why don't you join us for a cup of hot chocolate? Everyone else is busy doing other things, so we'd enjoy the company."

They fell into step together, and Patch ran ahead, chasing the white flash of a rabbit's tail as it vanished into the grass.

"Any news from Constable Redfern?"

"Not yet." Dolly couldn't keep the disappointment from her voice.

"Do you think Dominic has just gone to ground somewhere? If Mr Ferguson has left England, he'll probably never be brought to justice, and that other fellow has probably got away as well."

"I suppose, as long as none of them is around these parts, it doesn't really matter." A brisk wind rustled the trees around them, and Dolly pulled her shawl a little bit higher on her shoulders. "The thing I'm struggling with most is the thought that Dominic will want to try and get his own back on us somehow. I know his papa now sees him for what he really is, but Dominic is not the sort of man who likes to be beaten."

"Especially not by folks like us," Joe said, with a worried frown. "I'm inclined to agree with you, but I can't think how he could try and get revenge on us without drawing attention to himself again. Mr Smallwood said Dominic is a weak man who likes the finer things in life. We can only hope that he will disappear back to London and never bother us again."

"Has Billy been up to Dudbridge Manor again since the burglary?"

Joe's worried expression was quickly replaced by a broad smile. "Yes, he was there a few days ago, and apparently, Miss Shaw is overjoyed that her necklace was returned. It was all she could talk about while he was shoeing her horse, and he was dying to tell her how the jewels had been discovered, but I told him in no uncertain terms that he's never to tell a soul."

Dolly chuckled. "It was a good suggestion of yours…a discovery by an anonymous traveller passing through the area and handed into Constable Redfern for him to return to their rightful owners." Her heart skipped a beat again as Joe smiled down at her. "Hopefully, that will be enough for Lord Shaw to let the matter drop. As for the other wealthy folks who Dominic targeted, their jewellery will be long gone, but perhaps they are wealthy enough to be able to replace it."

"Do you think we might ever get some sort of reward?" Joe raised his eyebrows and gave her a curious look. "It would be nice to have a little nest egg to give us a more secure future."

Dolly wondered what he meant by that. *Marriage?* He hadn't even hinted at it since telling her he loved her, which left her feeling a bit confused. She thought about the idea of a reward as they emerged from the spinney of trees just before the spot where *The River Maid* was moored up. "I already have my reward," she said thoughtfully. "At one point, I was terrified I would be thrown into jail and never see my family again...or you, for that matter. So knowing that I still have my freedom is enough for—"

Before she could finish her sentence, a volley of barks from Patch just ahead interrupted them. Dolly felt her blood run cold as she looked past the dog at their narrowboat. There was a peculiar orange glow in the cabin that reminded her of...

"Fire!" Joe cried. "*The River Maid* is on fire!"

Chapter Twenty Two

Dolly picked up her skirts and ran towards the boat, feeling as if she was reliving the terrible nightmare of that night at Nailsbridge Mill.

"It's him, the same man!" she shouted at Joe as she caught a flash of his familiar red hair.

Ahead of them, the scruffy thug who had lived in her worst dreams jumped lightly off the deck of *The River Maid* onto the towpath. "Let this be a warning to yer!" he shouted with a smirk, before sprinting away.

"Get after him, Patch!" Joe yelled, pointing after the man. "Round him up."

"What about Amy? She's on the boat...I left her there, working on her flowers." Dolly felt a sob rising in her throat as the flames took hold.

"Fire up yonder!" Shouts from afar split the air as some of the other narrowboat families realised what was happening and ran towards them to help.

"Amy, where are you?" As Dolly stumbled to a halt on the towpath, she saw that Bob had already jumped onto land, driven off the boat by the crackling flames, which were licking up the cheerfully coloured curtains at the cabin windows.

She looked around wildly, desperately hoping to see Amy standing nearby, but she wasn't there. "She must have been asleep when he lit the fire," she sobbed. "I have to save her, Joe. I can't let her die in there."

Before she could leap onto the deck, Joe grabbed her arm and yanked her back. "What's that in the water?"

Dolly dragged her gaze from the fire, and a new wave of terror gripped her heart as she saw Amy's silk flowers bobbing on the surface of the canal. "She can't swim, Joe. If she jumped into the water to save herself, she'll drown."

Joe tore his jacket off without a moment's hesitation and plunged into the canal, swimming to where the silk flowers were with swift, confident strokes as Dolly watched on with mounting terror. He took a deep breath and dived below the water, but she knew that in the reeds and mud, it would be almost impossible to see where Amy was, even if she had only just jumped in seconds before they had arrived.

"Don't give up hope," one of the narrowboat men called as he arrived by her side, gasping from the run. Several other people arrived, carrying buckets, and they started scooping up water to douse the flames.

"Amy, where are you?" Dolly called again. Tears rolled down her cheeks, and she felt as though a shard of ice had lodged itself in her heart. They should have known that Dominic would want to exact his revenge. If the thuggish bully was capable of setting fire to Nailsbridge Mill, of course, it made sense for Dominic to send him to the canal to do the same again. It was Dominic's ultimate revenge. He knew that Dolly would never forgive herself and would have to live the rest of her life with Amy's death on her conscience.

"Amy...please tell me you're alright..." Dolly's heartfelt cry echoed across the water as Joe dived again, desperately trying to find her sister.

"Dolly! I'm alright... I'm here."

She spun around and sobbed with relief as she saw Billy and Amy hurrying along the towpath towards her.

"Thank the Lord...we thought you were in the boat...and then we saw your silk flowers in the water...and thought you had jumped in to save yourself...but I was afraid you'd gone under the water..." Dolly's garbled explanation came out in short gasps as Billy called to tell Joe that Amy was safe.

The acrid smell of burning timber filled the air, and Amy shivered with shock. "Billy came to visit, and we went for a walk along the towpath." Tears filled her eyes. "Did that horrible man start the fire? I'm sorry, Dolly, I said I would look after *The River Maid*, I should never have left."

Dolly shook her head, not caring about the damage the fire might do, and threw her arms around Amy again. "It doesn't matter. I'm glad you weren't here. Going for a walk with Billy probably saved your life. That man wouldn't have cared that you were in the cabin when he set fire to it." A surge of anger gripped her, and it took all her strength not to howl at the injustice of everything. "This is all down to Dominic. He took revenge because I didn't do what he wanted."

Amy took hold of Dolly's hands and squeezed them. "But now it's over."

* * *

BERT AND VERITY were told the news, and as all the other families rallied around to save what they could of *The River Maid*, dusk slowly crept up on them. There were blankets and hot, sweet tea brought for Joe and Amy, while Dolly told Constable Redfern exactly who she had seen fleeing from the scene.

Just as the moon appeared and darkness fell, one of the other constables came pounding down the towpath, his face wreathed with smiles.

"You'll be glad to know we've arrested the scoundrel who did this. That dog of yours gave him a nasty bite on his leg, and he was stupid enough to call at the Black Lion for a drink and some bandages. I know you and the villagers don't always see eye to eye, but they weren't going to let him get away with hurting someone like your Amy. The barmaid plied Mr McKenzie with ale to keep him distracted and sent her nephew to find me. Arthur's behind bars now, and that's where he'll be staying."

"Arthur McKenzie?" This was the first time a name had been put to Dominic's violent assistant, and Dolly's legs suddenly felt weak as relief swept through her.

"Aye...he's well-known for his criminal ways in London, I've found out. Been hiding out around Thruppley since he gave the police up there the slip, so you've done us all a service."

"Did you catch anyone else involved with this?" she asked hesitantly.

The constable shook his head. "Who did you have in mind?"

She looked at all her family and friends who had gathered to help and realised there was no point in mentioning Dominic Smallwood to the constable. He would never believe that such a wealthy, well-connected gentleman could have anything to do with these terrible crimes, and she had to trust that, without his henchmen to do his bidding, Dominic would finally slink back to his high society friends and leave them alone. She exchanged a smile with Joe, who she could tell knew exactly what she was thinking.

"It's nobody..." they both said in unison.

"That's good," the constable said, scratching his head, looking perplexed. "I'm just happy we've caught the man who did this, and he'll pay for his crimes, so we can all rest easy in our beds again at night."

"Speaking of beds," Sadie said, bustling forward, "you must all come and stay on our boat tonight."

"Aye," Isaac chimed in, "and first thing tomorrow, we'll all make a start on repairing *The River Maid*. It's a good thing you two turned up when you did," he said, grinning at Dolly and Joe. "The fire only really took hold on the bedding and curtains, but we think the cabin is salvageable." He patted the boat's roof and nodded defiantly. "We'll have the old girl as good as new again in no time, and until then, you needn't worry about getting your work done or having nowhere to live. Us narrowboat folk look after our own, and we'll take care of you."

"It's too late to start anything now," Bert said. He and Verity started following Sadie, who was already heading back along the towpath.

"I'll walk with you, Amy." Billy tucked her hand in the crook of his arm, looking slightly bashful as Dolly gave him an inquisitive look. "My intentions are honourable," he said hastily. "I didn't do anything untoward on our walk earlier, and there were plenty of people around to keep an eye on us, so it's not as if we were really alone."

Before she could reply, Amy tossed her curls and shot her sister an impish smile. "I'm only a few months off being sixteen, Dolly. Billy is my best friend, and he always has been. You can't stop us from walking out together."

"Mind you look after her," Dolly said, giving Billy a stern look, before dissolving into a smile. She knew she didn't need to worry about that.

As she watched them wander away, Dolly hung back, not quite ready to leave *The River Maid*, even though the fire was fully extinguished. She suddenly felt close to tears, overwhelmed by her tumultuous emotions and everybody's generous offers of help.

"It's been quite a day, hasn't it," Joe said softly. He had changed out of his wet clothes into a dry shirt and trousers, which Evan had brought for him, but his blonde hair was still sticking up at several different angles.

Without thinking, Dolly reached up and brushed his hair back into place with her fingers. "We've had more than enough excitement to last a lifetime," she agreed wearily. "I just hope that Isaac was right when he said *The River Maid* can be restored to working order. Without our boat, we won't be able to work, and that will be the end of everything."

"Maybe not the end…" Joe said hesitantly. "Perhaps this fire is a reminder that we shouldn't take things for granted." He ran his hand over the cabin of the boat, in the same way he did with Barnaby, as if it was a living creature, before turning back to face Dolly again. "I think perhaps I've been guilty of taking our friendship for granted."

"I don't know what you mean," Dolly said. The towpath had cleared, and they were all alone. There was a strange look on Joe's face, a cross between nervousness and hope, which made her heart pitter-patter in her chest.

"You know I'm not good with fancy words," Joe continued with a wry smile. He cleared his throat. "I don't mean that I've taken you for granted. What I meant to say is that—" He puffed his cheeks out with frustration and then laughed at himself.

"What exactly are you trying to tell me?" Dolly

looked up into his blue eyes, and a smile tugged at the corners of her mouth.

"Dolly, I know we haven't exactly been walking out together, but we've always been best friends, haven't we?" Joe didn't wait for her to reply, not wanting to lose his nerve. "I already told you that I love you...and I do, Dolly. I love you with all my heart. Would you do me the honour of becoming my wife?" He coughed again, and his cheeks reddened. "Or perhaps we could walk out first... but I'm not sure that we need to because I've already known for a very long time that I want to spend the rest of my life with you."

At last! Dolly's heart jumped with joy, but she couldn't say yes immediately. "Before I answer, I have to make sure of something. Ever since Pa died, I've promised myself that I will always look after Amy. Life can be difficult for her, what with not being able to see things as well as most of us. I'd never want her to feel she was a burden."

"Wherever we end up, Amy will always be welcome to live with us," Joe said hastily. "She's part of your family, and I never imagined it any other way."

"And I have to make sure that Aunt Verity and Uncle Bert are taken care of as well," Dolly continued. "I don't know how things will work with us having two boats between all of us. It's too much for Jonty to do the work alone."

Joe grinned. "We'll find a way to make it work, Dolly. Just look at everything we've already achieved together. Anyway, I wouldn't be surprised if Billy asks for Amy's hand in marriage at the earliest opportunity. He's been sweet on her for years.

"And I think Amy loves him dearly," Dolly agreed.

"I'll wager he's just biding his time for her to get a little bit older, and then he'll speak to Bert. Abe Wentworth has already promised Billy the little cottage next to the forge, which will make a fine home for them both."

Dolly considered his words and knew that Joe was right. They had overcome all of Dominic's attempts to ruin their lives, so what were a few challenges about restoring their narrowboat and figuring out who would live where?

"Please, Dolly, let's get married. You'll make me the happiest man on the canal…or should I say, in the whole of the West county."

Dolly burst out laughing, and then, with a nod,

stepped closer to the only man she had ever loved. "Yes, let's get married, Joe."

As the breeze dropped and the balmy late summer's evening fell quiet, Joe wrapped his arms around Dolly. She closed her eyes as their lips finally met in a tender kiss. Her heart soared with happiness as she realised that no matter what might happen in the future, they would always have each other.

"I love you, Dolly," Joe murmured.

She stood back slightly so their eyes could meet and felt herself being pulled irrevocably into his blue-eyed gaze. "I love you too, Joe, and I will for as long as I live."

Joe lowered his head to brush another kiss on her mouth when a sudden yap from Bob interrupted. He looked up at them, wagging his tail expectantly, and a moment later, Patch came bounding back along the towpath, wondering why they weren't following everyone else.

"I think they're telling us it's time to go and find the others," Joe chuckled.

They linked arms, and with one last backward look at *The River Maid*, Dolly sighed contentedly, and they strolled along the towpath where the sound of happy laughter drifted towards them.

EPILOGUE

Two Years Later...

"Look, Bert, somebody's finally moved into the lock keeper's cottage." Verity winced slightly as she climbed slowly up the cabin steps. Her knees were more painful than ever, but she didn't like to complain about it.

"About time, too," Bert replied. He was sitting next to the tiller, mending a rope, and he looked towards the cottage. "I wonder who it is? At least we'll have someone to help with the locks. It hasn't been the same since old Mr Murphy moved away to live with his daughter."

Dolly brought Jester to a stop in their usual spot near the oak tree. They were mooring up in Thruppley for two nights, which would give them a chance to stock up on supplies and spend some time with Gloria.

"Perhaps we should go and introduce ourselves," she said. Joe and Evan had already moored up, just ahead of them, and her heart lifted as she saw Joe walking towards them, just as it always did.

"Sounds like we're both thinking the same thing," he called with a wide smile.

"Maybe it's a young family," Verity said. There were some sheets draped over the washing line, drying in the early summer sunshine, and smoke curled up from the chimney. "I haven't got anything to take for them. Maybe we should wait until I've had a chance to bake a cake, I don't like to turn up empty-handed."

"I'm sure they won't mind," Dolly exchanged a secret smile with Joe, noticing that his eyes were gleaming with anticipation. "Why don't we go now while we know there's someone at home?"

Verity led the way, always keen to meet anyone new on the canal. Pink clematis was flowering around the door, and there was a generous garden behind the cottage. It looked overgrown, but it had promise, and the smell of freshly baked bread wafted out of the open window. She lifted the knocker and rapped sharply on the door.

"Gloria? What are you doing here?" Verity gasped with astonishment and confusion as the door opened, revealing Gloria standing there.

"Surprise!" Dolly and Joe cried.

"What on earth is going on, Dolly?" Verity fanned herself with a handkerchief, not knowing what to make of things.

Gloria stepped back and gestured towards the hallway and kitchen beyond. "Welcome to your new home, Aunt Verity and Uncle Bert."

Bert's mouth gaped open. "Have you had a nip of gin, Gloria? We couldn't afford a cottage like this even if we worked for another ten years, child, and you know it."

"We can explain everything," Dolly said. "I hope you've got a pot of tea ready for us?" she added, smiling at her sister.

Ten minutes later, they were all sitting in the surprisingly spacious kitchen, around the scrubbed wooden table, and Gloria had lined up enough cups and saucers for everyone, with several more to spare.

"Go on then, Dolly, we're all ears." Verity gazed around the cosy cottage, and Dolly could tell from her expression how much she liked it. There was a dresser along one wall, and a freshly blacked range, where Gloria had already cooked boiled ham and vegetables, thanks to Mrs Jones giving her a day off.

"Horace Smallwood invited Joe and me up to Chavenhope House last time we were in Thruppley," Dolly began.

"We wondered where you'd gone to," Bert said. "How is he getting on running all those businesses since his pa retired?"

"He's doing really well," Dolly said. "Mr Smallwood is enjoying his fly fishing, and quite happy to let Horace continue with everything. And now that Horace and Miss Shaw are soon to be wed, he has no desire to return to London."

"He told us that things have settled down since Dominic let them know that he's not coming back from America."

Bert harrumphed. "I don't suppose he would dare come back to England, not since word got out about his part in those robberies." His face clouded for a moment at the memory of what Dominic had put their family through, and Verity squeezed his hand.

"Apparently, he's married a wealthy heiress in Boston, so Edward has accepted that he'll probably never see Dominic again," Dolly continued. "That's partly what the meeting was about when we went up the other day. Horace wants to make some changes with the business, and more importantly, he wants our help."

"Are you sure? I thought there would be less work for us narrowboat folk, now that the steam trains are used more for hauling goods. Not as I agree with it." Bert's eyes lit up as Gloria put a lemon cake in the middle of the table and cut him a slice.

"You're right about that," Joe said, with a quick nod. "But Horace is branching out into other things."

"Well, we know about the hotel he's built on the outskirts of Thruppley. Very grand it looks, too," Verity remarked. "Perhaps we'll take tea and cakes there one day, with all them fancy London folk who come and stay here to enjoy our lovely green countryside."

Bert chuckled at the idea. "Let's not be getting

ideas above our station, Verity. We're a narrowboat family, remember."

"Or perhaps not, if Dolly is saying this is our cottage. Although it seems like a far-fetched idea if you ask me." Verity gazed around again, puffing out her cheeks in disbelief.

Dolly took a sip of her tea, enjoying seeing the anticipation on their faces, and then she relented. She had barely been able to keep the secret between herself and Joe these last few days, but it would be worth it to see the look of wonder on Verity's face. "Horace has given us the lock keeper's cottage," she exclaimed happily. "He and his pa always said they wanted a way of thanking us for saving Nailsbridge Mill, so this is it. If you're happy to accept it, Horace would like you to live here."

"Us? All alone?" Verity squawked. "Don't be daft, Dolly. This place is far too big for us, we'll be rattling around like two farthings in an old tin."

Dolly laughed out loud at the image Verity had conjured. "Joe and I were hoping you wouldn't mind us living here with you. Not only that, but we have another surprise to share."

"You're in the family way, aren't you?" Verity

said. Her eyes filled with tears which she hastily dabbed away with her handkerchief. "I thought as much, and of course, nothing would make us happier than to share this cottage with you and your family."

"Does that mean we won't work on the canals anymore?" Bert asked Joe. "I quite fancy turning my hand to being the lock keeper. It will be a shame to see *The River Maid* out of use, but you must do what's right for you and Dolly. It will be busy enough, working the lock."

Joe shook his head. "*The RiverMaid* will still be in use; don't you worry, Bert." He smiled broadly. "Horace has plans to turn it into a leisure boat. Apparently, the high society ladies and gentlemen coming to stay at his hotel have already been making enquiries about whether they could have trips up and down the canal. He wants us and *The Skylark* to be the narrowboats for his hotel guests, if you're in agreement?"

This time it was Dolly's turn to look shocked. "Do you mean we won't have to load and unload grain anymore?"

Joe and Jonty both nodded.

"It will be a bit strange to get used to being in

Thruppley every night," Joe said, giving Dolly a searching look. "Horace has assured us that the well-to-do folks from London will keep us more than busy enough. We should even be earning a bit more, and it means that once our baby arrives, I won't have to stay away at night, travelling down to Frampton Basin. Do you think we'll get used to being on land again?"

Before Dolly could reply, the cottage door flew open, and Amy and Billy walked in.

"Have you told them the news?" Amy asked breathlessly.

"So you all knew about the cottage, did you?" Verity chuckled.

Bert eyed Billy from under his bushy eyebrows. "Have you two been for another walk?"

Billy shuffled awkwardly and then stood a little closer to Amy. "Actually...there's...there's something I need to ask you, Mr Webster..."

Bert's face split into a wide smile. "Of course, you can marry Amy, Billy...I thought you'd never get around to asking me."

"This calls for a celebration," Gloria said, jumping up and rushing around the table to give Amy a hug. "I hope you're going to let me make your wedding gown. I had so much fun making Dolly's, that Betty is going to let me start offering wedding gown services to other ladies."

"I wouldn't dream of asking anyone else," Amy said, blushing, as Billy put his arm around her shoulder, with a beaming smile.

"Well, I'd better go and take Barnaby up to the common." Joe stood up reluctantly.

"I'll come with you," Dolly said. "Jester needs to go on the common as well."

As they walked arm-in-arm from the lock keeper's cottage back to their narrowboats, Dolly felt the first stirrings of the new life in her belly. She rested her hand over the faint swell under her gown and smiled as she looked up at Joe. "Everything turned out alright in the end, didn't it," she said happily.

Joe stopped under the oak tree and pulled her gently into his arms, pressing a tender kiss on her lips. "It did, and things are only going to get better. We have so much to look forward to, Dolly. A child of our own…a new lease of life for *The River Maid* and *The Skylark*. And our family and friends nearby."

A warm breeze rippled the surface of the canal,

and the sun glinted on the water, lighting it up like a golden thread as it stretched into the distance between the verdant green hills and honey-coloured cottages. This would always be their home, Dolly thought, together with Joe. There was nowhere she would rather be.

READ MORE

If you enjoyed The Narrowboat Orphans, you'll love Daisy Carter's other Victorian Romance Saga Stories:

The Snow Orphan's Destiny

As the snow falls and secrets swirl around her, Penny is torn between two worlds. Does a gift hold the key to her past, and will her true destiny bring her the happiness she longs for?

Penny Frost understands that she's had an unusual start in life. Taken in by a kind-hearted woman, she becomes part of the close-knit Bevan family of Sketty Lane.

Poverty is never far away, but they manage to scratch a living working for the miserly Mr Culpepper in the local brickyard.

READ MORE

Penny dreams of something better and never feels as though she quite fits in. And the fact that her mother never mentioned her own childhood only adds to the mystery of who she really is.

When she is bequeathed a piece of jewellery, Penny wonders if it might unlock the secret to her past. However, before she can find out, a shocking event one dark and snowy night brings her to the attention of the wealthy Sir Henry Calder.

Suddenly she finds herself swept into a world of privilege and comfort, far away from the Bevans and her best friend, George, and it seems as though her future is finally secure.

But not everyone wants Penny to succeed and will go to any lengths to get their own way, even if it means leaving her destitute.

Will the mistakes of the past be repeated and snatch Penny away from her true destiny?

Can she reclaim what is rightfully hers even though the odds are against her?

Torn between two very different worlds, Penny must decide whether to follow her heart or put duty first if she's to have a chance at love and happiness...

The Snow Orphan's Destiny is another gripping Victorian romance saga by Daisy Carter,

READ MORE

the popular author of Pit Girl's Scandal, The Maid's Winter Wish, and many more.

* * *

Do you love FREE BOOKS? Download Daisy's FREE book now:

The May Blossom Orphan

Clementine Morris thought life had finally dealt her a kinder hand when her aunt rescued her from the orphanage. But happiness quickly turns to fear when she realises her uncle has shocking plans for her to earn more money.

As the net draws in, a terrifying accident at the docks sparks an unlikely new friendship with kindly warehouse lad, Joe Sawbridge.

Follow Clemmie and Joe through the dangers of the London docks, to find out whether help comes in the nick of time, in this heart-warming Victorian romance story.

Printed in Great Britain
by Amazon